SHA

BETTER OFF
DEAD

SHAWN O'BRIEN
BETTER OFF DEAD

William W. Johnstone
with J. A. Johnstone

PINNACLE BOOKS
Kensington Publishing Corp.
www.kensingtonbooks.com

PINNACLE BOOKS are published by

Kensington Publishing Corp.
119 West 40th Street
New York, NY 10018

PUBLISHER'S NOTE
Following the death of William W. Johnstone, the Johnstone family is
working with a carefully selected writer to organize and complete Mr.
Johnstone's outlines and many unfinished manuscripts to create additional
novels in all of his series like The Last Gunfighter, Mountain Man, and
Eagles, among others. This novel was inspired by Mr. Johnstone's superb
storytelling.

To the extent that the image or images on the cover of this book depict a
person or persons, such person or persons are merely models, and are not
intended to portray any character or characters featured in the book.

All Kensington titles, imprints, and distributed lines are available at special quantity discounts for bulk purchases for sales promotions, premiums,
fund-raising, educational, or institutional use. Special book excerpts or
customized printings can also be created to fit specific needs. For details,
write or phone the office of the Kensington special sales manager:
Kensington Publishing Corp., 119 West 40th Street, New York, NY 10018,
attn: Special Sales Department; phone 1-800-221-2647.

PINNACLE BOOKS, the Pinnacle logo, and the WWJ steer head logo are
Reg. U.S. Pat. & TM Off.

ISBN-13: 978-0-7860-3567-0
ISBN-10: 0-7860-3567-6

First printing: March 2016

10 9 8 7 6 5 4 3 2 1

Printed in the United States of America

First electronic edition: March 2016

ISBN-13: 978-0-7860-3568-7
ISBN-10: 0-7860-3568-4

CHAPTER ONE

"Mister, you were warned to mind your own business and stay away from the foundry and you ignored me," the big man in the bowler hat said. "The gent you're looking for isn't here and it seems like we'll need to beat that fact into you."

Shawn O'Brien pushed himself off the saloon bar and faced four toughs, each armed with a hickory pickax handle. All wore bowler hats with goggles parked above the brims. Everyone who had cause to enter the Abaddon Cannon Foundry wore goggles.

"Maybe you will, Kilcoyn," Shawn said, clearing his gun. "But you'll step over your own dead to get to me."

He stood with his legs slightly apart, his gun hand close to the Colt on his hip. At that moment, relaxed, confident, significant, he looked like nobody's idea of a bargain. Tall, blond, his piercing blue eyes direct and unafraid, Shawn's frock coat and linen showed dust and wear from the trail, but their quality was unmistakable. The labels said Bond Street, London, and his riding boots, handmade in Philadelphia on a narrow last, were sewn sixty-four stitches to the inch with an awl so fine that an accidental piercing of the boot-maker's hand neither hurt nor drew blood. He wore a gold ring on the little finger of his left hand that bore the O'Brien family crest with its three lions and the motto, *Lamh Laidir an Uachtar,* "The Strong Hand From Above."

Valentine Kilcoyn was no fool. He was handy with a gun but first and foremost, he was a skull, boot, and fist fighter. The new breed of sophisticated gambler draw fighter was alien to him. He'd suspected that a hideout could be concealed under the man's frock coat, perhaps a derringer stuck in his waistband, but O'Brien had pulled back his coat and revealed an ivory-handled Colt and an expensive gun rig adorned with silver dragons that no ham-handed rube could afford. The bitterest lesson of all that Kilcoyn had learned in a past few moments was that this day might be his last. He could die with his beard in the sawdust because the man called the Town Tamer would be almighty sudden.

Kilcoyn had sand and there was no backup in him. He was primed and may have thrown down the ax handle and tried the draw. The kid beside him, a towhead with reckless eyes, seemed eager, but the other two company men held back and exchanged wary glances, wanting no part of what a fast gun like O'Brien could bring to a shoot-out.

The bartender put a stop to it. He leaned over the bar with a Greener scattergun in his hand and said,

"Val, you and your boys back on out of here, I don't want dead men messing up my place today."

"You taking O'Brien's part, Ambrose?" Kilcoyn said, his eyes ugly.

"I'm taking nobody's part." Ambrose Hellen's anger flared. "You damn fool, Kilcoyn. You'd be dead afore your hand even touched your gun butt and the others with you. You've lost today, so git and run your head under a water pump and cool off."

"Man gives good advice, Kilcoyn," Shawn said. "Besides, my lunch is getting cold. Either get the hell out of here or have at it and let's get our work in."

Kilcoyn tried to save face. "Next time we meet, O'Brien, you won't have a bartender with a shotgun to protect you."

Suddenly Shawn O'Brien was done talking. He felt weary, used up, and more than a little angry. "Kilcoyn, get the hell out of here right now or I'll drop you where you stand."

Kilcoyn saw the writing on the wall. He knew if he even twitched a muscle he was in for a moment of hell-firing gunplay that would have him shaking hands with eternity. "Let's get out of here, boys. Our time will come soon enough."

After the Abaddon men left, Shawn picked up his plate of Irish stew and walked to the other end of the bar, away from the door. He forked a piece of potato into his mouth and made a face. "Damn, it's gone cold. Didn't I say that would happen?"

"Here, let me get you another plate," Ambrose Hellen said. "There's plenty in the pot."

When the bartender returned with a steaming

plate, he put it on the bar in front of Shawn. "How's your brother Jacob?"

Shawn was puzzled. "How do you know—"

"I was bartending up El Paso way a few months back and he came into the saloon now and again to play the piano. I heard your name and put two and two together. But Jake don't wear fancy duds like you. I'd maybe give a dollar for everything he wore and ten for his horse."

"Jake is not one for sartorial splendor and he sits his ten-dollar horse like a sack of grain, never did learn to ride like a gentleman. Last I heard he was spending some time at Dromore, our father's ranch in the New Mexico Territory. He goes home now and then to say a rosary at Ma's grave. Other times, depending on where the wind blows him, he's spending time in a monastery or out in the wilderness bounty hunting. A time or two, he's gone on the scout after holding up a stage or a train. When Jake needs a grubstake, he's not one to care about getting on the wrong side of the law."

"He's a rum one is Jacob and no mistake," Hellen said. "He doesn't take any sass and he's mighty sudden with the iron."

Shawn smiled. "If it had been Jake here instead of me today, he'd have gunned two of those boys then beaten the other two to death with their own pickax handles. As you say, he doesn't take much sass."

"Mister, I don't think you take much sass either. How's the stew?"

"Real good. I think maybe I tasted better at the

Langham Hotel in London, but it's a close-run thing."

The bartender served another customer then returned to Shawn. "Val Kilcoyn called you the Town Tamer."

Shawn nodded. "It's a name I didn't seek, but folks seem to have cottoned on to it so there it stands and I live with it."

"What exactly do you want to tame in Big Fork? This town is the Abaddon Cannon Foundry and not much else."

The saloon door opened and Hamp Sedley, dressed in his dusty gambler's finery, stepped inside. He saw Shawn at the bar, stepped to his side, and ordered a beer. "Hell, there ain't a woman in the town by the name Doña Elena Maria Cantrell. With a handle like that, she'd stick out in a burg like Big Buck. Well, she doesn't stick out because she ain't here."

Shawn said to the bartender, "Ever hear that name around these parts?"

Hellen shook his head. "No, I haven't. The women we get in here are females of a certain vocation. In Mexico, only noblewomen are addressed as Doña."

"Yeah, well like I said, I didn't see one of them." Sedley tried his beer. "Warm."

"You want cold beer, head for Alaska." Hellen turned away as a couple customers stepped to the bar.

"You missed all the fun, Hamp," Shawn said. "Valentine Kilcoyn and his toughs tried to warn me off again. For a minute there, I thought it might come to a shooting scrape."

"What happened?"

"We had a nice little talk and then the bartender took a hand and Kilcoyn and his boys left."

"I say we blow this burg, Shawn. Are you sure you read Jake's letter right? He's not one to ask favors."

"Yeah, I've read it about twenty times and each time I read it right. He said Doña Maria was in Big Buck and that she thinks her runaway little brother is working in the cannon foundry. Jake wants me to find him . . . as a favor, one brother to another."

"How well does Jake know this gal?" Sedley asked.

"He slept with her. Is that well enough?"

"Oh."

"Yeah, Hamp, 'Oh.'"

Sedley shook his head. "Well, we've reached a dead end, seems to me. What the hell are you eating?"

"Irish stew."

"It looks like puke."

"Don't let the bartender hear you say that. He sets store by his stew and he's got a handy Greener scattergun behind the bar." Shawn laid his fork on his plate. "We'll give it another couple days. If we don't find Manuel Cantrell by then we'll head back to Denver and I'll write a letter of apology to Jake."

A big, soot-stained mechanic dressed in a heavy leather jerkin and pants, goggles pushed up on his head, walked into the saloon and looked around. His stare alighted on a small man wearing a claw hammer coat and top hat who stood alone at the end of the bar.

"Hey, Dorian Steggles. We got one for you," the big man said.

Steggles looked up. "In or out?"

"In."

"What happened?"

"He was shoveling coke for one of the blast furnaces and just fell over. Heart give out, I guess."

"But he's in you say?"

"In."

The undertaker took his goggles from the brim of his top hat and let them fall around his neck. "I hate it so much when it's in."

The big man shrugged. "I'm only a shift foreman. I can't control where and when the trolls drop."

Steggles sighed. "No, I suppose not, Mr. Breens. I'll get my assistants and be there shortly."

"Wait, Breens," Shawn called. "What's the dead man's name?"

Breens had a sharp answer ready to go, but when he took a good look at the tall, handsome man at the bar with a Colt on his hip he changed his mind. "Hell, mister, I don't know their names. He wasn't a white man, if that sets your mind at rest."

"I'm looking for a young Mexican man named Manuel Cantrell," Shawn said. "Have you heard that name? He's supposed to be working at Abaddon."

"Mister, there are three shifts at Abaddon, a hundred men to a shift, and I don't know any of their names. Try the front office."

"I did. They told me they'd never heard of him."

"Then he ain't there." Breens turned and walked out of the saloon.

"I want to take a look at that body," Shawn said.

"When?" Sedley asked, still beside him.

"Come nightfall when the undertaker's place is closed."

Sedley grimaced. "Well, that's something a man can look forward to."

"Why aren't you wearing your gun?"

"Don't see much point, Shawn. I can't hit anything with it."

"You can hit just fine at spitting distance. Make sure you wear it tonight."

CHAPTER TWO

Distracted by the flight of a hawk, Shawn O'Brien was looking skyward as he stepped off the boardwalk outside the saloon. At the last moment, Hamp Sedley grabbed his arm and yanked him back out of the path of a speeding horseless carriage. As the steam-powered monster flashed past, the handsome, middle-aged man in the backseat turned and glared at Shawn for having the audacity to get in his way.

Beside him a hard-faced but pretty blond woman yelled, "Watch where you walk, rube!"

By the time Shawn had recovered his balance, the steam car, trailing a billowing dust trail, swung in the direction of the foundry.

Shawn used his hat to pound dust off his coat and pants. "Who the hell was that? And what the hell was that?"

Another voice answered that question, but first, Mayor John Deakins stepped beside Shawn and introduced himself. "And according to what I was told by Ambrose Hellen, I'd say your name is Mr. Shawn O'Brien."

Shawn nodded.

"To answer your question, Mr. O'Brien, that gentleman is the owner of the Abaddon Cannon Foundry, maker of the finest instruments of mass destruction in this country or in any other, and he was driving a steam-powered horseless carriage, the vehicle of the future."

"What's his name? I reckon I'll tell him to slow down that contraption when he's driving through town," Shawn said.

"Ah yes, very commendable of you, I'm sure, but the owner is a man of mystery," Deakins said. "Very few people in this town know his name because he never, ever puts it out."

The mayor was a large-bellied, pompous man of impressive height, made more striking by his tall top hat with goggles above the brim. Shawn thought he looked like a more prosperous version of Mr. Dickens's Wilkins Micawber.

"Those like myself who do know the gentleman's name and have been invited to take a glimpse inside the foundry, a rare privilege, are sworn to secrecy," Deakins said. "I must confess that to me the foundry looks like a fire and brimstone haunt of the damned. Naked, sweating men toil in the glare of enormous furnaces and massive boilers bang and hiss like steam locomotives. But then doesn't every factory in our modern industrial age present such a fearsome aspect, even though its fortunate workers prosper like never before?"

"One of those prosperous workers died in there today," Sedley said.

"Alas, accidents happen, especially when one casts iron cannons that weigh many tons," the mayor said.

Shawn said, "The man dropped dead, or so his foreman told the undertaker."

"The work is hard and now and then a weakling will perish, but none of them are white men, so their deaths are hardly worth getting concerned over." The mayor took a magnificent gold skeleton watch from his vest pocket and consulted the time. "Well . . . Mr. O'Brien . . . I must be on my way. Business matters press me closely. But a word to the wise before I leave. The wealth of Abaddon trickles down to the people of Big Buck. Before the foundry arrived, we were just another dusty little cow town lost in the wilderness of southwest Texas. Now we have a railroad, the stores and the saloon are thriving, and we no longer depend on cattle but on steam engineers, mechanics, cannon borers, tradesmen of all kinds, and railroaders. This is why we don't pry too deeply into what goes on behind the walls of the foundry and neither should you."

Mayor Deakins smiled and pointed to the goggles on his top hat. "You will see many people in Big Buck wearing these. We wear them to show our solidarity with the foundry owner and his workers. Now good day to you both, gentlemen—and I do hope you heed my advice."

Shawn said, "Mayor, wait. We're looking—"

Without turning, Deakins waved a hand as he stomped away. "I said good day to you, sir."

Shawn ended his pursuit of Deakins when he

bumped into an old lady who stood at the door of a hardware store. The woman wore a black shawl over her head and her face was lost in shadow.

He touched his hat. "I'm so sorry. That was clumsy of me."

Without lifting her veiled face, the woman shoved a scrap of paper into Shawn's hand and walked away, showing a brisk enough pace for such an old-timer.

The old dear's action involved secrecy of some sort and Shawn didn't look at the paper until he and Sedley sought the privacy of an alley between a general store and a bakery. The note was short and to the point.

Midnight. Meet me at the hangman's tree.

That was it. There was no signature.

"No signature," Sedley said with his usual knack of stating the obvious. "Maybe the old woman has some information on Manuel Cantrell. Or somebody paid her a few dollars to bait a trap."

Shawn agreed. "There's only one way to find out."

"You'll go?"

"Sure I will, once I know where the hangman's tree is located. Stroll with me, Hamp. I want to take another look at the foundry."

CHAPTER THREE

The Abaddon Cannon Foundry was a massive, rectangular building with a steeply angled roof dominated by three tall chimney stacks that constantly belched black smoke. The steel frame structure was sheathed with sheets of corrugated iron that had once been painted red but then faded to a dirty brown color, blackened with streaks of soot. There were a dozen outbuildings. The two largest were the dormitory and the adjoining canteen. Railroad tracks lay on the west side of the building where a loading dock was located and the line headed all the way into Old Mexico. Abaddon cannons cast in iron and bronze were considered the best in the world and served in the artilleries of all the European powers as well as the Chinese Imperial Army and many South American republics.

It was said that old Queen Victoria, on being introduced to a 9-pounder Abaddon cannon that had recently caused great execution among a native army, patted the barrel and declared that the artillery piece was "one of her most precious children." This caused one of the queen's more irreverent regiments of artillery to call their Abaddon 9-pounders *Vickie's Bastards*, until using that term was made punishable by court-martial.

In bad weather, rain fell around the foundry dirty with soot and the building's sulfur, hot tar, and smoked ham stench permeated the plains country for miles in every direction. It would be no exaggeration to call the factory an annex of hell, as many of its unfortunate occupants did.

Day and night, armed guards surrounded the foundry. Four of them gathered in front of the main entrance and gave Shawn and Sedley hard, unfriendly stares. The men had the look of brawlers and in a scrap, they'd be a handful.

"I don't think we're wanted here," Sedley said under his breath.

"Seems like," Shawn said. " I wish the place had glass walls. It would make finding Manuel Cantrell a hell of a lot easier."

"If he's even there. He might just as likely be down Mexicali way sparking some pretty señorita."

"Maybe the old lady can tell us something."

"Yeah, she'll tell us that our boy Manuel is sparking some señorita—"

"Down Mexicali way," Shawn finished. "I get the point, Hamp."

"Uh-oh. I think we've got trouble. Sure glad I went back to the hotel for my revolver."

The four guards—one of them the blond kid with the reckless eyes from the saloon—crossed the rutted wagon road outside the foundry, Winchesters in their hands. They walked toward Shawn and Sedley, kicking up dust with every step.

The sun was high and the day was hot. Their leader, a well-built bruiser wearing a bowler hat and goggles, red suspenders holding up his pants, leveled his rifle at Shawn. "What the hell are you doing here?"

"Admiring your fine factory," Shawn answered. "It's truly a wonder to behold. I bet you make some real nice cannons in there."

"Don't tell me any damned lies," Suspenders said. "You're spying."

"Spying on what? All I see is a building the size of a small mountain and four hardcases set to guard it."

"Only four hardcases, is it? Look across the road, bully boy."

Shawn did. Another five riflemen stood in line, their rifles trained on him and Sedley.

"Seems like you got the drop on us, so we'll be on our way," Shawn said. "We'll come back another day when you're in a more hospitable frame of mind."

"You were warned to stay away from the foundry," the big man said. "Better you'd left and shook the dust of Big Buck off your boots, Mr. O'Brien. You were told the man you hope to find doesn't work at Abaddon. Maybe you just don't hear so good."

Shawn frowned. "You have my name. Who are you?"

"What difference does it make?"

"I might meet you in a saloon one day. I'll buy you a drink and we'll talk about the old happy times we had in Big Buck."

"Name's Blaine Keeners, but I'll never drink with a fine setup gent like you, not when it would take me a year to save enough to match the coat like the one you're wearing."

"He thinks we're trash, Blaine," the towhead said, grinning. "I can see it in his eyes."

"Trash is it, mister high and mighty?" Keeners said.

"You said it, not me." Shawn never saw it coming. He had expected Keeners to make a pistol play of some kind, but it was the towheaded kid who moved.

He grinned and fired from the hip, and Shawn felt that he'd just been hit on the right side of his head with a sledgehammer.

Suddenly the ground rushed up to meet him and he fell facedown in the dirt. He heard the sound of a Colt—Sedley getting off a shot—then boots slammed into his face and ribs and he was lost in a world of pain. He tried to fight to his feet, but a kick to the face put him down again. *Thud! Thud! Thud!* Boots pounded into him.

Mercifully, the ground opened up under him and Shawn found himself tumbling headlong into the bloodred depths of a bottomless pit.

Shawn O'Brien woke to the concerned face of an angel. For a moment, he thought it was Judith, his dead wife, welcoming him to eternity. As his vision cleared, he realized it was not Judith, but another woman, just as beautiful but not an English rose, rather a dark-eyed señorita with tender hands.

A man's voice said, "I thought he was done for. It's a miracle he survived after the beating he took."

Shawn recognized the voice of Ambrose Hellen the bartender. Then he heard a croak, like a lime green frog beside a pool, and it took him a moment to realize that it came from his own throat.

"He's far gone," the woman said. "I hope I can bring him back."

"Do what you can, Maria," Hellen said. "If God wills it, O'Brien will pull through . . . or he won't."

Shawn raised his head and tried to talk again, his broken lips working.

The woman said, "Hush now. We can talk later." She lifted Shawn's head and helped him drink something bitter from an earthen cup. "Now you will sleep. The herbs will lower your fever but they may make you dream."

She was right. Shawn lowered his battered head and immediately fell deep into troubled slumber . . .

A moon as thin as a slice of cucumber hung high above England's Dartmoor Swamp, its wan light glittering on the hoarfrost that enameled every tree, bush, and blade of grass.

Shawn O'Brien's breath smoked in the air as he turned to Sir James Lovell and said, "Did you bring your revolver?"

His father-in-law, wearing a caped riding cloak and top hat, nodded. "I have an Enfield, my old service revolver."

"Then keep it close. I have a feeling that before this night is out you may need it."

Alarm showed in Sir James's face, but he said nothing. Under the shadow of his hat brim, his eyes were haunted.

Shawn rose in the stirrups and studied the bridle path though the marsh. In the moonlight, it looked like a twisting white ribbon fallen from a woman's hair. "The tracks of

Judith's horse are headed west as though she headed straight for the tor. We'll search there first."

"Shawn, Drago Castle is a couple miles west of the tor," Sir James said. "Judith may have been overtaken by darkness and headed to the castle to spend the night. She and Lady Harcourt have been friends since childhood."

"The tor first." Shawn's face was grim, lines of concern cutting deep like wires. "If I was an escaped convict, that's where I'd hole up. From the top of the hill, a man could hide among the rocks and scout the moor for miles around."

"There are other tors on the moor, Shawn."

"I know. And I'll search each and every one of them."

Sir James reached inside his coat and produced his pocket watch. "It's almost midnight. There are storm clouds coming in from the north. Soon it will be too dark to see."

"Then let's press on. Now every minute counts." Shawn saw the exhaustion on his father-in-law's face, the deep shadows under his eyes and in the hollows of his cheeks. Sir James was no longer young and the search for his daughter was taking a toll on him.

But he was a proud man and it didn't enter into Shawn's thinking to suggest he turn tail and head for home. Sir James Lovell would be wounded deeply by such urging, a terrible slight to his honor that he would neither forget nor forgive.

"I reckon we should leave the horses here and cover the rest of the way to the tor on foot. The police inspector said the convicts had raided the prison armory before they broke out, and they may have rifles."

Sir James nodded. "A sound plan, Shawn. We're sitting ducks on horseback. Damned Afghans taught the British army that lesson."

As gently as he could, Shawn asked, "How are you holding up?"

"Oh I can't complain, old boy. Elderly English gentlemen with weak hearts love to take midnight strolls on dangerous moors in the middle of winter, don't yo know?"

Shawn managed a slight smile. "To say nothing of hunting down dangerous escaped convicts."

"Oh, yes, I'd quite forgotten about those," Sir James said.

But he hadn't, of course . . . and neither had Shawn O'Brien.

Both had a feeling, for better or worse, the dreary, dreadful night would end with men dead on the ground.

The tor was a rugged outcropping of bare granite rock that rose fifteen hundred feet above the surrounding mire. Scoured by the winds, snows, and rains of many centuries, the treeless hill looked like the skeletal backbone of an enormous hound. Gray mist hung above the marshes like smoke and ice fringed the mud puddles. The hard night air was saw-toothed with frost and painful to breathe.

Shawn suddenly stopped, took a knee, and closely studied the bridle path. "Whatever happened, happened right here." His face was bitter. "Damn them. Damn them to hell."

Even Sir James, never schooled in the tracker's art, could read the sign plain. "Judith was dragged from her horse at this spot. There are boot prints of several assailants." He looked like a man who'd just read his own death notice in The Times of London.

Shawn nodded. "Three men. Judging by the depths of their boot prints and the lengths of their strides, all of them are tall and heavy."

"Just the kind who could kill their guards and escape from a prison," Sir James said.

Shawn nodded, studying the tracks, most already obscured by snow and ice. "They dragged Judith toward the tor and one of them led her horse."

Sir James suddenly looked old and tired. "Shawn, there are two hundred tors on Dartmoor. This may not be the one."

"It's the one." Even in the gloom, Shawn's eyes gleamed with blue fire. "There can be no other."

Sir James looked confused. He'd never understood, or quite believed, the Celtic gift of second sight.

Cursing the ability, Shawn did not consider it a gift, for it imposed a terrible burden—the faculty to sense death, be it near or far. He felt death reach out to him, its thin fingers as cold as the night, and he knew in that single, awful moment that his wife was no longer alive.

Sir James Lovell watched the change in Shawn's face, saw his son-in-law's skin draw tight to the bone, the mouth become a hard line. Shawn had a fearful, haunted look, as though a wild, ancient war song heard in a dream had intruded into his waking consciousness.

And then the older man knew what Shawn knew. "We're too late, aren't we, Shawn? My daughter is dead, isn't she?"

Shawn had no answer, or at least none he wished to make. He opened his coat and drew his Colt from the leather. With numb fingers he fed a round into the empty chamber that had been under the hammer and holstered the revolver again. "Let's get it done."

Sir James remembered words like those from his time in the West, said by hard men committed to following the code of an eye for an eye, a tooth for a tooth, no matter the cost or the consequences.

When uttered by a man like Shawn O'Brien, there was no turning back. Not now. Not ever.

It was Sir James who first saw the man walking along the path through the mire, appearing through the mist like a gray ghost.

Shawn, the instincts of the gunfighter honed sharp in him, saw the older man's eyes narrow and he swung around to face the danger, the Colt coming up fast.

"No shooting!" the stranger yelled, his voice croaking from cold and frost. "It's only harmless old Ben Lestrange as ever was. I mean harm to no one but goodwill to all."

"What the hell are you doing here?" Shawn growled. "I could've plugged you square." He knew the ragged, bent old man was not one of the convicts, but he wanted to kill him real bad. It was as though an unwelcome stranger had walked into a private funeral.

"What am I doing here, ye say. And I answer that old Ben has walked this moor, man and boy, for nigh on fifty year." Lestrange laid the pack he carried on his back at his feet and winked. "I know the secret places and where the ancient bodies lie buried."

"Did you see men on the tor?" Sir James asked, his breath smoking in the frigid air. The moon was high and white as bone. "Come now, man, speak up."

Lestrange's wrinkled face, weathered to the color of mahogany, took on a sly look. "What old Ben seen was a dead 'un, squire."

"Where?" Shawn commanded. "Was it a man or a woman? Tell us."

"At the foot of the tor. It wasn't a man." Lestrange shook his head. "Oh dear no, she were a lady." He reached inside his filthy greatcoat and brought out a silver chain with a heart-shaped locket. "Took this from her, and if it's what

you're wanting, well, it's old Ben's, not yours. Finders keepers, that's the way of Dartmoor."

"Let me see that." Sir James reached out his gloved hand.

Lestrange turned away, the locket pressed against his upper chest. "It's old Ben's. Why would a fine gentleman like yourself want to steal what's mine?"

"I warn you, my man, let me examine the locket or I'll have you in the dock at the next assizes, charged with vagrancy and theft from the dead," Sir James said. "You'll end your days at a penal colony in the West Indies."

Lestrange angrily shoved the locket at Sir James. "Here, take it and damn you for a thieving toff."

Sir James ignored that and examined the locket, turning it over in his gloved hands.

"Is it Judith's?" Shawn asked. "It's not something I've seen her wear."

"No, it's not Judith's. The chain is silver, but the locket is cheap, made of tin." Sir James opened the locket, turned it to the pale moonlight, and stared at it for a long while.

"What do you see?" Shawn asked, stepping closer.

"Two people and I recognize their likenesses." He held out the open locket to Shawn. "It's George Simpson the blacksmith and his wife Martha. Their daughter Mavis was abducted from the village shortly after the convicts escaped."

Shawn swung on Ben Lestrange. "Take us to the girl."

"I told you, she's a dead 'un. You need have no truck with her, young gentleman."

"Take us to her," Shawn said. "Show us where she lies."

Lestrange looked sly. "Do I get my chain back?"

"Here." Sir James dropped the locket into Lestrange's hand. "I rather fancy that Mavis has no further use for it."

The old man grinned, knuckled his forehead, and picked

up his pack. "Follow me, gent. Mind you don't step into the mire"—he cackled—"or you'll end up dead 'uns like poor Mavis Simpson, God rest her."

The girl's plump, naked body lay tangled in a gorse bush at the base of the tor. That she'd been badly abused and raped was obvious.

"Found her lying there," Lestrange said. "There's frost all over her and that's why at first I thought she was a silver woman. There are some who will pay plenty for a woman made out of silver."

Shawn's bleak eyes searched the top of the hill, then he lowered them to the tramp. "Go away. Get the hell out of here."

"Can you spare me a shilling, squire? Then you'll never see old Ben again."

"No, Shawn!" Sir James placed his hand on the younger man's gun arm. "Killing this poor, demented creature won't bring Judith back to you."

For a moment, Shawn teetered on the edge, breathing hard. Finally he brought himself under control. To Lestrange he said again, "Just . . . go away."

Sir James fished in his pants pocket and came up with a coin. "Here, Lestrange, take this and go. You've done us a service."

The tramp stared big-eyed at the gold sovereign in his palm and knuckled his forehead. "Thankee. You're a real gent, as old Ben knowed when he first set eyes on you." After a quick, frightened glance at Shawn, the old man shuffled quickly down the path, the moonlight casting his rippling shadow on the frozen earth.

"I'd say the girl was murdered and then her body was thrown from the crest of the tor," Sir James said.

Shawn nodded. *"Seems like."*

The older man was quiet for a few moments as though he was taking time to choose his words carefully. Finally he said, *"Shawn, let me go alone. I can use a revolver quite well."*

"Why do you say that?"

"Because"—Sir James searched for the words—*"because I don't want you to see Judith like"*—his eyes moved to the girl's stark body—*"like her."*

"You're her father. Do you think that you can stand it?"

"No. No, I can't. But I'm an old man. You are young, Shawn. If you don't keep seeing one terrible picture in your mind, you can recover from this."

"Recover if I don't see what happened to my wife? Is that it?"

Sir James floundered, his face strained. *"Something like that."* He shook his head. *"Be damned to it all, Shawn, I just don't have the words."*

Shawn looked at the sky. *"It will rain soon and we'll lose the moon to clouds."*

"Then we both must face what's before us and drink grief's cup in full measure," Sir James said. *"Are you sure there can be no sparing you?"*

"No, I can't be spared. There's no stepping away from it."

Sir James nodded. *"Then let us climb the hill together."*

The way up the tor was difficult, especially in darkness and a cold, ticking rain. Shawn and Sir James scrambled through gorse bushes and grabbed the twisted limbs of stunted birch trees to navigate the icy slope. Every now and then, the moon entered a break in the black clouds and afforded a view of the granite rocks at the crest of the tor. Nothing moved and no sound carried in the rising wind.

After fifteen minutes of climbing, the top of the hill still seemed a long way off and Sir James stopped on a flat ledge of rock to take a breather.

The rain had turned to a slashing sleet, carried on the knifing north wind. The night grew colder and darker. After scanning the tor, he pulled the collar of his coat closer around his face, like a turtle retreating into its shell "There's a wild sheep on the tor. Would it remain there with armed men around?"

"I don't know," Shawn said. "Show me."

"There," Sir James said, pointing.

Shawn saw what the older man had seen, but with younger, farseeing eyes. Suddenly, everything inside him died. He looked broken.

That was no sheep on the tor.

It was the slender white body of Lady Judith Lovell, spread-eagled on a flat slab, a naked sacrifice to the lusts of men who were not fit to breathe the same air as the rest of humanity.

"Oh, my God," Sir James whispered, reading Shawn's face. He buried his face in gloved hands. "Oh, my God . . ."

Shawn did not cry out in his pain and rage. He was silent, filled with an icy, calm, his hands steady, as is the way of the gunfighting man when there's killing to be done. Without waiting to see if Sir James followed, he climbed the hill.

Shawn kissed his dead wife's lips. They were cold and lifeless as marble. Pain beyond pain knifed through him and he wanted to turn his face to the torn sky and scream his grief.

Biting sleet cartwheeling around him, he stood in

moon-splashed darkness, gun in hand, and watched the dull orange glow of a fire among the rocks ahead of him.

He was aware of Sir James stepping beside him. The man no longer wore his coat. Shawn accepted what that implied without comment.

Then in a whisper he said, "They're camped out among the rocks, sheltered from the wind."

Sir James nodded.

"This will be real close," Shawn said. "When you get your work in, aim low for the belly. A bullet in the gut will stop any man."

Again Sir James nodded and said nothing. His eyes were lost in shadow.

His face a stiff, joyless mask, Shawn said, "Then let's get it done."

Their steps were silent on the slushy, uneven ground. Half hidden behind the shifting shroud of the sleet, the two men advanced on the rocks. Shawn smelled wood smoke, the heavy odor of wet earth, and the sword blade tang of the sleet itself, cold and raw and honed sharp.

Three convicts sat between a pair of massive boulders, and had pulled over their heads a makeshift roof of thin sheets of black shale. Vicious predators who for too long had stalked a peaceful, pastured land with impunity, they were dressed in blue canvas jackets, pants of the same color, and heavy, steel-studded boots.

A draw fighter schooled by draw fighters, Shawn O'Brien stood above them. He was no pale, puny, prattling prelate who'd just watched them rape his wife and loot his village church's poor box. He was death.

Startled, the convicts dived for the Martini-Henry rifles propped against the boulders . . . but they never made it.

At a distance of less than six feet, Shawn O'Brien didn't miss.

He thumbed three fast shots and all three men went down, hit hard. He scored two headshots, killing the convicts instantly. The face of the third crashed into the fire, erupting flame, sparks, and a scream of sudden agony. Then silence. His booted feet gouged the ground as he cringed away from the visitation from hell. He had taken Shawn's bullet in the throat. The side of his neck between earlobe and shoulder was a mass of red, mangled meat that pumped blood.

Sir James, gun in hand, stepped beside Shawn and looked into the smoke-streaked hideout.

In a wet, gurgling voice the wounded convict screamed to the older man, "Help me! I'm hurt bad and I need a doctor!"

Sir James, in shock, turned to Shawn. "He says he needs a doctor."

Shawn nodded, thumbed back the hammer of his Colt, and shot the man between the eyes. "He just got one."

Shawn spent the rest of the long night with his dead wife in his arms, holding her close to his chest as the slanting sleet bladed around him.

Come the dawn, Sir James, his face gray as ash, gently tried to take his daughter from Shawn's arms. "I'll bring the horses."

"No. I don't want the horses." Shawn lifted Judith's body, her face as beautiful in death as it had been in life. "I'll carry her. I'll carry my wife home."

He turned his face to the black, uncaring sky and called out in terrible agony, "Judith! Judith! Judith!"

* * *

"It's all right, Shawn. I'm with you."

Shawn pried open his swollen eyes. The dark-eyed woman bent over him. A lamp burned somewhere in darkness and spread a dim orange light. "I . . . it was a dream. . . ."

"Yes. It was a bad dream. Banish those visions of the past from your mind and sleep now. Sleep, Shawn. Sleep."

Shawn O'Brien closed his eyes and knew no more.

CHAPTER FOUR

Jays quarreled in a tree, kicking up a fuss and waking Shawn O'Brien. He heard the distant sound of a clanging locomotive bell as a fly buzzed around his face. It was only when he lifted a hand to swat the pest away that he realized how badly he was hurt. His hands, arms . . . his entire body ached and the pain in his chest when he breathed warned him that he could have broken ribs. Only one of his eyes would open, but it was enough to tell him that he lay in a tent of some kind. Its canvas flapped in a strong breeze, the oil lamp hanging from the ridgepole moved back and forth, and the glass chimney chinked quietly.

He tried to sit up, but the effort was too much for him. Defeated, he groaned and lay back again, weak as a day-old kitten. He had no memory of his dream. It had come and gone like a mist.

The tent flap opened and a woman stooped inside. She wore a black taffeta skirt that rustled, black high-heeled ankle boots, and a boned red corset tied up the front with a black lace. Her hair, dark and glossy as ink, tumbled over her bare shoulders and the top of her breasts. Her wide, expressive mouth was bright red, as though she'd been eating strawberries. She smiled, her teeth white. "You are with us again, Shawn."

"I reckon. What's left of me at least."

"How do you feel?"

"As bad as I look." Then, "Hamp?"

"He's outside tending to the coffee. He wasn't beaten as badly as you."

"Why didn't they finish me?" Shawn asked.

"I would say because your father is rich and influential and you have Jacob O'Brien as a brother. They want you gone, not dead."

"Are you—"

"I'm the old lady who bumped into you on the boardwalk."

"Then you're Doña Maria Cantrell?"

"None other. But please call me Maria."

Shawn tried to think, his head reeling. "Old lady, young lady . . . I don't understand."

"It's simple, really," Maria said. "I came to Big Buck and started to ask questions about my brother, but I was told to go back to Mexico or I'd find a grave out in the thorn brush. I left and came here, but I still go into town disguised as an old crone."

"And have you learned anything?"

"No. That's why I wanted to talk with you."

Shawn winced. "All I know is that whoever the man is who owns the cannon foundry isn't partial to people poking their noses into his business."

"Manuel is there. I know he is. For weeks Abaddon was all he wanted to talk about. He said he could make his fortune and return to Mexico a rich man. He said he would restore the Cantrell family's honor and fortune."

Isolated in his own pain and misery, Shawn made no answer.

Maria continued. "Once, the Cantrell rancho was the biggest in all of Mexico. My father and mother drove in a carriage drawn by four fine horses and our cattle numbered in the tens of thousands. A hundred guests at a time were entertained at our hacienda and my father would have the fountains flow with wine. The name Cantrell was honored and respected throughout the land."

"What happened?" Shawn grimaced. It even hurt to talk.

"My father gambled it all away. When he was young, he was lucky with the cards and dice, but as he grew older his luck changed. It took several years, but we lost everything. My mother died from nothing more serious than a summer cold, the doctor said, but it was from a broken heart. A year later, when he finally lost the hacienda, my father took his own life. I use the title Doña before my name because my mother always did, but I have as little right to it as any peon."

"And Manuel hopes to change all that?" Shawn asked.

Maria nodded. "He said there was big money to be made in the cannon foundry, enough to give us a new start. It was the foolish dream of an eighteen-year-old boy. To restore what we had would take millions of pesos. If you lost Dromore, how much would it take to rebuild what you have now?"

"A fortune, I guess." Shawn's voice was barely a whisper. "Unless my pa was content to start small."

"I would be content with that, but Manuel has big plans." Then, slowly, as though a memory was painful, she said, "I have to tell you something, Shawn. A week before he left Mexico, my brother killed a man who wished to use me for his pleasure. Manuel took it as an affront to the Cantrell honor, sought out the man, and shot him. How many more men will he challenge until he himself is killed?"

"Maria, don't build houses on a bridge we haven't crossed yet," Shawn said. "Let's find him first."

"You've done enough for me as it is. I will find Manuel."

Shawn shook his head, and then as pain spiked at him, he wished he hadn't. "I'm not doing this for you, Maria. I'm doing it because my brother asked me to. The O'Brien family loyalties also run deep and there's no getting away from that."

Hamp Sedley ducked into the tent. His left arm was in a makeshift sling and his battered face looked like a strawberry pie that had just been stepped on by a drunken baker. "How are you feeling, Shawn?"

"Terrible. And you?"

"Can't complain. Maria is an excellent nurse." He held out a tin cup. "Here, drink this. It's beef tea."

"What's beef tea?"

"A chunk of beef brought to the boil and simmered for hours. Drain off the meat, add a little salt and pepper to the liquid and you've got yourself beef tea. I read one time that Lillie Langtry swears by it. Says it brings roses to her cheeks."

Maria supported Shawn's head as he sipped from the cup. "Tastes like ordinary old beef broth to me."

"Don't tell Lillie that," Sedley said. "She calls it beef tea because that's what old Queen Vic calls it. Or so they say."

"The arm, Hamp. What happened?" Shawn asked.

"After the towhead kid fired his rifle I drew and got a shot off. I didn't hit anybody though. Next thing I know I'm on the ground and a bunch of big Irish micks are laying the boot into me. Ambrose Hellen put an end to it and brought what was left of us here."

"He's the only person I trust in Big Buck," Maria said. "He's a good man."

"So what about the arm?" Shawn asked again.

"It isn't broken. Just badly bruised."

"Hamp, I want you to do something for me that I'm in no shape to do for myself."

"Name it. By times, I'm a real obliging feller."

Shawn named it and Sedley's hair stood on end.

CHAPTER FIVE

As the clocks of Big Buck chimed midnight, Hamp Sedley made his way across the waste ground at the east of town. The night was cloudy and there was little moonlight. He walked carefully, calculating each step. In the distance, the sky was on fire above the Abaddon foundry and thick columns of smoke stood dirty gray against the darkness. The Abaddon thugs had taken his Colt and the weight of Maria's derringer in his pocket did little to reassure him. If he ran into trouble, he could do little damage with a belly gun unless he was hugging close.

Coyotes hunting near the town yipped into the night as he angled toward the cemetery. "Look for the whitewashed pillars of the gate," Maria had told him, but his eyes were badly swollen and he saw little but a curtain of darkness ahead. He stumbled on, walking though the canyons of the witching hour like a man lost. But he could hear just fine.

And the man hidden in the gloom stated his intentions loud and clear enough. "Hold up right there, sonny, or I'll blow your damn head off with this here Greener cannon I got in my hands. She's both wife and child to me and I don't miss with her."

Sedley heard grass rustle underfoot, steps coming toward him.

"What you doing out here at this unchristian hour of the night when the hurting dead walk?"

Frozen in his tracks, Sedley answered, "I'm looking for the graveyard."

"Hell, boy, you're standing on it," the hidden man said.

"I couldn't see the gateway," Sedley explained.

"That's because the gate ain't here. It's a fair piece down thataway to the west. What you doing here? Answer plain and short and make no fancy moves. I ain't what you might call a trusting feller."

"The answer is that I'm here to find a grave. Then I aim to find a shovel and plan to dig up a body."

"There ain't no shovels around. Where did you expect to find one?"

"Figured there had to be a caretaker's hut or something."

"Well, there ain't and I'm the caretaker. Here, you ain't one of them resurrectionists are you, digging up bodies and selling them to medical men?"

A small, skinny old man dressed in an ancient gray overcoat and bowler hat stepped out of the shadows. He held a scattergun so that the muzzles pointed at Sedley's belly. Alarmed by the voices, an owl questioned the night and at a distance, a terrified thing squealed, a small death in the darkness.

"I'm no body snatcher. I'm a gambler, born and bred." Sedley stood in a glimmer of moonlight. "And

I'd be obliged if you pointed that there widowmaker somewhere else."

"Maybe I will and maybe I won't," the old man said. "What body was you interested in, like?"

"The man carried out of the Abaddon foundry yesterday."

"He was buried this morning just after sunup. I seen him. You work for them Abaddon people?"

"No, I don't."

"May be just as well because iffen you did, I'd feel inclined to let you have both barrels in the gut. Just lettin' you know."

"Look at my face," Sedley said. "Abaddon toughs did this."

"It ain't pretty."

"Yeah, well my friend's face is even worse."

"What name does he go by?"

"Shawn O'Brien. He's out of the New Mexico Territory."

"And what's your handle?"

"Hamp Sedley."

"You said you're a gambling man."

"Yeah, but I'm running from a three-year losing streak. So far, it's been catching up with me."

"It happens. I know an O'Brien from up New Mexico way, big Jake O'Brien. He's two shades meaner than the devil himself but plays the piano real sweet."

"Jake is Shawn's brother," Sedley said.

The shotgun barrel lowered and the old man said, "Name's Crop Hermon. I ain't really the caretaker here, but I camp nearby. It's real quiet and well away from the noise and stink of the damn foundry."

"You say you saw the dead man this morning?" Sedley asked.

"Yeah, I did. But you come with me afore you break a leg or something. I got coffee on the bile."

Crop Hermon had set up his camp within a stand of wild oak near a thin-running stream. He'd made himself a lean-to from timber scraps, canvas, and whatever else he could find. His coffee was good and his information better.

"I seen the body after Dorian Steggles rolled it out of a sheet and it laid there all naked on the ground." Herman's eyes met Sedley's in the firelight. "I fit Yankees, Comanche, Apache, and one time a Ute nearly took my hair up in the Yampa River country, so I've seen my share of dead men. But that Abaddon feller couldn't rightly be called a man, more like he was a living skeleton when he was alive." Hermon took time to light his pipe. "Look at your wrist, gambling man. Well, his arm was no bigger around than that. His jaws were so sunken you'd have thought he was grinning and his ribs showed, stood out all in a row, if you catch my drift."

"What did you think when you saw him, Crop?"

"Well, here's how I saw it. Either that man was mighty sick with a cancer or he'd been starved to death. There ain't no other explanation for how he looked, at least none that I can come up with."

"How many Abaddon workers are buried in the cemetery?" Sedley asked.

"A handful, just to make things look good. Afore

he disappeared, I had some talk with Sheriff Asa Chapman. He was a nice, older feller who was sheriff here even before Abaddon got built. Asa told me that a lot of fellers die in the foundry and that most go up the chimney, some of them only half-dead when they was thrown into the furnaces. God rest him, Asa planned to investigate and that was the last anyone ever saw or heard of him. That's the reason I hide out here. If Abaddon finds out that Asa spoke with me, I'm a dead man."

Sedley smiled. "You're taking a risk telling me, Crop."

"If you're a friend of Jake O'Brien's brother then you're true blue in my book, Hamp. He's a wild one is Jake, but honest as the day is long when it comes to ordinary folks. Ah, here's Trigger. Where have you been, boy?"

A black-and-white collie dog emerged from the darkness, greeted Sedley politely, then jumped on his master's lap and smothered him with sloppy kisses.

"I smell jackrabbit on your breath, boy," Hermon said. "You just ate supper, did ye?"

Feeling like an intruder, Sedley rose to his feet. "Thank you for the coffee and information, Crop. Now I got to be getting back."

"One word afore you go, gambling man," Harmon said, talking over his dog's head. "Jed Rose arrived in town yesterday by the three o'clock train, him and Hank Locket, the one they call the El Reno Kid."

"Who are they?"

"Better ask Shawn O'Brien. His brother knows them both." Hermon rubbed Trigger's ears and said, "They ain't nice people."

CHAPTER SIX

It was two in the morning when Hamp Sedley, a judicious man, stopped walking toward the tent glowing a dull orange and called out, "It's me. Coming in." He bent and entered the tent.

Shawn lay on his back, his battered face showing the signs of the beating he'd taken. Maria Cantrell continued her vigil over him. She wore a filmy black nightgown and a pocket watch on a silver chain hung around her neck. Her long legs were tucked under her as she dabbed at Shawn's face with a wet cloth.

"What happened, Hamp?" Shawn grimaced as he got up on one elbow. "Did you learn anything?"

"Yeah, there was no shovel left around for digging up dead folks," Sedley said.

"I wasn't in my right mind when I suggested that. I'm still not. Too many kicks to the head, I reckon."

"Well, I did learn something. I spoke to a man who saw the body before it was buried." Sedley told of his encounter with Crop Hermon and the man's description of the dead Abaddon worker. "You were right, Shawn. It looked to Crop that the man had been worked to death on mighty short rations."

Shawn nodded. "Slave labor. I had a feeling that was the case."

"It seems like men enter the Abaddon foundry but none ever come out again. A few of the dead are buried in the cemetery, but Hermon said most go up the chimney." Sedley lightly touched Maria's hand. "I'm sorry."

"We don't know for sure Manuel is there," Shawn said.

"He's there," Maria said. "I know he is."

"Crop told me something else, Shawn," Sedley said. "He says two men arrived in town yesterday, said you might know them. Jed Rose is one of them, but I can't recollect the other feller's name."

"Does Hank Locket ring a bell?" Shawn asked. "Sometimes goes by the El Reno Kid?"

Sedley's face brightened. "Yeah, that's him. Crop says your brother Jake knows them."

"My brother Jake knows everybody. Rose and Locket work as a team. They're guns for hire and surefire killers. A couple years back, Jake shot Jed Rose in Paddy Murphy's saloon in a town called Gray-cott up in the Panhandle. I don't remember all the details, but Rose was laid up for a three month and barely made it through. He was one dangerous hombre before he got shot and now he's a sight worse. As for Locket, he's fast on the draw and shoot. Last I heard, he'd killed eight men, but he's proba-bly added to that total since. Locket is poison, a man without a conscience or a shred of decency."

Sedley frowned. "Why are they here, you reckon? Because of us?"

"Maybe, but I doubt it. I think the Abaddon toughs made it pretty clear that they don't fear us."

"Then who?" Maria's gown had slipped off her beautiful shoulders and ringlets of jet-black hair fell over her forehead. At any time and in any place, she would be considered a breathtakingly beautiful woman.

"Rose and Locket are contract killers, very expensive." Shawn looked to Maria. "Maria, who else knows you're here?"

"No one except Ambrose Hellen."

"And you trust him?"

"Yes, I do. Shawn, are you trying to tell me that the hired guns might be after me?"

"It's possible. Unlikely maybe, but just possible."

"Now you're scaring me, Shawn," Maria said, her lovely black eyes haunted. "I mean, really scaring me."

"Best we all stay scared for a spell," Shawn said. "It will make us more careful."

The telescope was located in a crow's nest at the very top of the Abaddon building, but set in a lofty pillar away from the worst of the smoke and heat. Round like a castle turret, supported by massive steel beams, the nest could rotate on its base so that the brass telescope, large as an Abaddon cannon, could be used to scan the terrain for miles around in all directions.

The gray-haired man at the eyepiece pushed his hat and goggles higher on his head and intently studied the ground to the east, in particular the cemetery. After a couple minutes, he smiled. "Good, the foreman Anstruther Breens was right. There is a man living up there."

Breens had said he saw another man with him, though because of the darkness and the distance involved he couldn't be sure. The big foreman had stepped out to smoke a cigar, not scout for spies. Still, it was probably nothing, just a couple tramps looking for a place to sleep for the night. But it was an irritation, and Caleb Perry could not afford to be irritated, not when there was so much at stake.

Perry stepped to the speaking tube and told his secretary to send up the two guns he'd just hired. He'd meet them in his office just off the foundry's main gantry.

Jed Rose and Hank Locket seemed dazed when they were ushered into Perry's office. Abaddon had that effect on people. It was a smoke-filled, massive black and scarlet cave with enormously high ceilings, massive, flaming furnaces, boilers three times the size of those on oceangoing steamships, the steady overhead passage of gigantic cannons amid a hellish cacophony of clanging, roaring, hissing clamor that could make sane men mad. Among it all toiled starved, half-naked laborers, their tight skins gleaming with sweat, driven on to ever-greater efforts by the brawny foremen with their whips and billy clubs and savage faces.

"Ah, gentlemen, how nice of you to visit. Can I interest you in a refreshment?" Perry smiled, revealing canines as large and gleaming as those of a lobo wolf.

"The preferred tipple of the Abaddon foundry is black rum, but you may have anything you wish."

The gunmen opted for rum and Perry filled a pair of fluted glasses to the brim. "Please be seated." He looked over his latest hires and liked what he saw.

Rose was a tall, gaunt man with the eyes of a carrion eater. Like Locket he carried only one gun, a plain blue Colt in a shoulder holster. Locket affected the dress and demeanor of a country parson and wore spats over his buttoned ankle boots. Both men had been given goggles as a protection against flying sparks and they hung loosely around their necks.

"I have a job for you gentlemen, a killing," Perry said. "It's hardly worthy of your talents, but it will be the first of many, I'll be bound."

"Bless you, sir, and we are willing and able to do your bidding. For us, no job is too large or too small," Locket said in the pulpit drone of a preacher. "When justice is done, it is a joy to the righteous but terror to evildoers." The gunman smiled. "I quote from the Book of Proverbs."

Rose said, "Who do you want us to kill?"

"No one important. Just a vagrant who seems to be living in the cemetery," Perry said. "He might be a spy but probably not. Still I don't want to take any chances. I have much at stake, as you gentlemen will learn."

"When?" Rose asked.

"This evening would be fine."

Rose nodded. "Then we'll get it done. A straight-up kill? No fire? No cutting?"

"Just blow his brains out. I've got nothing personal against the man, whoever he is. We'll reserve the torture for people I don't like, and that includes just about everybody."

An adjoining door opened and a woman stepped into the office. She wore a tight corset of brown leather, laced at the sides, over a short frilled dress and knee-high boots adorned with half-a-dozen brass buckles. A mane of blond hair fell over her naked shoulders and pushed-up breasts and her scarlet fingernails were painted the same shade as her pretty, pouting mouth.

"Ah, here's Lizzie at last," Perry said, clapping his hands. "Gentlemen, may I introduce you to Miss Lizzie Skates? She'll entertain you while I get on with my paperwork. Oh, and good hunting tonight. It should make for some fine sport."

CHAPTER SEVEN

To say that big Jacob O'Brien was irritated would be something of an understatement. In fact, he was boiling mad. Combined with his uncertain temper and deadly gun skills, that made for a dangerous mix.

The rail journey from the New Mexico Territory had been ordeal enough. He'd kicked his heels in out-of-the-way rail stations in one-horse cow towns and waited for trains that were always hours late. That and eating bad food and drinking worse coffee took its toll on a man. And just as the train crossed the border into Texas, the locomotive had lurched to a clanking, steam-hissing halt.

And the guard had just stuck his head into the car and yelled, "Road agents! It's a holdup!"

Across from Jacob, a slender young girl in a gray silk travelling dress, a straw boater hat perched on her upswept auburn hair, looked back at the door, her pretty face alarmed. He rose to his feet. A big-shouldered, unshaven man dressed in whatever shabby duds he could patch together, he indicated the seat beside him and said, "Here, miss, sit by the window near me."

Intimidated by his bulk, rough-hewn face, and bristling black mustache, the girl hesitated. "Will . . . will the bandits rob us?"

"Not if you're sitting by me they won't," Jacob said.

A shot racketed from outside the train and the girl changed seats with amazing alacrity. She smelled of wildflowers.

Jacob liked that. "Now you just sit there real quiet and let me do the talking."

"Will there be more shooting?" the girl asked.

"Well, I guess that all depends on how the talking goes," Jacob said.

A few moments later, the door at the opposite end of the carriage crashed open and three armed men rushed inside, their lower faces covered by bandanas. One of the three carried a burlap sack. "All donations are welcome folks. Money, rings, watches, whatever you got. Come now, don't be shy."

The dozen or so passengers complained and threatened the robbers with the law, but the presence of Colts pointed at their heads soon silenced them and the sack began to fill.

Then came Jacob O'Brien's turn.

The man with the sack stared at Jacob for a while and then his mouth moved under the bandana. "Jake! Jake O'Brien! What the hell are you doing here?"

"Getting robbed, seems like."

Quickly pulling down his bandana before replacing

it again, the man said, "It's me, Jake. Elmer Oddlin as ever was."

"Hell, I thought you were still in the bank robbing profession," Jacob said.

Oddlin shook his head. "It's getting too crowded. It's becoming a game for amateurs and now the law is always on guard when strangers ride into a town. The glory days of Jesse and them are over."

"How's your ma and your brother Newt?" Jacob asked.

"Apart from the rheumatisms Ma's fine. Newt is back there robbing folks in another car. Who's the young lady?"

"My niece. I'm escorting her to a burg called Big Buck down the Pecos River way."

Oddlin lifted his hat. "Right pleased to meet you, miss. You sure are purty."

The girl blushed. "Thank you, sir."

Oddlin turned his head and called out to his two companions, "Hey, Sam, June, look who's here. It's Jake O'Brien, headed down to the Pecos country with a pretty gal."

A great deal of handshaking, backslapping and grinning followed. "We got to be going, Jake." After a moment's hesitation, Oddlin said, "Jake, I really hate to ask you this, but I'd be right honored if you could see your way clear to dropping something in the sack. It's a thing I could tell my grandkids one day."

"Gather around, kids, and let me tell you about the day I robbed Jacob O'Brien, huh?"

"Yeah. It would be a fine story to tell and robbing

you would be a great honor, Jake. Sam, June, ain't that right?"

"Sure is," Sam said. "It would be the acme of our outlaw career an' no mistake. And your ma would be so proud, ain't that so, Elmer?"

"Proud? Why she'd strut around like a gobbler at layin' time," Oddlin said.

"All right, just this once," Jacob said, raising his hands. "Don't shoot." He took a silver dollar from his shirt pocket and dropped it into the sack. "How's that?"

"Damn it all, Jake, it was perfect." Oddlin's eyes above the bandana were misted by tears. "I always said you was a white man through and through and as true blue as a man ever was."

"Well, good luck with the new profession, Elmer," Jacob said. "And give my regards to Newt and your ma."

"I sure will, Jake. And Newt will be right sorry he missed you. Good luck to you too, Jake. Good luck."

The girl got off at a whistle stop just south of the Texas border where she planned to care for an ailing aunt. She gave Jacob a kiss on the cheek before she left and that pleased him greatly.

Amid the hubbub generated by the robbed passengers and the placating talk of the guard, Jacob reread Maria Cantrell's letter for the hundredth time. Yes, the town was Big Buck, no mistake about that, and Shawn was probably already there. He'd sent his brother to do a job he should have done

himself, all the time knowing that Shawn was easily
led astray by a pretty face or a well-turned ankle and
could easily land himself in all kinds of trouble. But
during his last stay at Dromore, Jacob had buried
himself in a deep depression as all the demons that
haunted him returned to demand their due. He had
confined himself to his room, talked to no one, and
hit the bottle pretty hard.

Finally Luther Ironside, his father's grim old se-
gundo, had taken him aside. Jake gave some thought
to their conversation.

*"Jake, your pa won't tell you this, but I will. As I see it,
you got two choices: You either just give up now and blow
your brains out or you go to Texas and see what you've done
to Shawn. The decision is yours."*

*"You're telling me that I've cast a dark shadow over
Dromore long enough. Is that the way of it, Luther?"*

*"Damn right. That's the way of it," Luther said. "When
you were a boy, I'd have taken a willow switch to you before
now, but you've grown too old for that, so heed me. I've lived
long enough around Irishmen that some of how they think
and feel has rubbed off on me. Like your saintly mother, may
God rest her, I've had dreams, bad dreams that Shawn is in
trouble. For some reason, I was given a glimpse into hell, a
flaming, roaring place where the damned toil naked among
the fires. It's a dream no good Presbyterian man should
ever have."*

*Jacob nodded. "It's an Irish dream, all right, Luther, and
it speaks a prophecy to you in your sleep. It must have been
a terrible dream."*

"Yes, it was a terrible dream. Go to Texas Jake, and by the good God that made me, I pray you will not be too late."

Jacob had left Dromore that very day.

He shook off the memory, folded Maria's letter, and put it back into his pocket. "Damn this train. How much longer before I reach Big Buck?"

CHAPTER EIGHT

"Damn this lying on my back." Shawn O'Brien sat up and his world, shrunken to the four walls and roof of a tent, spun around him. The pain of his broken ribs stabbed at him and he decided he couldn't place a dime on any part of his body that didn't hurt.

Hamp Sedley was gathering firewood, planning to drag a bundle behind his horse, and Maria Cantrell had gone to bathe at the nearby creek. Left to himself, Shawn was determined to stand on his own two feet like a man should. It took him fifteen minutes to pull on his pants and stomp into his boots and by that time, he felt as though he was ninety years old and ailing. Buttoning on his shirt over his bandaged ribs was out of the question and bending to get through the tent flap took a good deal of thought before he attempted the task.

Finally he made it outside. Since his Colt had been taken, the Remington derringer that Sedley had left behind was in his pocket, but it offered little consolation. After the flat land stopped bucking and wheeling around him, Shawn took a few steps.

"So far so good." He walked with little pain, though his bruised, swollen eyes were sensitive to the morning sunlight.

He no longer heard Maria singing as she bathed at the creek and he decided to head that way and walk back with her. He smiled to himself. Make that *toddle* back with her. His hesitant baby steps could hardly be called walking.

Maria had said she used the water every day at a spot shielded from prying eyes by an abandoned stage station and scattered wild oaks. There was no sign of Sedley, who had a tendency to wander, and the only sound was the scuffing of Shawn's boots through dry summer grass. After a few minutes, he came to the old stage road, much overgrown by brush, but it gave him a path to follow that was surer underfoot. The Comanche had known the area well and their uncomfortable coming and going was probably what led to the abandonment of the stage station. The Comanche had left no sign of their presence, no scars on the land, nor had the Apache who'd followed them. Away from Maria's campsite, it was a lost, lonely place, a haunt of owls and herons that humans rarely visited.

Shawn stopped in his tracks, every nerve in his body taut as a fiddle string.

Ahead, he heard a man talking, his voice rough and husky with lust, a tone old Luther Ironside called a cathouse growl. Shawn heard Maria plead with the man. The only answer was a laugh as cruel and painful as a slap in the face. Weak and hurting as he was, armed only with a belly gun, Shawn knew he was in no shape for a fight. He'd come out the loser and most probably be dead.

Maria shrieked and Shawn reached a decision. No matter the odds he had it to do. There was no one else.

He tottered forward, his breath coming in short painful gasps. He felt dizzy in the morning heat but tried to increase his pace. Maria's shrieks were louder and came more often as she tried to fight off her assailant, a man with violent rape on his mind.

The stage station was just ahead, only two adobe walls and the sagging relic of a pole corral still standing. Scattered wild oak and a single cottonwood grew along the creek bank. He saw a sudden white flash of a woman's naked body on the ground and a man standing over her, his pants and underwear around his ankles.

Trying to make as little sound as possible, Shawn advanced on the creek, keeping the walls of the station between himself and Maria's attacker. He stepped around the ruin, walked through the oaks, and saw the man. He was a big-bellied brute with massive shoulders and arms and a thick mane of yellow hair. His plug hat, goggles above the brim, and his holstered revolver lay on the ground where he'd dropped them.

Noticing Shawn, the unshaven man, dirty with soot, realized that he was at a disadvantage. Maria, naked as a seal, used her legs to push away from him and he did nothing to stop her.

The big bruiser's eyes flicked over Shawn and he grinned, his few teeth green and black at the gums. He saw a tall, slender young man, his chest swathed in a bandage, his face swollen and discolored from a terrible beating. Best of all, he saw no gun.

"Damn you, boy, get away from here until I finish with that." He nodded in Maria's direction.

She looked terrified and tried to cover her breasts with her hands.

"And if I don't?" Shawn said.

"Then I'll . . . hell, I'll show you what I'll do."

The big man, overconfident, pulled up his pants and made a major mistake. He came at Shawn, planning to beat him to death with his fists and boots and left his holstered gun where it lay.

Luther Ironside's words came rushing back. Lecturing Shawn and Jacob on the ways of the shootist, he had said, *"When the history books are written about gunfights the feller still standing when the smoke clears is declared the winner. How he killed his man, front, back, while the ranny was a-saying of his prayers, or bouncing a baby on his knee doesn't amount to a hill of beans. You boys remember . . . never fight fair in a shooting scrape. Fight to win . . . whatever it takes."*

Shawn remembered, pulled the derringer from his pocket, and thumbed back the hammer. The big man hesitated.

Shawn said, "Maria, did he . . ."

"No. You arrived just in time."

"What you gonna do with me?" the big man asked. "I got friends in this town."

"I'll make you a deal. You . . . you . . ." A strange darkness crowded in on Shawn and he felt the ground rock under his feet . . . and then he was falling . . . falling.

Maria saw the derringer drop from Shawn's hand

a moment before he fell. She got to her feet and ran to the gun. Too late. The man was on top of her, the smell of his breath rancid in her face. Grinning, he pinned her down with his weight as he started to pull his pants down. She screamed and tried to fight him off, but her strength was no match for his and her head lowered to the ground in defeat.

Shawn revived slowly, his senses returning. His first instinct was to pull the man off Maria, but weak, sick, and dizzy as he was he knew he would never make it. At that point, she was probably stronger than he was. As he tried to get to his feet, his fingers touched the cold steel of the derringer. With no time for thought, no time to consider the right or the wrong of the thing, Shawn pointed the Remington at the man's temple and pulled the trigger.

At close range, the .41 round from a short barrel was devastating. The would-be rapist paid dearly for the lust that made him underestimate Shawn O'Brien's resilience and died without a sound, the hole in his temple trickling blood.

Maria pushed the startled corpse away and rose to her feet. She stepped back into the creek and used soap to wash the dead man's stink off herself. Without a word, Shawn picked up her robe and held it up for her until she'd soaped and scrubbed every part of her body. Only then did she allow him to place the robe around her shoulders.

"Did you know him?" he asked.

"I've seen him around town," Maria said. "He's one of the Abaddon slave masters."

"I didn't give him much of a chance," Shawn said.

"And what chance would he have given me? After

he finished with me, he would not have let me live. I believe the rape of a woman is still a hanging offense, even in this town." Maria's face showed her concern. "Shawn, I need to get you back to the tent. You must rest."

"I guess. I feel pretty used up, but I want his guns and his horse. What about burying the dead man?"

"We'll drag him off into the brush and leave him to the coyotes. He's no longer a man. Now he's carrion."

CHAPTER NINE

"My dear Count Von Jungen, think of the potential," Caleb Perry said. "You can strike at the enemy's heartland, topple tall buildings with a broadside, and send populations fleeing in terror for their lives. 'Peace at any price' will soon become the credo of governments all over Europe."

"My fellow industrialists are very interested." Werner Von Jungen smiled. "Leveling London with an air weapon has its attractions to many European governments. Not least, my own."

"London and beyond," Perry said. "After a few years of further development on the steam engines, New York and this country's entire eastern seaboard could be laid waste. Once the frightened American government sues for peace, your honorable self could be the most powerful man in the world."

"A laudable ambition." Von Jungen was a tall, gaunt man who looked good in a military uniform but not in his present gray broadcloth. "This chaotic world needs a strong master who will bring order, by the gun if necessary. I can fulfill that role by subjugating lesser races all over the globe."

Perry nodded. "On that subject, we are of one mind. Black, brown, or yellow, their backs can be bent to serve the empire."

"May I see the prototype?"

"Of course, *mein lieber Graf*, but bear in mind that it is only one quarter the size of what future terror frigates will be."

"I believe I can visualize the finished product, Herr Perry."

"Yes, yes of course you can." Perry opened a desk drawer and handed the German a pair of goggles. "Since we will walk through the foundry I must ask you to wear these. There are many hot sparks in the air."

Von Jungen's smile was wintry. "In Germany, I have visited the Krupp Foundry in Essen many times and I'm aware of that hazard." He settled the goggles into place.

Perry thought that the count looked like an ogre. "They become you," he lied. "Now, if you will please follow me."

The walk to the bay where the weapon was stored took them across a section of the foundry floor where the doors of enormous, blazing furnaces yawned open like the jaws of dragons. A dozen naked men shoveled coke in unbearable heat and Count Von Jungen was forced to remove his coat.

He yelled into Perry's ear above the roar, "Slave labor?"

"Of a sort," Perry yelled back. "The laboring trolls are Mexicans. The white men are overseers."

The German smiled again and nodded, approving what he believed was the natural order of things.

A steel door accessed the construction bay where the frigate was kept and inside was much quieter, the background noise kept to a dull growl.

Speaking in a normal voice, Perry said, "If you'd care to examine the gondola first, we can later climb the stair to the gantry and you can examine the canopy."

Von Jungen stroked his chin as he examined the gondola, a sleek, wooden craft that looked like a Viking longship but for the four cannons mounted on each side. Toward the stern were the miniaturized boiler, furnace, and the steam engine that drove a massive two-bladed propeller.

"Iron cannons, as you can see, Count," Perry said. "I would like to use bronze, but they are heavier."

"And the speed of the air frigate?" Von Jungen asked.

"At least ten to twelve knots. Maybe more, depending on the wind."

"And there will be eight cannons on the finished weapon?"

"No. I've asked my designers and engineers to provide for twenty-four on the full sized ship, the equivalent of six batteries of cannon." Perry smiled. "A few well-placed broadsides and the walls of London will come tumbling down."

"And how large a crew?"

"The full-sized, eighty-foot-long airship will be manned by six officers and a hundred airmen plus a few boys as powder monkeys. Unfortunately, the crew must be large because of the need to serve the guns."

Von Jungen thought for a while and then said, "Can you increase the length of the frigate to accommodate marines? There are adventurous governments that may wish to kidnap the English queen and assassinate her advisors."

"I will talk with my engineers, but making room for a score of marines should not present too great a problem."

"Then let us take a look at the canopy," Von Jungen said. "By the way, the name of the first frigate delivered will be *Graf Von Jungen*. His royal highness Prince Rudolf of the Rhine, my company's biggest shareholder, has graciously granted me that honor." An industrialist, a man of iron and steel, Von Jungen had little interest in the dirigible's canopy except to say, "Will it stand up to small arms fire?"

"Yes indeed. Even at maximum elevation, there is little threat from our most modern cannons. And in any case, by the time a ball reached"—he bowed as he flattered—"the *Graf Von Jungen*, she would be long gone."

"How long to produce twenty of the steam frigates?"

"I can deliver in a year," Perry said.

"I want them delivered in six months," the German said. "I can see concern in your expression, Herr Perry, but let me just say that a certain central European power is anxious to launch an attack on London that will bring England to its knees and with it the British Empire. Six months from now will be spring, the campaign season. A Channel crossing in force will follow the aerial bombardment and Queen Victoria's fat neck will be under the heel of the Prussian boot. Do I make myself clear?"

"Perfectly, *mein lieber Graf,*" Perry said. "I will hire more men. Just this morning, there were a score of Mexicans lined up at the door looking for work. I can find many others."

"And the price per frigate?" Van Jungen asked, now the shrewd businessman.

"I can deliver for a cost of just over a million dollars per unit. Say twenty-five million for the twenty-ship fleet."

Von Jungen nodded. "That is quite acceptable, but cut costs where you can as far as the slave labor force is concerned. Feed them starvation rations and work them to death. That is how overheads are reduced in this modern age. Gruel and the lash, Herr Perry, a combination that never fails."

"It shall be done. And Count Von Jungen, when you and your fellow industrialists are masters of the world, remember my humble contribution."

"*Mein lieber* Perry, stick a pin in the map of the United States or Europe and you will be governor of that region with dictatorial powers. You have my hand on it."

As he shook hands with the richest man in Europe, Caleb Perry was the happiest man on earth.

CHAPTER TEN

In the West, saloons were storehouses of information, not only for local news but farther afield. National and political reports were keenly followed, as were the doings of notable gunslingers and outlaws. In many towns, desperadoes like John Wesley Hardin, Wild Bill Longley, and the James boys became household names.

With that in mind, Jacob O'Brien dismounted outside the Alamo Bar & Grill and dropped the reins at the hitching post. He had little fear that his hammer-headed yellow mustang would be stolen. Unlike his brother Shawn, who rode like a Comanche and sat his blood horse like a king on parade, in the saddle Jacob had all the grace of a sack of grain. He was known to fall off now and again, a gleeful occasion for the mustang that believed in kicking a man while he was down.

After one last lingering look at the gigantic cannon foundry that dominated the town like a dark mountain, he stepped into the saloon. After the glare of the sun, he stood in the doorway and let his eyes grow accustomed to the gloom before he stepped up to the bar and ordered a rye.

Ambrose Hellen ran a cloth over some spilled beer, laid a shot glass on the counter, and poured the whiskey. "Welcome to Big Buck, Jake. It's been a long time."

"Ambrose Hellen. Not so long that I've forgotten your name."

"I appreciate that. Makes a man feel like he's worth something."

Hellen took note of Jacob's shapeless hat, washed-out blue shirt, frayed canvas suspenders, and the bandana tied loosely around his throat that had once been red but was any color you'd care to name. *Same old Jake*, he decided. "You passing through?"

"Looking for somebody, Ambrose," Jacob said.

"I reckon you are, but don't say the party's name out loud. He has enemies here."

"He all right?"

"Took a bad beating, but he'll recover."

"Not like him to lose a fight."

"Easy to do when there's a bunch of them putting the boot in."

Jacob was rough as a cob, but he had God's gift in his fingers. He looked around. "Me and the man I can't mention are here looking for someone."

"I know. And if he's in the foundry . . . well, the only way a man leaves there is through the chimney. His sister is in town."

"Maria?" Jacob was surprised.

Hellen nodded. "You'll find her and that other party by the old stage station south of town. Jake, I advise you to—" Hellen shut his mouth abruptly as three men stepped into the saloon.

As the newcomers bellied up to the bar, Jacob decided they were worth a second look. All were big men, muscular in the chest and shoulders, and each carried a holstered Colt. They wore plug hats with goggles on the front of the crown, a sight that Jacob thought was mighty unusual. He pegged them as fist and boot fighters, not gunmen, but reckoned they'd be dangerous in any kind of scrap. *Are these the toughs who'd beaten Shawn?*

Ignoring Hellen's warning glance, Jacob ordered another rye and pretended to be what he was not, just another saddle tramp riding the grub line. The biggest of the three men, who'd been steadily watching him in the mirror, detached himself from the others and stepped beside him "Howdy."

Jacob nodded but said nothing.

"Looking for work, are ye?"

"You could say that. But I'm done with cowpunching if that's on your mind."

"Hell, I don't blame you none. Cowboying is something a man does when he can't do anything else. Name's Val Kilcoyn. You ever make cannons before?"

Jacob smiled. "No. I guess that's a job I never got around to doing."

"Good. You don't need to know anything about cannons to work at the Abaddon foundry. How does two hundred a month sound to you, plus grub, booze, and a woman when you need one?"

"Sounds a hell of a lot better than the nothing I'm earning right now. What's the job?"

"Shift foreman. You oversee the labor, mostly men doing shovel work, stoking the furnaces, stuff like that. You'll weed out slackers and those unfit for work and drive the rest with a bullwhip or club if you have to. Being a foreman is not work for the faint-hearted. Think you can handle it?"

Jacob O'Brien hesitated only for a heartbeat. "I can handle most anything."

"You ever kill a man before?"

"Yeah. Yeah, I have."

"Then you won't have any problem working at the Abaddon Foundry. What do you call yourself?"

"Buck Ross, out of the New Mexico Territory."

"Glad to meet you, Buck." Kilcoyn stuck out a hand. "Come over and meet a couple of your fellow foremen."

What Jacob O'Brien would always remember was how ordinary and normal all of the Abaddon men were. They would not hesitate to beat a slave laborer to death with their bare hands if they deemed him no longer fit for work. Yet when they talked about their wives and families or aged parents budding tears appeared in their eyes. The dozen or so kitty cats on factory floor rat patrol were constantly picked up and petted by foremen and often the hands that had just beaten the life out of a slave stroked a cat's soft fur with the tenderness of a woman.

Jacob thought it a perfect plan that he work for Abaddon and search for Maria's brother without suspicion. But perhaps if he'd known the horror that lay in store for him, he would have changed his mind.

CHAPTER ELEVEN

As the day shaded into evening, Hamp Sedley rode into camp, dragging a bundle of firewood behind his horse.

Shawn saw the gambler's face and knew he carried a heavier load on his shoulders. Even before Sedley drew rein, Shawn said, "What happened?"

"Crop Hermon is dead. They hung him, Shawn. Shot his old dog." Sedley's face was ashen. "Now why would they do that? Why would they shoot his dog? And Crop's feet were just inches off the ground. He strangled to death . . . his, his tongue was hanging out . . . and . . . and . . ." Sedley was obviously in shock and Shawn gently urged him to dismount.

Maria Cantrell emerged from the tent with a glass of whiskey. "Drink this, Hamp. You need it. Sit by the fire and tell us what happened."

"I told it." Hedley didn't touch the whiskey. "They hung Crop and shot his dog. I liked the old man and thought I'd ride over and visit a spell." He held up blistered hands. "I buried them side by side, Crop and his dog. His name was Trigger and he was just a dog."

Shawn finally got Sedley to sit beside the campfire. "You see anybody, Hamp?"

The gambler shook his head. "Nobody. There were boot tracks around the wild oak where they hung him, but a lot of men wear boots." He fished into the pocket and produced an empty shell casing. "I reckon Trigger was killed with a rifle, .44-40 caliber. Plenty of those in Big Buck."

"When you first spoke to Crop Hermon about the body from Abaddon, did anyone see you, Hamp? Anyone at all?" Shawn asked.

"I don't know."

"I think he was killed because he told you about the condition of the dead man," Shawn said. "Strange that it would happen right after a couple paid assassins like Jed Rose and the El Reno Kid arrived in town."

"It could have been them, maybe so," Sedley said. "As I told you, I just don't know. All I know is that Crop Hermon got hung."

Shawn made a quick decision. "Maria, we're striking camp, getting out of here. Now. Tonight."

"You're in no condition to ride, Shawn," Maria said.

"I can make it. The Abaddon assassins found Crop, and I can almost guarantee that we'll be next."

"Where will we go?" Sedley asked.

"The one place they'll never suspect—Crop Hermon's old camp."

"Hell, Shawn, it's a two-hour ride," Sedley said. "You can't sit a horse that long."

"I can if my life depends on it. And it does."

Sedley drained his glass. "God help us."

* * *

The trip to the Hermon place, undertaken in darkness, took far longer than Shawn had anticipated. Because of his weak condition, he had to stop and rest often. The sudden appearance of a belligerent black bear spooked his horse and he was thrown to the ground with an impact that rattled every aching bone in his body. It took an hour to recover and even then, he was hurting bad.

Sedley, a man with an eye for the ladies, would normally have enjoyed the sight of Maria Cantrell's shapely thighs as she hiked up her black skirt to straddle her horse, but the death of Crop Hermon had affected him so badly he hardly noticed.

The first light of dawn had banished the long night when they rode into the Hermon camp. Exhausted, Shawn stretched out in the lean-to and immediately fell asleep. He slept so soundly that he was unaware that Maria changed the bandage around his broken ribs and cleaned blood and grit from his face.

They'd used the dead Abaddon man's mount as a packhorse and Sedley set up the tent and started a fire for coffee. After that, he scouted around the camp as far as the graveyard but saw no one.

When he returned Maria said, "All we can do is hide out here until Shawn recovers. I can go into town in disguise to buy food."

"You're taking a big risk of being recognized," Sedley said, pouring himself coffee.

"We have coffee for two days, food for three. I don't have any choice."

"Then I'll go," Sedley said.

"You're badly hurt yourself, Hamp, and the Abaddon toughs are sure to recognize you as one of the men they beat. No, I'll do it. I've done it before. Oh, my God. What is that noise?"

Sedley put down his cup and slowly rose to his feet. He drew the dead man's Colt and looked around him, trying to pinpoint the direction of the sound, a steady, pulsing drone louder than a highballing steam locomotive. The racket grew as the thing . . . whatever it was . . . drew nearer, causing the hairs on the back of his neck to stand up.

Maria grabbed the rifle that Sedley had propped against an oak and racked a round into the chamber. "Is it an *oso*?" she said, her beautiful eyes wide. "Is it a big growly bear?"

Sedley shook his head and yelled above the increasing din, "No, it's not an *oso*, it's a machine! Look!" He pointed to the sky above the wild oaks.

Maria turned and stared upward. "A flying machine!" she yelled above the roar. "It's a flying machine!"

The dirigible was a beautiful sight. Under a bright scarlet balloon hung what appeared to be a graceful wooden boat and at the stern of the craft, a spinning disc gleamed silver in the morning sunlight. Adorning the bow was a large bronze anchor and amidships a single chimney belched black smoke and showers of sparks. Small cannons lined both sides of the aerial ship, betraying its purpose as a weapon of war. A man wearing a closefitting leather helmet and goggles looked over the side at Maria and Sedley and made a rude gesture with the middle finger of his gloved hand.

Then slowly, a rudder at the end of the canopy swung to its right and the machine made an elegant turn and headed west at speed.

For a while, Sedley and Maria watched the flying machine until it disappeared into the distance, then she said, "What is that thing?"

"It's a flying warship, is what it is. And it means big trouble for somebody, maybe us."

"I don't like it, Hamp," Maria said. "The thought of a flying machine scares me. It's a monster."

Sedley smiled. "You're not alone. It scares the hell out of me as well."

"What do they call it?" Maria asked.

"My dear, they call it the future."

CHAPTER TWELVE

"She flew extremely well, Mr. Perry," the pilot said. "She has an excellent turn of speed and maneuvers like a cutting pony."

"We'll try her with a third of her eventual crew," Perry said. "We must deploy and fire the guns, Mr. Killick. For every action there's a reaction and I fear that, say, a full port broadside could send the craft hurtling out of control across the sky on her starboard track."

"And away from any target," Egbert Killick said.

"Exactly. I'm an accountant, not an engineer, but I believe it could happen."

"She's ready for such a trial. She's a ship sailing on air, not water, but I'm convinced she'll act like a man o' war and remain stable when her cannons fire. Send me the gun crews and a couple overseers and I'll get it done." Killick was a small, wizened man who wore a leather coat fastened with buckled straps. He'd switched his helmet for a top hat and goggles and his blackened leather gauntlets in the shape of his hands lay on his lap like massive paws. He spent all his time tinkering with his steam engines, didn't drink, and never lay with the Abaddon women offered to him. "The sooner we carry out the trial the sooner you can put your concerns to rest, Mr. Perry."

"Should anything go wrong, the test crew is expendable, but I can hardly afford to lose you, Mr. Killick."

"And you won't, Mr. Perry. I am so confident that the air frigate will perform flawlessly that all souls onboard, myself included, will return safely to earth. I'm quite certain of this."

"Then I must hope that is the case," Perry said. "I will arrange for a test crew at the earliest possible moment. Now, how was your voyage?"

"Just a routine cruise at treetop level with a few tight turns."

"See anyone of note?"

"No. There was a man and a woman by the cemetery, that was all."

Perry frowned. "Mourners?"

"No, they seemed to be camped. I took them for rootless trash."

"Still, they might be worth investigating."

"Better safe than sorry, I suppose."

Perry smiled. "Now, Mr. Killick, are you sure I can't interest you in a couple hours with Lizzie Skates? Call it a little reward for your outstanding efforts on what will soon be the world's most fearsome terror weapon."

"That is very kind of you, Mr. Perry, but I think I'd rather spend time with my engine and the rudder assembly. She's a bit tardy answering the helm."

"Suit yourself, but you're missing a rare experience. Lizzie is a very inventive girl."

"I'm sure she is," Killick said, but felt no sense of loss.

If a man died and wakened up in hell he would have found himself in the Abaddon cannon foundry, Jacob O'Brien decided. It was a place without windows, a vast cavern of darkness lit only by the glare of cascading torrents of molten iron and bronze, sparks filling the air like fireflies. The sweating men, thin as matchsticks, toiled under the eyes of foremen, hulking, whip-wielding brutes who had the power of life and death over them.

Jacob O'Brien was part of it and the thought horrified him.

Valentine Kilcoyn pushed workers out of his way as he led Jacob across the foundry floor to the bay where the flying machine was kept, opened the steel door, and clanged it shut. "Since you're a new man you're getting an easy job to start, Buck. This is where the flying machines will be built." He nodded in the direction of the prototype. "Like that one, only four times bigger."

"What the hell is it?" Jacob said, his eyes moving over the dirigible.

"They call it a steam frigate, but it doesn't sail on the ocean. It flies through the air."

"What's its purpose?"

Kilcoyn smiled. "You're an innocent, Buck, for sure. The flying machine—squadrons of them will be built right here—is designed to destroy cities and their populations from the air. The owner of the foundry calls it a terror weapon and I guess it is."

"Don't tell me the United States is buying these," Jacob said, appalled.

"No, not yet, but I can tell you the frigates will be delivered to a foreign government." Kilcoyn gave Jacob a long look. "That's all you need to know."

Wary of pushing too hard, Jacob smiled and nodded. "I'm a curious man. Gets the better of me sometimes."

"A word of advice. When you're at Abaddon, don't let your curiosity get the better of you. You'll live longer that way."

"I got your drift, Val. From now on I'll keep my questions to myself."

That statement drew yet another assessing glance from Kilcoyn. But then the big man's face cleared. "Well, you're new and everything seems strange at first. You'll get over it. Right here in this bay you'll oversee the laborer trolls and you'll also be dealing with steam engineers, mechanics, and carpenters, all of them white men."

"How can I tell my laborers from the rest?" Jacob asked.

Kilcoyn gave a lopsided smile. "You'll be able to tell, Buck. The ones that have to stand up twice to cast a shadow are yours."

"When do I start?"

"A couple days from now. In the meantime, feel free to walk around the foundry and get acquainted with how it works. You can ask the foremen questions but don't talk with any of the laborers. Most of the Mexicans won't understand you and the others that know some English won't answer. We have a canteen, a saloon, and a brothel and all three are free to the foremen. I'll show you your living quarters later."

Kilcoyn opened the small burlap sack he had been carrying. "Wear these at all times," he said, handing Jacob a pair of oversized goggles. "If you're eating, drinking, or screwing, push them up on your hat." He pulled out a pocket watch. "This is set to factory time. Wear it around your neck. And finally and most important"—he pulled out a small gun—"slip this Remington derringer in your pocket. You may be called upon to dispose of a sick or rebellious worker and the belly gun has a more discreet bark than the Colt you're wearing on your hip." His gaze was searching. "Any more questions?"

"No. I guess you laid it out just fine."

"Good. Then I'll talk to you later."

Jacob O'Brien watched Kilcoyn leave and his face was troubled.

In Dante's *Inferno* the Seventh Circle of Hell's outer ring is a river of boiling blood and fire where the damned suffer for eternity. Jacob wondered if the great poet had the Abaddon foundry in mind when he wrote those verses.

CHAPTER THIRTEEN

Without of word of explanation, Hamp Sedley walked into camp, picked up the coffeepot, and threw its contents into the fire. He stamped out the few remaining embers and only then said, "Riders in the cemetery."

Shawn O'Brien raised himself painfully on one elbow. "How many?"

"Two that I could see."

"Recognize them?" Shawn was hidden in darkness.

"Nope. Maria, where's the Colt?" Sedley said. "And the Winchester."

"What are your intentions, Hamp?" Shawn asked.

"I aim to stop those two men getting at you and Maria. They're looking for us, Shawn, sure as shooting."

"Hell, Hamp, you can't hit anything in daylight. You'll be even worse in the dark."

"They'll be here soon," Sedley said, taking the Colt and rifle from Maria. "I got it to do."

"No you don't got it to do," Shawn said. "Gunfighting is my line of work."

"Shawn, you're not fit to take on two men in a gunfight." Maria still wore her boned corset, skirt, and knee boots. "I'll go with Hamp. I'm a pretty good shot with a rifle."

But Shawn was already on his feet. He'd rested and seemed steadier. "If the riders are really a danger to us, I'll get my work in fast and close. Let's hope it's only a pair of lost punchers. If it is, and knowing cowboys like I do, you can bet the farm they're spooked at finding themselves in a graveyard. They'll be riding hell for leather and long gone by the time I get there."

"Suppose it's Jed Rose and the El Reno Kid?" Sedley put in.

Shawn frowned. "Those two won't spook worth a damn and I wish you hadn't said that. Load all six chambers, Hamp, and give the Colt to me. Quickly now."

Sedley did as he was told and Shawn shoved the revolver into his waistband. "Maria, you see me hightailing it in this direction it means there will be two men with bad intentions chasing right after me. Don't worry about me, just cut loose with the Winchester. Got that?"

The woman nodded. "I'll cut loose all right."

"Well, maybe not too loose." Shawn turned and walked unsteadily into the perilous night.

His breath wheezing in his chest and feeling lightheaded and weak, Shawn was glad to see, against the backdrop of stars, the silhouettes of two riders sitting their horses at the edge of the cemetery. He could stop walking, or as he told himself, *staggering*. He stood still, listened into the night, and caught the end of a conversation between the men.

". . . that is if the woman is pretty. If she ain't, we'll just gun her with the man."

"What did Egbert Killick say about her?"

"Hell, he didn't say anything about her. He don't set store by women, if you catch my drift. Now let's get it done. I'm looking forward to spending some mattress time with that little Lizzie Skates gal." The man kneed his horse forward.

Shawn said, "You boys hold up right there."

The man drew rein, sat forward in the saddle, and peered into the darkness. "Show yourself."

"So you can drill me? Uh-uh." Shawn moved a couple steps to his right as silently as he could. He didn't want anyone shooting in the direction of his voice.

"We got no quarrel with you," a younger voice said. "Stand aside and give us the road."

"I'm only guessing, mind," Shawn said, "but I'd say your name is Hank Locket, the El Reno Kid. And the ranny beside you must be Jed Rose."

Silence stretched for a few moments, then, "Yeah, I'm Rose. Who the hell are you?"

"Name's Shawn O'Brien. One time my brother Jake near blew your guts out. Remember?"

That was met with silence again then Rose said, "Is Jake out there hiding in the dark with you?"

"Maybe, maybe not. That's a thing you'll need to find out for yourself."

Shawn knew he had to get closer. Sick and puny as he felt, shooting in darkness, his aim would be an uncertain thing. He took a few steps closer until he could see the faces of the two gunmen.

The El Reno Kid wore dusty range clothes and looked like a harmless young, freckle-faced puncher. But no thirty-a-month cowboy could afford his horse and saddle and none had his poised self-confidence, like a rattler waiting to strike. By contrast, Jed Rose wore the frock coat garb of the gambler and at a time in the West when men wore mustaches or beards, his jowly face was unshaven.

"Well, look what the cat dragged in," Rose said, looking Shawn over. "We're facing a dead man."

"Correction. I'm only half dead."

"You look like hell, O'Brien, all beat-up and bandaged. And I don't like shooting a man who isn't wearing a shirt. It's ain't mannerly." Rose stood in the stirrups and yelled, "Jake, you back there? Don't have me send you to hell as a god-cursed yellow belly. Come out where I can see you. Have some pride, man."

"He isn't there," Shawn said. "I'm by myself."

"Sorry to hear that," Rose said. "I'd like to even the score with ol' Jake. I'm still carrying his lead and I'm looking forward to payback time."

"Seems like you'll have to settle for me. I'll settle Jake's score," Shawn said.

"Hell, do I have to draw down on a sickly man? Yeah, I guess I'll have to." Rose went for his gun.

Shawn drew, but ignored Rose, figuring that the El Reno Kid was faster. He shot the Kid's horse to take him out of the fight and then took a step back into darkness. Rose, wearing his gun high, horseman style, had to pull his Colt from midway between his waist and armpit, slowing his draw to a full second.

Aware of that, he hurried the shot. In the uncertain light and distracted by the Kid's downed horse, Rose was still the consummate professional and his bullet stung Shawn's left ear.

But sick and woozy as he was, Shawn O'Brien was still a shootist of the first rank. He fired and fired again, both shots sounding as one. He scored two hits. Rose took a bullet in his upper chest, then as Shawn's Colt lifted higher in recoil, the second slammed into the gunman's throat and exited at the back of his neck, punching out flesh and splinters of bone.

Shawn didn't wait to see Rose fall from the saddle. The El Reno Kid was on his feet, but groggy from the tumble he'd taken when his mount went down. He was scrambling for his gun when Shawn shot at him. The Kid was a few steps too far away, half-hidden in gloom, and the shot was a clean miss.

Locket made a bad mistake. His draw fighter instincts drove him to close the distance and he staggered a few steps forward, firing as he went. Shawn took a hit, a painful burn across the inside of his left thigh, but he stood his ground and fired steadily— three shots, two scores—one a grazing wound to the Kid's shooting arm, the second a solid hit to the chest, dead center and fatal. Locket, knowing he was a dead man, screamed out in anger and pain and fell.

His ears ringing, gray gun smoke drifting around him, Shawn stared at the destruction he'd caused in the space of less than ten seconds. Two men dead, a horse kicking in its death throes, and that strange, green curling in the belly that happens to a man after a gunfight. His gun was empty. He picked up Rose's revolver and put the wounded horse out of its misery.

The darkness parted and Maria Cantrell stepped to Shawn's side, the Winchester in her hands. "Are you all right, Shawn? Are you wounded?"

"I'm fine."

"Are they . . . ?"

"Yeah, they're dead. Jed Rose and Hank Locket, the one they called the El Reno Kid. They had sand, both of them."

"I think they were the men who killed old Crop Hermon," Maria said.

Shawn nodded. "I reckon they were the ones all right. Maria, tomorrow I want to drop off a note at the Abaddon foundry. You'll need to go in your old lady disguise."

"We need coffee and some other things. I'll do it then."

"Be careful."

The woman's beautiful eyes lifted to Shawn's face. "Tell me, is my brother still alive? Is all this for nothing?"

Shawn shook his head. "I don't know, Maria. I just don't know."

"I'll help you get back to camp." She stared at him. "What are you thinking? I can see something in your face."

Shawn's smile was slight. "It was a wish, is all . . . a wish that my brother Jake was here. I could sure use his help."

"Maybe he'll come, Shawn. Stranger things have

happened and Jacob is such an odd man to begin with."

Shawn's smile grew. "My feeling is that he's gone from Dromore and is holed up in a monastery someplace, maybe in Tibet."

"I loved him once, and I think he loved me, but one morning he had to flee from his demons and he just saddled up and left." She nodded. "Yes, he could be in Tibet, a place at the edge of the world where he has nowhere else to run."

"You can run in this direction anytime, Jake," Shawn said, staring into the night. He shook his head. "Listen to me. I've lost so much blood in the last few days I'm getting downright silly."

CHAPTER FOURTEEN

"Both of them dead?" Caleb Perry cried.

"Yeah, shot dead. And a horse," Valentine Kilcoyn said.

Perry slammed his fist onto the desk in frustration. "Hell, I don't have time to deal with this right now. I have twenty steam frigates to build and at the same time maintain cannon production. Damn it, who killed them?"

"As of this time, I don't know, Mr. Perry. Rose and the El Reno Kid were the best shootists in Texas or anywhere else for that matter. We're dealing with a gun here and I don't know who the hell he is or where he comes from."

"Then we must find him, Mr. Kilcoyn. Find him and kill him. But not right now. I need all my foremen right here at the foundry. Once the first full-sized frigate is launched, maybe then. What about the man and woman I sent Rose to exterminate? Could they have been the ones that killed him and the Kid?"

"You heard what Egbert Killick told us. The

woman was dressed like a saloon girl and the man looked like a down-on-his-luck snake-oil salesman. They didn't outgun Jed Rose and the El Reno Kid. Not a chance in hell."

"Maybe it was a private quarrel," Perry said. "Maybe someone we don't even know ran into them on the trail and settled an old grievance."

"I don't think that's likely. Those two were our best with the iron," Kilcoyn said. "We need to find their killer. The man is dangerous."

"Yes, yes, but later. Let me see that damn note again."

Kilcoyn dropped the scrap of paper on the desk and Perry read it.

Graveyard. Pick up your dead.

"It tells me nothing," Perry whined. "Anybody in town could have written this." He thumped his desk again. "Who delivered the note?"

"Some old woman. She says a black man paid her a dollar to deliver it."

"A black man?"

"That's what she said."

"I can't believe a black man killed Rose and the Kid. Maybe he works for somebody. Hey, what about that O'Brien fellow, the one they call the Town Tamer? They say he's fast with the Colt."

Kilcoyn's lips curled into a contemptuous smile. "Him? He was nothing. Blaine Keeners kicked his ribs in and then put the crawl on him. He's long gone."

"Blaine Keeners?" Perry asked.

"Junior foreman. A good man," Kilcoyn said.

"How is he with the laborers?"

"He's killed a couple slackers and sent a few of the sickly up the chimney."

"Good. Promote him and send him to the airship construction bay."

"I already have a foreman there. New feller by the name of Buck Ross. He'll work out after he gets over his shyness."

"We can always use another foreman and he can help the new man figure things out."

"I'll get it done," Kilcoyn said. "What about Rose and the Kid?"

"Set that investigation aside for now, Mr. Kilcoyn. Our main purpose is to build the steam frigates and that takes priority over all else. Do you understand?"

Kilcoyn nodded. "I understand."

"Good man. Now be about your business and let me be about mine."

Maria Cantrell stood on the boardwalk in her guise as a little old lady, a shopping basket over her arm, and watched a door swing open at the side of the Abaddon foundry. A moment later, a powerful steam horseless carriage roared outside and took the road through town, its attendant dust cloud trailing behind the back wheels.

A stocky man with iron gray hair sat in the backseat beside a woman Maria knew, the hard-bitten little blonde Lizzie Skates. In contrast to Maria's shabby dress and moth-eaten shawl, Lizzie wore a dark blue corset, buckled as tight as the bark on a bois d'arc tree, that left her shoulders and the top of her breasts bare. She flashed her legs in fishnet tights under a flimsy taffeta skirt that barely covered her thighs. Both she and Caleb Perry sported cloth caps and goggles and between them a magnum of champagne cooled in a silver ice bucket.

Perry's driver showed his usual reckless disdain for pedestrian traffic as the carriage, belching smoke, hurtled at a high rate of speed along Main Street. Maria watched the steam car until it was lost in distance and dust. She felt a great sense of disappointment. If only . . . if only she'd been carrying a revolver, she could have shot Perry and ended the horrible business and perhaps seen Manuel walk out of the foundry a free man.

Maria Cantrell made a vow. Never again would she tread the boardwalks of Big Buck without a gun.

CHAPTER FIFTEEN

The young stoker shrank back from Jacob O'Brien in terror, his thin body trembling.

Jacob tried again, *"Es el nombre de Manuel?"*

Raising his shovel like a shield, the man shook his head. His black eyes were huge, fearful, uncertain. A moment later, the young Mexican lay on his back among the coke, felled by a powerful blow to the side of his head.

Anstruther Breens lowered his meaty fist and glared at Jacob. "You don't talk to these people. If they're slow to carry out your orders, hit them. If they're still slow, kill them."

Fighting down his anger, Jacob couldn't blow his cover, not yet. "I'm new here. I haven't learned the ropes yet."

"What's your name, mister?" Breens said.

"Buck Ross."

"Yeah, Val mentioned you. You'll be working in the air frigate bay."

"That's right."

"Well shape up, Ross, or you won't be working

anywhere." Breens prodded the young Mexican with his toe. "Get that one back to work and keep your conversations for the bar girls. Understand me?"

Jacob nodded. "I'll remember. I don't forget easily."

Breens gave him a slightly puzzled look then said, "See you do remember." He walked away, his muscular body highlighted by the demonic crimson glare of the furnace.

Jacob helped the felled man to his feet. The right side of his skeletal face was badly bruised and blood trickled from the corner of his mouth. Without a word or a glance at Jacob, he went back to work, shoveling coke into the roaring furnace. Overhead, a conveyor belt of finished cannons headed for the loading bay. They were long and enormously heavy and moved with the slowness of a funeral procession.

As Jacob turned to walk away, a small, bald man carrying an oilcan walked past him. Out of the corner of his mouth, he said, "Try workers' canteen. Carry bread." And then he was gone.

"You're new here, huh?" The young mechanic's goggles were perched on his forehead and like Jacob, he wore a watch on a chain around his neck.

"Yeah. Name's Buck Ross. I just got in today."

The mechanic stuck out his hand. "Pleased to meet you. My name is Garrett Mallard. I work on the foundry's steam engines." He smiled. "Those things with the huge gears and drive wheels."

"I've seen a few of those today," Jacob said. "I'd thought I'd stop in for a cup of coffee."

"Coffee and meals are available here twenty-four hours a day. Day or night, you can order a steak and eggs, chops, stew, whatever takes your fancy. The coffee is down this way." Mallard led Jacob past rows of tables and benches to a counter where half a dozen men dressed like Le Cordon Bleu chefs worked on various stages of food preparation. "These boys have a lot of hungry men to feed. They seem to work nonstop around the clock."

A blackened coffeepot about the size of a rum keg hung on a post from the ceiling and was hinged so that it was able to tilt by means of a handle at its back. Mallard held a cup to the spout, tilted the pot, and filled Jacob's cup. "All the comforts of home. Enjoy."

Jacob looked around him. A dozen men sat at various tables, eating. A few others nursed coffee. All wore bowler hats with goggles above the brim that marked them as foremen or mechanics. A woman wearing a frilly dress, thigh-high boots, and a top hat let out a brassy laugh at everything a foreman said. She wore a black patch over her left eye that was decorated with a scorpion picked out in rhinestones. The counter where the chefs worked was loaded with deep trays of various dishes kept hot by spirit lamps. Between them were baskets heaped with bread rolls. After the fire and brimstone stench of the foundry floor, the canteen smelled like a fine Boston or New York restaurant.

"Do the workers eat here?" Jacob managed to

make his voice sound like his next sentence would be, *Perish the thought.*

"The trolls, you mean?" Mallard smiled. "That's what we call them. No, they have their own place. Come, I'll show you. Bring your coffee."

"Let me grab a bread roll," Jacob said. "I feel the need of a snack."

"Help yourself. We go this way." Mallard led the way out of the canteen and along a lit passageway that led to one of the outbuildings. He made a turn into a narrow corridor with doors opening to the right and left. He chose the one on the left and Jacob followed him into a dingy, dark room that stank of man sweat and boiled cabbage. The room was larger than the foremen's canteen but lit only by scattered lamps that cast shadows everywhere. At one end of the room was a counter where a young, dark-eyed man stood stirring a large cauldron of what seemed to be soup.

"This is also the troll sleeping quarters. As you can see, they sleep anywhere they can, wallowing in their own filth. Lord, but greasers are disgusting people." Mallard led the way to the counter. "What's the soup today?" he asked the dark-eyed man. It was a rule at Abaddon that any man wearing a hat had to doff it to a superior with the rank of foreman or mechanic and above. The cook wore a round hat that he removed before he said, "What it is every day, soup made from the leftovers from the foremen's canteen."

"Good, good." Mallard sniffed the steaming vessel. "Ah, I can detect pork in the mix."

"The pork was added last week," the cook said. "When it was already rotten."

But Mallard wasn't listening "Good, excellent. Well carry on. You've got a lot of hungry men to feed."

"I have a lot of dying men to feed," the young man said

If that remark had been made to a foreman, the young cook would have been soundly beaten for impertinence. But the mechanic let it go.

"Health through hard work is the key." Mallard turned to Jacob. "If you want to poke around the trolls, can you find your own way out? My shift starts in"—he consulted his watch—"five minutes. I have to go."

"Sure, I'll manage," Jacob said. "I'll see you later."

Big as it was, there must have been a hundred men jammed into the place, sleeping on every tabletop and corner. The smell was almost unbearable.

After Mallard left, Jacob took the bread roll from his pocket and laid it in front of the black-eyed man. "For God's sake, put your hat back on your head."

The man did.

"Now, eat the bread I brought you."

The young man wolfed the roll and then carefully picked up crumbs from the counter and fingered them into his mouth.

"What's your name?" Jacob asked.

"In this place, there are no names, only numbers."

"Is it Manuel?"

When the young man looked surprised, Jacob, looking equally surprised, said, "Are you Manuel Cantrell?"

"Yes. But how did you—"

"Maria is here in Big Buck. She asked me to find you."

"Is my sister well?"

"I reckon so. Worried, but well."

"And you are?"

"Just call me Buck Ross. The man who plans to get you out of here."

"The only way out of here is up the chimney. A few tried to escape, but all were caught and thrown alive into a furnace. Now, nobody attempts to break out of Abaddon. It would be easier for the damned to storm the gates of hell."

"I'll find a way to do it and keep both our skins intact," Jacob said. "Now listen up, this is important, Manuel—"

"Don Manuel. If you please."

Jacob might have been irritated, but allowances had to be made in the man's case and he merely smiled and nodded. "Don Manuel it is. If a foreman asks if you've had any experience shooting cannons, you tell him that you have. Understand?"

"What you said is easy to understand, but why tell him I've shot off cannons?"

"Because I want to get you into the flying machine building bay where I'll be one of the foremen. The ships are to be armed with cannons and they'll need men to test fire them. You'll be one of the cannoneers."

"I don't know how to fire a cannon," Manuel said, his dark eyes sunken in his pale, starved face.

"It's easy. You put in a charge of gunpowder and a ball and then touch off the fuse. You learned how to do it in the Mexican army. Savvy?"

"If anyone asks me, I'll tell him that." Manuel nodded, but still looked uncertain.

"You may have to volunteer. But the chances are they'll come round asking for men with artillery experience. And you have it in spades, Don Manuel. You got that?"

The Mexican nodded again. He seemed less unsure.

"It will work out all right, don't worry," Jacob said.

Manuel managed a smile. "Look around you, Buck. If it doesn't work out, what do I have to lose?"

The obvious answer was Not a damned thing, but Jacob didn't say it.

CHAPTER SIXTEEN

A week passed. With the amazing resilience of Western men, Shawn O'Brien began to recover. The swelling left his face and when he shaved off a seven-day growth of beard and trimmed his mustache, Maria Cantrell declared him, "The handsomest man in Texas."

He grinned. "West Texas maybe?"

"No, all of Texas."

"Don't let Jake hear you say that, Maria."

"Jacob is many things, both good and bad, but one thing he is not is handsome."

"He favors our pa's side of the family," Shawn said.

Maria smiled. "That, I will not touch."

Shawn didn't answer as his eyes reached out to distance. "Hamp coming in at a gallop."

Sedley drew rein and dismounted into a cloud of following dust. As he brushed his hands over his coat, he said, "Posse on the way, Shawn. Them boys are looking for somebody and it could be us."

"Let them come. We haven't broken any laws."

"The only laws around these parts are Abaddon's laws and we've broken plenty of them."

Shawn buckled on a dead man's gun belt and holstered Colt, his attention directed to the approaching dust cloud. At least six riders, maybe more. Maria Cantrell stepped beside him, the Winchester in her hands. She was dressed for war in a red and black laced-up corset, a mid-thigh red skirt, and black knee boots fastened along the outside with a row of seven silver buckles.

Despite the imminent danger, Shawn was amused. "How many clothes do you have in that trunk of yours?"

"A lady knows how to pack, and corsets don't take up much room. That is, if the lady's waist is slender like mine."

Sedley grinned. "I'm about to get hung, but I still think you look wonderful."

"I have another ten trunks of clothes back in Mexico, Hamp." Maria's black eyes stared right ahead of her. "Let's hope I get a chance to wear them."

Shawn took a step in front of the others as the posse swung into sight and halted about ten yards away. Mayor John Deakins, in a tan duster and top hat with goggles above the brim, was in the lead.

"What can we do for you, Mayor?" Shawn's eyes moved along the line of horsemen and stopped at the smirking towhead who'd taken a shot at him outside the Abaddon foundry. He wore Shawn's gun belt and ivory-handled Colt and had made no attempt to cover the rig with his slicker.

"I'm hearing bad things, Mr. O'Brien," Deakins said. "Not half a mile from here two men were killed in the dead of night and no one to answer for it. Would you know who was responsible?"

"Who sent you, Deakins? The owner of the Abaddon foundry?" Shawn asked.

"That's neither here nor there," the mayor offered. "The culprit or culprits must be found."

The towhead smirked. "Enough damn talk. We know it was these three that done it. The hanging tree is right there"—he pointed—"I say we string them up and have done." He looked around him. "Are you with me, boys?"

Maria levered a round into the chamber of the Winchester as Shawn said, "I can drop half of you. You want to give hanging me a try?"

"There's no need for violence," Deakins said. "In the absence of a sheriff, I am conducting an investigation here. O'Brien, if you're not the guilty party, just say so and we'll be on our way."

"The hell with that," the towhead declared. "There must be a hanging."

In a soft, almost conversational tone, Shawn said, "What's your name, mister?"

"What's it to you, back-shooter?" The towhead's eyes were ugly and he grinned as they slimed like slugs over Maria's voluptuous body.

Shawn didn't back down. "You're wearing my gun. I want it back."

"The hell with you," the man said, but he looked worried.

"Mister, I reckon you're all paw and beller without any real sand," Shawn said. "Unbuckle the gun belt and let it drop."

"Here, this won't do," Mayor Deakins said, urging his horse forward.

Despite his wounds, Shawn O'Brien moved with amazing speed and grace for a big man. He stepped around Deakins's mount, reached up, grabbed the towhead by the buckle of the gun belt, and yanked him out of the saddle. He tried to draw but couldn't clear leather and then tried to fall and grab for his gun, but Shawn held him upright and backhanded him hard across the face. Blood and saliva flew from the man's mouth as his head snapped violently to one side. He tried again for the Colt, but Shawn grabbed his wrist in an iron grip and forced him to drop it.

Then it was payback time.

Every punch Shawn landed felled the towhead and a tremendous right hook rolled him between the legs of the posse's horses. Shying and rearing, the mounts tried to scramble out of the way. Ignoring hooves and a few kicks from the riders, Shawn dragged the towhead into the open and systematically gave him a terrible beating, pulping his face into a scarlet mask of blood.

Mayor Deakins sought to end the slaughter. He drew his gun then squealed as Maria's rifle bullet blew the top hat clean off his head. Badly discouraged, Deakins swung his restive horse away from the mayhem and yelled for calm.

By then, Shawn was done, the rage leaving him like an ebb tide. He leaned over the groaning towhead, stripped him of *his* gun belt and Colt, and left him lying there. The other riders, cowed by Maria's Winchester and Sedley's leveled Colt, had seen enough. None of them were Abaddon men. They were townsmen who'd agreed to do the mayor a favor. Some favor. After what had happened to Deakins's hat and the towhead's face, their sense of adventure had faded fast. They wore belted guns but kept plenty of space between them and their hands.

Shawn turned to them, the knuckles of the hand that held his gun belt skinned and red. "What name does that piece of trash go by?"

Deakins, some of his pomposity returning, directed one of his men to pick up his perforated top hat before answering, "His name is Zedock Stubbings. He's a foreman at the Abaddon factory and now there will be hell to pay."

"Take him back to Abaddon with my compliments," Shawn said.

An older rider with gray sideburns said, "Hell, mister, there ain't hardly enough left of him to take anywhere."

"Well scrape him up the best you can and tell him the next time I see him, I'll shoot him on sight."

"I don't think he'll want to see you again, mister," Sideburns offered.

"Get Stubbings on his horse," Mayor Deakins said, studying the front and aft bullet holes in his hat. He jammed the topper onto his bald head and turned to Shawn. "You haven't heard the last of this, O'Brien. As of this moment, you're facing a double murder charge over the deaths of Jed Rose and Hank Locket. I assure you that you will be brought to justice."

Shawn glared. "Deakins, go back to the Abaddon foundry and tell your boss what happened here. Tell him if he wants the job done right to come himself."

"You're damned impertinent, O'Brien," the mayor said. "If I was a younger man, I'd take a horsewhip and thrash you to within an inch of your life."

"If you were a younger man, I'd let you try," Shawn said. "One more thing, Deakins. Tell your lord and master that I want him to release one of his workers, a man named Manuel Cantrell."

"Who?"

"You heard me."

"Mr. Perry would never—"

"Perry is it?" Shawn interrupted. "So he's the mysterious owner of Abaddon? Not such a mystery by the way—everyone in town knows his name."

"Yes, damn you. Caleb Perry. And as I was about to say, he would never hold a man against his will."

"Notify him, Deakins. Tell Perry that if he doesn't let Cantrell go, I'm coming after him."

Suddenly Deakins's face blackened with rage. He pointed at Shawn, turned to a rider beside him who had the brown face of an outdoor worker, and yelled, "Arrest that man!"

"You want him, arrest him your ownself." The man turned his horse and drifted away with the other riders, a groaning Zedock Stubbings slumped in the saddle.

Deakins attempted to save face. "I'll be back, O'Brien. Depend on it."

Maria Cantrell smiled. "Tell us when you're coming, Mayor, and we'll have cake and ice cream."

"Go to hell."

CHAPTER SEVENTEEN

Mayor John Deakins always felt uncomfortable in Caleb Perry's office and he felt no different at the moment. The man's cold blue eyes and steady stare had him off balance.

"You sure it was O'Brien?" Perry said. "My boys say they roughed him up and put the crawl on him."

"It was him all right," Deakins said. "He was on the prod and beat Zedock Stubbings into a pulp."

"And that's why Stubbings doesn't work for me anymore. I have no regard for weaklings." Then Perry asked, "Who the hell is Manuel Cantrell?"

"O'Brien seems to think the man works here," the mayor said.

Perry turned to his head foreman. "Mr. Kilcoyn, do you know this Cantrell person?"

"I don't know their names, boss, but I'm sure I can find him."

"Yes, do that. See what his connection is to O'Brien."

"Want me to pay a social call on O'Brien, boss?" Kilcoyn smirked.

"No. Just ask around about this Cantrell person and we'll go from there. As I told you already, we can even scores once the first frigate is built. Until then, I need you and all the other foremen right here. How's the new man working out?"

"Ross? Fine. I have no complaints."

"Good. I want to come down to the construction bay later and check on the progress of the frigate."

"The keel's laid, sir, and—"

"Wait," Perry said. "Mayor, you can go now."

"I was hoping I could spend a little time with Lizzie Skates," Deakins said, his flabby face eager. He smiled. "Even a happily married man has his needs."

"No. Your failure at O'Brien's camp hardly merits a reward." Perry added a small punishment. "Besides, Lizzie says you're too fat to be lying on top of her and you smell." He smiled. "You can leave now, Mayor."

Deakins's eyes met Kilcoyn's amused stare and he rose from his chair and stomped out of the office. He felt two feet tall.

There were so many men working in the building bay that the steam-powered retractable roof was wide open to the sky to let in fresh air. Swarms of carpenters and their mates, aided by skinny, half-naked laborers, were adding the ribs to the keel of the new frigate. From where Jacob O'Brien stood on the gantry above the floor, the gondola was already taking the shape of a Viking longship. He reckoned that when she was armed with her cannon and steam engine, she'd be a formidable weapon.

Valentine Kilcoyn stepped beside him and he too stared at the skeleton of the frigate. Above the constant noise of hammers and saws, he spoke into Jacob's ear. "Hey, Buck, you know the names of any of the trolls?"

Playing for time to collect his thoughts, Jacob said, "Huh?"

Kilcoyn spoke louder. "I'm looking for a troll goes by the name of Manuel Cantrell. You know anybody by that handle?"

Jacob shook his head.

"Well, if you hear the name let me know. Mr. Perry wants to talk with him."

In fact, Manuel was already working in the bay, laboring for a carpenter. It was none of Jacob's doing, just a routine change of job for a worker who looked reasonably healthy enough to do hard labor. Manuel kept his head down, did his work, and nobody noticed him. He was just one half-starved Mexican troll out of hundreds and for now Jacob wanted it to remain that way. Volunteering as a cannoneer would come later when the new frigate was ready to float through the open roof and take to the skies.

For the first time since his arrival at Abaddon, Jacob sat at the upright piano that Caleb Perry had provided for the canteen, though nobody ever played it. He carefully settled a roast beef sandwich on the top board and began to play.

Chopin's Nocturne in E-flat Major told its tale of love and loss and to Jacob's surprise the hundred or so foremen, carpenters, mechanics, and steam engineers present stopped their talk to listen. Over to one side where four females sat at a table, he saw Lizzie Skates dash tears from her eyes as the piece rose to its passionate climax before ending in relative calm and reflection.

When he stood and regained his sandwich, he got an enthusiastic round of applause and Lizzie Skates crossed the room—her high heels thudding—hugged him close, and whispered in his ear that he played like an angel, to come see her sometime soon, and she'd do something nice for him.

Jacob smiled, said he'd be sure to do that, then sat at a table and began to eat. As men passed him on their way out, several patted him on the shoulder and told him he'd played real good.

Then Valentine Kilcoyn sat beside him . . . and the news he brought was mighty bad.

CHAPTER EIGHTEEN

"I got a job for you, Buck," Valentine Kilcoyn said. "I didn't know you could play like that. Heard it all over the foundry floor. I hear that Shawn O'Brien feller has a gunfighting brother who plays the piano." Suspicion shined in his eyes. "You ain't kin by any chance?"

Jacob shook his head. "Heard about him, but we've never met. He plays better than I do. Or so I was told."

"Well, you play pretty damn good," Kilcoyn said. "Hey, do you know 'Saggy Maggie from San Antone'? It ain't as hifalutin as what you just played, but it's real pretty."

"Can't say as I do." Jacob grinned. "But I might have met Saggy Maggie a few times."

"Well, as it so happens I'm right partial to that song so I'll teach it to you some time."

"What's the job you have for me, Val?"

"That Shawn O'Brien feller I was talking about? Well he crawled the hump of one of our foremen, took his gun away, then beat the crap out of him, damn near bedded him down permanent."

"Why did he do that?"

"Because the foreman, his name is Zedock Stubbings, kicked O'Brien's ribs in about a week ago. Well, him along with three others."

Jacob frowned. "So where do I come in?"

"Mr. Perry won't have a yellow belly like Stubbings work for him. He wants you to take him outside and put a bullet in his brain. I reckon the boss is testing your loyalty, Buck. This is a good chance to prove you've got what it takes to be an Abaddon foreman and earn those goggles and pocket watch." Kilcoyn's voice became matter of fact. "You don't need to take Stubbings far. A mile or so out in the scrub will do before you scatter his brains. Hell, you don't even have to ride a horse."

"Why not do it right here?" Jacob asked.

"Because Mr. Perry doesn't want it done here. Don't question the boss, Buck. Just do as you're told." A searching look came from Kilcoyn. "Don't tell me you ain't game."

"I'll earn my wages," Jacob said. "When do you want it done?"

"Wait until sundown and then pick Stubbings up at the infirmary. Tell him you're taking him to a doctor. Tell him anything the hell you want. Just make sure Mr. Perry won't see his shadow come morning."

Jacob nodded. "I'll get it done."

Kilcoyn rose to his feet. "If Stubbings doesn't die real fast, that will be all right with Mr. Perry."

"You mean gut shoot him?"

Kilcoyn shrugged. "Whatever you want. Use your imagination, Buck. Earn your goddamn salary."

The Abaddon infirmary treated only minor injuries, usually burns.

The person in charge was a tall, pleasantly plump woman who identified herself as Nurse Clementina Rooksbee. She looked Jacob O'Brien up and down and made it clear that she wasn't impressed by what she saw. "You've come to take Stubbings?"

Jacob nodded. "That's the plan."

"Stay there. I'll get him."

When Jacob saw the man's battered face he was horrified. Shawn was not a forgiving man and he obviously hadn't pardoned Stubbings. He shook his head. *Shawn, why the hell didn't you just shoot the man and be done?*

"This man is taking you to a doctor." Nurse Rooksbee had obviously been primed by Kilcoyn. "I can do nothing more for you here."

"I know where he's taking me," Stubbings said. His broken mouth had trouble forming words.

She glared at Stubbings with wintry eyes the color of ocean shallows. "Good, then what happens won't come as an unpleasant surprise to you, will it?" She held out a paper sack to Jacob. "Would you care for a butterscotch humbug?"

Jacob pushed Stubbings through a door to the left of the construction bay that led to the rear of the building and into seemingly endless heaps of black slag stretching into the distance like rows of black pyramids. Iron production generated vast amounts of slag and Abaddon simply dumped it where it was close and convenient . . . at its own back door.

"Is this where you're going to kill me?" Stubbings mumbled.

The slag heaps cast arrowheads of shadow in the fading light and the air smelled of coal dust and of the constant rank stench of chimney smoke.

"No, not here," Jacob said. "Somewhere else."

"Get it over with, damn you. Shoot me in the head. It's quick."

"I'll consider that. Now get going."

"Where are we headed?"

"The loading dock. And that's your last question."

Stubbings took a step. "Should I care? I'm already a dead man."

A massive locomotive, sooty and weatherworn, stood at the dock and hissed and steamed like an angry dragon. The engine's headlight was lit and illuminated the track a ways, gleaming on the bright V of the narrowing rails. The drab engine's elegant cowcatcher, painted bright yellow, added a splash of color, as did the golden hue of the bronze cannons stacked and chained on the flatcars.

At the end of the train was a single boxcar just before the caboose. The car's doors were open and Jacob O'Brien looked around him before he pushed Stubbings in that direction.

The towhead read the writing on the wall. He was to be taken into the boxcar and gut-shot. His body would be found in Mexico hours or maybe days later.

A bullet tearing up his belly might take him that long to die.

Jacob grabbed Stubbings's arm and shoved him into the boxcar. A short length of canvas strap from a packing case lay in a corner and he used it to tie his prisoner's wrist to a steel staple hammered into the car wall. Stepping to the door, he looked toward the locomotive, seeing that the engineer had already climbed into the cabin. His fireman followed. A few moments later, the train lurched and then slowly clanked and hissed into motion.

Jacob turned to Stubbings.

The man's eyes were wide with fear in his battered face. "Make it quick."

"Have a good time in ol' Monterrey, Zedock," Jacob said. "If I ever see you around here again, I'll do my job and kill you."

He jumped onto the platform and from the boxcar he heard Stubbings shout, "You go to hell!"

Jacob laughed. *Damn, but that towhead had sand.*

CHAPTER NINETEEN

"This was their camp all right," Edmund Lute said. "Do you concur, brother?"

"Indeed I do," Marcellus Lute said. "And now it looks as though it's been deserted for some time. I fear it will make the task dear Mr. Perry set us that much more difficult."

Edmund removed his bowler and rubbed his hairless scalp. "No matter. We'll find them. Happy day that Mr. Perry sent for us. I was becoming quite bored without a contract. I'm ready to kill a man for the merest slight or the wrong look in my direction."

Marcellus concurred. "Well, no matter, brother, we have killings at hand and a chance to again practice our craft. Mother dearest is most insistent that we kill them. Nothing less will do."

"I was led to believe that our new client said dead or alive," Edmund remarked. "Or did I mishear?"

"You heard correctly, brother. But Mommy says dead is simpler, that Bang! Bang! is more direct than jaw-jaw-jaw, you understand."

"Sensible Mommy, Edmund, is she not?" Marcellus's

cherubic face broke into a grin and he did a little jig
and sang.

> *My mommy is so smart,*
> *That's why she stole my heart.*
> *She taught me how to kill,*
> *And that was such a thrill.*

Edmund Lute laughed and then he too sang.

> *Fiddlesticks and candlesticks,*
> *And voices o'er the lea,*
> *Aren't we a happy pair*
> *That Mum loves thee and me.*

When the singing concluded the twins indulged
in an outbreak of mirth. It was so heartfelt that their
horses jumped in surprise when the brothers clutched
their little potbellies and rolled around on the grass.
Mr. Lewis Carroll when he wrote *Through the Looking-
Glass* could have used the Lute twins as models for
his Tweedledee and Twedledum characters. Both
stood an inch under five feet with small round faces
that in repose looked like ripe Georgia peaches.
Stout little men, they each had a round protruding
belly and were as bald as crystal balls. Their voices
were high and shrill like the squeals of teenaged girls
and when they laughed, they had a habit of covering
their mouths with their pudgy hands.

Acting together, the Lute twins had killed twenty-
eight men and were the most sought-after paid assassins in the West. Their weapon of choice was the
Remington Rolling Block rifle in .45-70 caliber and

both were acknowledged marksmen with that arm. Forehead shots at a hundred yards were their specialty, though they would draw a bead on the heart or lungs if they deemed it necessary.

The driving force behind the twins was Mommy. Unfortunately for Edmund and Marcellus, they possessed only her embalmed head. She had been hanged for poisoning seven of her eight husbands and when the twins, then teenagers, arrived to claim her body, only her decapitated head had remained. Why this happened was never explained to the twins' satisfaction. In the end, they had to accept the governor of New York's explanation that a misunderstanding had occurred and that they could have the head with his compliments.

The Lute twins did nothing without opening the reliquary—her head was kept in a jar of embalming fluid—and asking her advice.

Since Edmund was a full ten minutes older than his brother, the honor of talking to their deceased parent fell to him. In fading daylight under a few sentinel stars, he reverently removed the reliquary from a pannier hanging over the flank of the gambler's ghost packmule. He untied the neck of the soft leather bag that held the relic and removed the jar with all the reverence of a medieval monk handling the head of John the Baptist.

Marcellus stood apart at a respectful distance as Edmund spoke to Mommy. The woman's head was well preserved since the hangman, before the governor frustrated him, had intended the relic for P.T. Barnum's Greatest Show On Earth. Barnum had intended to showcase the head as *Nelly Lute, the*

Deadliest Female Poisoner Since Locusta of Ancient Rome Or *The Black Widow of Bandit's Roost,* but all that came to naught.

Despite her notoriety, Mommy Lute had been an ordinary-looking woman with gray hair, slightly protuberant blue eyes, and a receding chin. The mark of the hangman's rope still scarred her throat.

Edmund's lips moved as he whispered to his mother and then after a few minutes he fell silent and began to nod as though absorbing her every word. Finally, he rose to his feet from his kneeling position, lifted the reliquary, and kissed her through the glass. He replaced it in the leather bag and tied the back tightly again. "Marcellus, shall we camp here tonight?"

"What does Mommy say?"

"She says we should."

"Then we will. What else did the dear say?"

"That we pick up tracks come morning and then move in for the kill."

"Excellent advice. You make up the fire, brother, and I will prepare dinner. We have plum cake, don't forget."

"Yummy. I never forget plum cake."

"Now I remember," Marcellus Lute said, snapping his fingers. "That Shawn O'Brien person Mr. Perry wishes discarded has a reputation as . . . oh, what do you call it? Ah yes, a draw fighter. Apparently that's a Texas term for a thug who's quick to bring a belted revolver into play."

Edmund removed a crumb of plum cake from the corner of his mouth. "Really? Is that how he gets his work in? With a pistol?"

"Apparently so, brother. I remember reading about him. He's called the Town Tamer and he had an equally murderous family of brothers. At one time, this Mr. O'Brien was married to an English lady, but she died or he murdered her. I can't recall which."

"I hate cold-blooded killers with a passion," Edmund said. "We eliminate undesirables, brother, and that's a vocation, like a call to the priesthood or politics. That last one—"

"Ah yes, Porry Blunt. The penniless pastor who wanted to wed the rancher's daughter."

"Yes. Now he was a classic case of an undesirable who had to be removed from this world. The impertinence of the man, daring to ask for the hand of the daughter of one of the richest men in Texas."

"He was easy to eliminate, riding out on a mule all the time with his Bible in his hand, the knave."

"And now poor Mr. Perry also has such a thorn in his side," Edmund said.

"O'Brien will be easy to dispose of. Honest rifle men have little to fear from . . . I spit on him . . . a draw fighter."

"Yes indeed. Mommy said that very same thing."

CHAPTER TWENTY

Still with healing to do, Shawn O'Brien chose a secluded campsite three miles east of Big Buck at a lonely spot in rough and broken country away from the trails and the well-traveled wagon road into town. The place was called Anderson's Draw, named after prospector Herb Anderson, who had settled nearby. The ruin of his adobe cabin still stood. Some said Comanches had done for him, others that he'd just walked away from the place when the gold panned out. Whatever the reason, the draw offered shelter and good water. A narrow creek fed by an underground spring lay just half a mile away.

As darkness fell and the coyote chorus began, Shawn, Maria, and Sedley shared a meal of broiled jackrabbit, pan bread, and coffee. The subject of the whereabouts of Manuel was mentioned again.

Maria brought up Manuel's whereabouts from a different an angle. "Shawn, if you weren't here eating tough rabbit and drinking weak coffee, where would you be?"

He smiled. "Well, if I wasn't back east somewhere, I reckon I'd be at the Windsor Hotel in Denver accepting Baby Doe Tabor's hospitality."

"Who is she?" Sedley asked.

"The wife of Horace Tabor the silver millionaire. They own the place. Last time I was there Baby Doe refused Calamity Jane service at the Bonanza Bar because she got drunk and refused to act like a lady."

Sedley said, "And then what happened?"

"Well, Calamity drew her hogleg and shot six holes in the ceiling. She played so much hob it took four Irish bartenders and Baby Doe herself to throw Calamity out into the street. But neither she nor Baby Doe held a grudge. When Calamity came back the following night, she wore a dress and was a perfect lady. She even checked her six-guns at the front desk."

Maria looked as though she didn't want to smile, but she did. "Shawn, how much does a room at the Windsor cost?"

"With its own bath, I guess about five dollars a night."

"It's a rich man's lodging, then?" Maria asked.

"I never thought about it in those terms, but yes, I suppose it is."

"Shawn, you should be there, at the Windsor in a room with its own bath, not here in this godforsaken wilderness sleeping on rocks," Maria insisted.

Shawn was genuinely puzzled. "What brought on this change of heart?"

"Because you've done enough and you've been hurt enough. Because my brother is dead and it's time for me to admit that fact and call a halt." Maria wiped a tear from her cheek. "It's over, Shawn."

"If I can get inside Abaddon—"

"No, Shawn. If you try that, they'll kill you. Your face is too well-known to them. You wouldn't last an hour. And you wouldn't either, Hamp."

"Don't worry, I've no intention of doing that," Sedley said. "I plan to stay as far away from the place as I can. Hiding out in the draw suits me just fine."

Shawn frowned. "Maria, are you sure this is how you want to play it?"

"Yes. I'm going back to Mexico."

"Back to what?"

"I still have relatives there I can live with until I find something to occupy my time."

"I won't let you do that," Shawn said.

"And I won't let you stand in my way, Shawn." Maria lifted her nightdress and scratched a red blotch on her shapely thigh. "Mosquito bite. That's all I do—scratch mosquito bites and wait around for a dead brother to show."

"Maria, I'll find Manuel," Shawn said. "I just need time."

"Shawn, there is no more time. The longer we remain around Big Buck, the greater the chances all three of us will be killed." She was silent for a few moments then said, "Shawn, I'm just not as brave as you are."

"Or as pigheaded," Sedley added.

Maria rose gracefully to her feet and stepped into the ruined cabin where she'd spread her blankets. "Get out, Shawn"—she turned back—"while you still can."

* * *

At first light, Shawn shook Sedley awake. He held up the coffeepot. "I'm going for water, Hamp. Walk with me."

"Damn it, Shawn. I only just got to sleep."

"I don't want to wake Maria. Walk with me."

Grumbling, Sedley rolled out of his blanket and buckled on his gun. "Lead the way. I'll hold your hand."

After they'd walked half the distance to the spring, Shawn stopped. "I'm not going to cut and run, Hamp. I took on this job and I aim to finish it. I'm telling you this because you've no call to stay. It was me Jake asked to find Manuel Cantrell, not you."

Sedley's answer was to dive at Shawn and force him to the ground. Immediately, two racketing rifle shots shattered the quiet morning. Sedley grunted as both bullets thudded into his back and he fell limp on top of Shawn.

Shawn pushed Sedley off him, rolled, and came up shooting, aiming at two drifts of smoke that rose from a brush-covered rise about a hundred yards away. The distance was too great for effective Colt work, but it sent the message that the bushwhacker's target was still alive and dangerous.

Making himself almost invisible among the twisted roots of a mesquite, Shawn lay on his belly and waited for the ambushers to force the next move. It never came. Sedley groaned behind him and the back of his shirt was covered in blood, but Shawn fought the impulse to go to the man. He scanned the ridge, searching for the slightest sign of movement, but there was none. Wary, he waited for a full fifteen minutes as the morning sun slowly warmed the land around him.

He kneeled beside Sedley, removed his bloody shirt, and examined the gambler's wounds. The two heavy rifle rounds had punched great holes in Sedley's back. Both bullets had exited through his chest, not a hand's breadth apart, and had done massive damage.

Sedley's eyes fluttered open and he smiled. "Saw the shine of a rifle barrel, Shawn. I mean me, who's as blind as a snubbin' post. Ain't that funny?"

"You saved my life, Hamp," Shawn said. "I won't ever forget it."

"I'm finally cashing in my chips. This is where my losing streak ends." Sedley was silent for a moment then spoke, his voice very weak. "Shawn, this is where you step in and tell me I'm going to be just fine."

"I can't say that, old fellow. You're hit hard and I think it's time to make peace with God."

"We ain't exactly been on speaking terms, Him and me. Doesn't seem right to try and patch things up when I'm at death's door."

"I'm sure He won't mind, Hamp."

Sedley was quiet for a long time and then the death shadows gathered in his cheeks and eye sockets. "Shawn, bury me with my gambler's ring." Slow and soft, he said, "Good luck, Shawn O'Brien. It's been a fun trip . . ." and all the life that had been in Hamp Sedley left him.

Shawn, filled with grief for a friend lost, reached into his pocket and found his rosary. His lips were moving, the beads still clicking through his fingers when Maria found him an hour later.

Shawn and Maria buried Hamp Sedley with a pair of dice in his pocket and his silver ring on his finger. They were his only mourners, two more than most gambling men could ever count on.

CHAPTER TWENTY-ONE

"He took both our bullets, the rogue." Edmund Lute shook his head. "I saw it plain as day. He died for his friend."

"When O'Brien went to ground, our cause was hopeless, for that day at least," Marcellus said. "As Mommy often says, one can't shoot what one can't see."

Edmund stepped to the hotel window and looked into the street. "Humble as this dark, grimy town may be, it looks quite festive at night."

Gas lamps lighted Big Buck's saloons and reflector lanterns lined the boardwalks. Arm in arm, couples promenaded with eyes for only each other and a few cowboys from outlying ranches were in town to spend their wages.

"Perhaps, but I'm not in the mood for festivity," Marcellus said. "Mommy says we must confess our failure to our employer."

"Temporary failure, brother. We will kill O'Brien tomorrow or the next day. But Mommy is correct. We must talk with Mr. Perry. A two thousand-dollar contract is enough money to make this morning's miss a serious matter indeed."

"Who was the scoundrel?" Marcellus questioned. "An acquaintance of O'Brien's I presume."

"A close friend I'd say. Casual acquaintances don't take the bullet."

"Oh dear, what will Mr. Perry say? I do dislike trying to explain away a miss."

"We don't have many, brother. In fact I think today was only the second failure of our career."

"Yes it was. The first was that awful Mary Jane Wedge person. Remember her? We put two bullets into a dappled gray brewery horse that day."

Edmund turned from the window. "She was lucky the brewery wagon happened to be passing. As I recall, it was a five-hundred-dollar contract, not much, but then how much value is a pregnant harlot?"

"That was dear Mr. Mulladay, the banker's contract. A streetwalker like Mary Jane Wedge shouldn't threaten to expose a happily married man and church deacon." Marcellus rose from his chair, did a little jig and sang a tune.

> *He knocked her up,*
> *We knocked her down,*
> *And the dirty deacon*
> *Lost his frown.*

Edmund giggled, his round belly jiggling, and also launched into song.

We shot a gray horse
And then a plump whore.
The horse is dead
And the whore is no more.

This last occasioned so much jollity that the Lute twins laughed themselves into tears and only when Edmund gave his brother a sobering reminder that on the morn they had to beg Mr. Perry for a second chance did the merriment finally end.

"I had hoped for better news, gentlemen," Caleb Perry said. "One out of two is only half the job done. You came so highly recommended that your performance is quite frankly something of a disappointment."

"Pray you, sir, let us try again," Marcellus Lute said. "We will kill the O'Brien person later today or tomorrow. That, sir, is a guarantee."

Lizzie Skates lounged on a sofa in a revealing lace skirt, boned scarlet corset that pushed up her large breasts, and red leather boots. She wore a top hat with jeweled goggles on the crown and a bored expression. "Perhaps the brothers Lute have lost their marksmanship skills. I'm told that Shawn O'Brien is a big man and hard to miss."

Perry grinned. "There's a thought. Have you boys been spending your time with harlots and not at the rifle range?"

Marcellus glared at Lizzie with obvious distaste. "Mr. Perry, Edmund and I do not take pleasure in fallen women. On our mommy's advice, we spend our leisure time reading Father Butler's *Lives of the Saints* and from time to time we also peruse the various works of Mr. Charles Dickens."

"Really?" Lizzie said, one plucked eyebrow arched. "I bet I could change your mind. I'll take on both of you little toby jugs for ten dollars. How's that? No? Well, let's test your marksmanship before Mr. Perry renews your contract."

"That's so silly," Edmund said. "Apart from Mommy, you women are so silly, silly, silly."

Perry, sensing a good lark, said, "Miss Skates makes a good point. I have only the word from your past clients that you boys can shoot. I'll pick the target and we'll see if you can hit it."

Lizzie pouted. "Caleb, let me pick the target."

Perry nodded. "All right, you can pick it. That's only because at the moment I'm pleased with you."

"We didn't bring our rifles," Marcellus said.

"That's all right, I'll loan you one." Perry rose from his desk chair and lifted a .44-40 from the gun rack. "It's loaded . . . so which of you boys wants to try?"

"If we must go through with this charade, Edmund is the older and I will defer to him."

The gantry outside Caleb Perry's office had an unobstructed view of the foundry floor, but as always, the men below worked in infernal darkness.

Lizzie Skate's chosen target was a black man. "There, the one shoveling coke into the furnace."

"Why him? He seems healthy enough," Perry

said. "Choose one of the skinnier trolls. They're harder to hit."

"The black man looked at me in a certain way," Lizzie said. "In Texas, his kind doesn't look at a white woman like that."

Perry turned to Edmund. "Can you kill him from here?"

"Yes, it's an easy shot."

"There, Lizzie, Mr. Lute says he can kill him real easy. We'll let it go at that. I'm short of workers as it is."

Lizzie frowned. "Caleb . . . he . . . looked . . . at . . . me."

Perry sighed and shook his head. "Lizzie, sometimes you're a trial and a tribulation to me." Then to Edmund, "All right, the black man it is. Make it a head shot."

Edmund threw the rifle to his shoulder, barely taking time to sight, and fired. The black man dropped like a stone, the bang of the Winchester barely heard above the foundry din. A foreman ran to the fallen man, his whip raised. He looked at the fatal head wound, raised his eyes to the gantry outside Perry's office, and walked away.

"A good shot!" Lizzie Skates yelled, clapping her hands. "Very well done."

"It was no great feat of marksmanship," Edmund said.

"Easy-peasy-lemon-squeezy, Edmund made the shot look easy," Marcellus rhymed.

"All right. You've earned your second chance, boys." Perry smiled.

CHAPTER TWENTY-TWO

Two shots, two drifts of gun smoke. Shawn O'Brien was on the trail of a pair of bushwhackers. He believed them to be a couple of Caleb Perry's draw fighters masquerading as ironworkers . . . yet he had a niggling doubt. Shoes as small as a woman's had left the tracks he'd discovered at the top of the rise, dainty almost, and the ejected shells, both .45-70 caliber, suggested target rifles, not a common weapon among Texas's hired gunmen.

Something at the back of Shawn's mind tugged at him and gave him no peace. He rode under the shelter of a wild oak out of the morning sun and built a cigarette, the tobacco and papers one of Maria Cantrell's thoughtful purchases, and the smoke sharpened his concentration.

Was it Jake who'd said . . . no, not Jake . . . somebody else . . . somebody . . . He remembered. It had been Luther Ironside, back at Dromore. Much to Colonel Shamus O'Brien's dismay, Luther had taught his sons much about draw fighting, tracking, fallen women, whiskey, profanity, the exploits of famous gunmen and nothing, in the Colonel's mind at least, of scripture and devotion to Holy Mother Church.

Memory came flooding back to Shawn. On his last visit home, just after the death of his wife, he recalled Luther talking about the best pair of contract killers in the West, sharpshooting twins who could knock a man off his horse at two hundred yards. According to Luther, when the twins rode into a town, the local law went fishing. A sheriff who'd think nothing of facing off against an all horns and rattles revolver fighter feared men who could kill him stone dead before he even heard the report of their rifles. And there was something else . . . something Luther had said about the twins' mother being the brains of the outfit. *Had it been her footprints he'd seen on the rise? Had a woman been one of the shooters?*

Shawn had figured two small men and a pack-mule. But it was possible that the pair's mother was a third rider. Jake would gun the woman without giving it a second thought. As Shawn rode out from under the oak, he was troubled. Killing a woman had never entered his thinking, but soon he'd be faced with it . . . and he'd no idea how he'd respond.

Tracking the twins, if that's who they were, was easy. Fearing nothing, they'd left plenty of signs behind and their direction pointed right at the town of Big Buck.

Main Street was busy with shoppers and horse traffic when Shawn rode into town. Smoke from the cannon foundry's chimney cast a pall over everything, like the London fog he remembered from his time in England. He bypassed the Rest and Be Thankful

Hotel, rode directly to the livery stable, dismounted, and stepped inside.

A tall thin man emerged from the gloom at the back of the stable. "Stall and hay, two bits. Oats ten cents extry." Studying Shawn's bruised face, he said, "Hell mister, did you ride into a tree in the dark?"

"Something like that."

The man's eyes slid to the Colt on Shawn's hip. "Looking for gun work at the foundry? Seems there's a lot of fellers doing that nowadays."

"No, I just want to look around town."

"Not much profit in that."

Shawn spun a dollar that the man caught deftly. "I need some information."

"If I got it, you got it," the liveryman said.

"Did a woman ride in on the white mule? Did she have two men with her?"

"Two little men with big rifles rode in on the horses you see over there in the stalls. The only thing on the mule was pack."

"Did they give you a name?"

"Lute. They didn't put out their first names. They said they'd left their ma at the hotel, except they called her *mommy*. Who the hell calls his ma *mommy*?"

"The Lute twins, I guess," Shawn said. "Are they at the hotel?"

"No. I saw them two boys head for the foundry. Looking for work, I guess, except"—the man placed his hand palm-down at waist level—"they're only this tall. Sure don't look like ironworkers . . . or shootists either . . . but something about them bothered me. Once upon a time, I was a peace officer and I guess I still have the instinct for spotting danger because right off, I pegged those little men as trouble."

Shawn nodded his thanks. "Take care of my horse and give him a double scoop of oats. I'll be back later." He stepped to the livery door, but the man's voice stopped him.

"You ever hear anybody play a lute? Like they did back in the olden days?"

"Yeah. Once in my life in England," Shawn said.

"My guess it that if you go after them two little men you'll hear somebody playing the harp, and it could be you."

Shawn said nothing, but his face asked a question.

"Mister, I've been in the West for a long time, a lot of years, and in my day I've seen gun hands of all kinds. I can sense them, like I figured you for a feller who's killed his man."

Shawn raised his eyebrows. "And?"

"Them two little men are surefire killers and they're a few bricks shy of a load. I reckon they don't carry Remington rifles taller than they are for show."

"Something to remember."

The tall man nodded. "Just step careful, draw fighter."

His jingle-bob spurs ringing, Shawn walked into the cool dark lobby of the hotel and stepped to the desk.

The clerk had a long gloomy face as though he'd never been told a joke in his life. After a glance at Shawn's Colt and the obvious good quality of his blue shirt and canvas pants, he said, "What can I do for you, mister?"

"Two little white men standing this high. What room?"

"I'm afraid I'm not at liberty—" The clerk looked cross-eyed at the revolver muzzle shoved into the bridge of his nose.

"Last time. Two little white men standing this high. What room?"

"Room twenty two upstairs," the clerk said, his prominent Adam's apple bobbing. He took a key from a hook behind him.

"I'm much obliged." Shawn climbed the stairs, unlocked the door to the room, and stepped inside. The mattress of the unmade bed still showed the imprint of two fat little bodies. Two canvas rifle cases stood propped against the far wall and a large leather bag containing something round lay on the table by the window.

Realizing that he might be recognized and that the clerk was probably already squealing like a stuck pig, Shawn acted quickly. He removed the Remingtons from their cases then pried the lead out of two .45 cartridges. Using a short piece of iron rod he'd picked up at the abandoned cabin as a dowel, he used the butt of his revolver to hammer a bullet a couple inches into the barrels of the rifles. He then placed the rifles back in their cases and leaned them against the wall again.

His time was running out. The last thing he wanted was to get into a gunfight in the middle of Big Buck, but the leather bag on the table intrigued him. If it was a jug of whiskey he'd take it with him. He untied the bag's rawhide string and . . . almost yelped in fright.

Suspended in the jar was the pickled head of an old woman, her blue eyes staring at him in lifeless accusation. The man at the livery said the Lute twins had left their ma at the hotel. The head must belong to the woman they called *mommy*. It seemed that the Lute boys were asking the advice of a dead woman.

Shawn tied up the bag and took it with him as he made his way back to the desk. To his surprise, the clerk was still there, . . . wearing a bowler hat and goggles as though about to leave. The man gave the leather sack a sidelong glance but said nothing.

"I want you to give the Lute twins a message from me," Shawn said.

The clerk grabbed a notebook and mechanical pencil. "All right. Let me have it."

That was an unfortunate choice of words, but Shawn let it pass. "Write this. I've taken Mommy for a ride. You can meet her again at the spot where you murdered Hamp Sedley."

"Do you want to say who it's from?" the clerk asked.

"Yeah. Just sign it Shawn O'Brien."

The clerk's eyebrows climbed up his forehead like hairy caterpillars, but he said nothing except, "I'll make sure the gentlemen get it."

Shawn nodded. "Good. They'll be so pleased."

CHAPTER TWENTY-THREE

Heartrending was the lamentation of the Lute twins when the clerk handed them Shawn's note and they rushed upstairs to find Mommy gone.

Marcellus and Edmund fell on each other's shoulders and cried and cried, like two little potbellied bookends bereft of books.

Through his sobbing, Marcellus said, "Mommy is in terrible danger. She's in the hands of the barbarian." This brought on more wailing and then he said, "We must save her from the ogre."

Such was their grief that the twins fell to the floor, rolled around, tore at their clothing, and screeched in a torment of sorrow. A pounding at the door ended the proceedings.

A ladies' corsets drummer suffering from a rum punch hangover entered. "Hell, boys, I've been listening to your racket. If your ma's been kidnapped, saddle up and go after her and leave a man to his sleep."

Marcellus spoke up, choking a little on his sobs. "That's just the advice Mommy would have given us."

"You bet it is," the drummer said. "Now, stop acting like a couple maiden aunts at a cat's funeral and ride. That's the ticket, boys."

And so it was that the Lute twins rode out after Shawn O'Brien . . . who'd left a trail so obvious a rube could have followed it.

Shawn left his rifle behind with his horse as he stepped out of the wild oak into the open. He wore only his Colt and stood relaxed, a pose to reassure the Lute twins who were coming on at a walk. Knowing they'd nothing to fear from a revolver at distance, Marcellus and Edmund dismounted when they were still a hundred yards away.

Only then did they see Mommy's head at Shawn's feet, pieces of the smashed jar lying around it.

Enraged, Edmund yelled, "You fiend!" He dropped his pants, turned, bent over, and flipped up the tails of his claw-hammer coat, exposing his round white butt.

"Take that, you demon!" his brother yelled. "That's what we think of you."

Shawn waited, praying that the bullets stuck in the barrels of the Remingtons would soon turn them into wall hangers. To hurry the agenda, he placed his booted foot on Mommy's gray head and watched the Lute twins turn completely loco.

Edmund pulled up his pants and they slid their rifles from the boots and got down on one knee in front of their horses. "In the belly!" he yelled. "Because you're smelly!"

"In the heart because you fart," Marcellus hollered.

The twins threw the Remingtons to their shoulders and Marcellus nodded off a count . . . one . . . two . . . three . . .

They fired in unison and the result was devastating.

It all happened so fast it took Shawn a few moments to realize what destruction he had wrought. He saw the breech of Edmund's rifle explode and the little man shrieked and staggered back, his hands to his face. The barrel of Marcellus's Remington had bulged and then peeled back like a banana. The screaming man dropped the rifle like a hot brick. His hands and cheeks were black with powder residue and his pants had fallen around his ankles.

Shawn O'Brien drew his Colt and his long strides quickly covered the distance between himself and the howling twins. He looked at the little men and was horrified. Edmund's eyes had been blown out of his head and he stumbled around with his arms outstretched . . . a blind man. Marcellus had lost the thumb and two fingers of his shooting hand. He stared at the bloody stumps in horror and then his gaze lifted to Shawn, seeing him for the first time.

"All this is for my friend Hamp Sedley, the man you murdered," Shawn said.

"He stepped in front of my bullet," Marcellus said. "He was a fool."

"Who paid you to kill me, Lute?" Shawn spared a glance for Edmund, who was on his hands and knees, blood dripping from his shattered face.

"A nicer man than you," Marcellus yelled.

"Who? Tell me or I'll shoot off your other hand," Shawn threatened.

"It was Mr. Perry who made us merry."

"Your poetry stinks, little man."

"Then kill us and be done," Marcellus said. "Take your revenge, damn you to hell, O'Brien."

"I already have. You and your brother can ride away anytime you feel like it. I suggest you find a good doctor. You two badly need one and so does your mommy."

Marcellus said above the wailing of his twin, "O'Brien, you're a hard, unforgiving, and vengeful man."

Shawn nodded. "Yup. I was raised among those."

Maria Cantrell poured a shot of Old Crow into Shawn's coffee. "Why didn't you kill them?" She wore a black corset, a long scarlet skirt, and high boots.

Shawn thought she looked like a cross between a fine Spanish lady and an East End of London streetwalker. Either way, she was a breathtakingly desirable woman. Returning his mind to her question, he said, "The punishment of the Lute twins is only beginning. Neither of them will trigger a rifle again. They'll go somewhere and they'll die."

"It's sad in a way."

"No, it's not. When they murdered Hamp, they brought down a reckoning. And there's a reckoning on the way for Caleb Perry."

"So you're not leaving?"

"Not until Perry is dead and Big Buck returns to being what it was before, a cow town clinging to its

railroad spur like a drowning man clings to a lifebelt."
He tried his whiskey-laced coffee. "This is good. And
what about you, Maria?"

"Hamp's death changed everything. If you're staying, then so am I." She touched the back of Shawn's
hand with her fingertips. "It's difficult for you, isn't
it Shawn?"

He saw something in the woman's eyes and understood what she meant. "Yes, Maria. It's difficult."

The woman smiled and placed his hand between
the swell of her breast and her collarbone. "Then
sleep in the cabin with me tonight, Shawn. Tonight
and every night."

Shawn held Maria close and kissed her. There was
no need for words.

CHAPTER TWENTY-FOUR

"First Stubbings and now the two best hired assassins in the country. Does this man O'Brien have a charmed life?" Caleb Perry snapped.

"Seems like, boss," Valentine Kilcoyn said.

"Is it bad?"

"You mean for the Lute twins?"

"Yes, yes, is it bad for the Lute twins?"

"It's bad. Marcellus got most of his gun hand shot off and his brother lost both eyes."

"O'Brien did that?" Perry sounded on edge.

"Yeah. He did that and then he let them go. He knows they'll crawl away and die somewhere."

"Damn it all, man, where are they?"

"Well, an hour ago they were at the doctor's office with big Buck Ross guarding them. I told Ross after the doc finished to take them to the hotel and stay there himself in case O'Brien decides to come back and finish the job."

"Maybe it would be better for us if he did," Perry said.

Lizzie Skates had been probing between her

breasts for a lost earring. She gave her attention to
Perry and said, "Send them up the chimney, Caleb. I
hated those two little gnomes."

Perry smiled. "Because they refused mattress time
with you, Lizzie?"

"Fancy boys if you ask me." She sniffed.

Perry nodded. "Do as Lizzie says, Val. Bring the
twins back here and shoot them. You know what to
do with the bodies."

"Fat little goblins like them two will burn like
torches," Lizzie said.

"Don't involve Ross," Perry said. "Let's keep some
things secret for now. He might be a man who blabs.
We don't know."

"Sure thing, boss," Kilcoyn said. "An hour from
now, all that's left of the Lute twins will be black
smoke."

Nurse Clementina Rooksbee raised icy eyes to Val
Kilcoyn. "Not here, you won't."

"But your office is private and no one will notice,"
the big foreman said. "Hell, this is the quietest place
in the foundry."

"I'll notice when I have to wash blood and brains
from the floor," Nurse Rooksbee said.

"Get a troll to do it."

"A troll won't clean the floor to my satisfaction."

Kilcoyn was suddenly angry. "Damn it, woman, I
have to shoot them someplace. I don't want to drag
them into the middle of the floor and shoot them
there. It upsets the trolls."

"Where are they?"

"Outside, wailing and kicking up a fuss. They want you to repickle their ma's head."

"Repickle? What in the world does that mean?"

"It means you stick her head in a glass jar with embalming fluid, I guess. Anyway, once I shoot them you won't have to do it. Mommy's head will go in the furnace."

"Who's with them?"

"Buck Ross, the new foreman."

Nurse Rooksbee shook her head. "There's a better way. Send the foreman away and bring the twins inside."

Kilcoyn frowned. "What are you going to do?"

"I'll give them something to relieve their pain"—the woman smiled, revealing teeth the size of yellowed piano keys—"permanently."

Kilcoyn smiled. "Now I catch your drift. I'll tell Ross to beat it and I'll bring them boys in."

Had Valentine Kilcoyn been listening at the door, he would have heard a snippet of conversation between Jacob O'Brien and the Lute twins.

"I've heard about him," Jacob said. "And you're right, Shawn O'Brien is a dastardly villain. Did he have a woman with him?"

"No. Just a man, the one we shot." Marcellus was in terrible pain and he gasped as he spoke.

Next to him, sightless Edmund screeched, "He has destroyed us."

"The savage!" Jacob agreed. "Where did this happen?"

Kilcoyn opened the door, and the exchange

ended. "Buck, go back to the construction bay. I'll take care of these boys now."

Jacob could only nod and leave, questions unanswered. *Where is Shawn? And is Maria Cantrell with him?* He felt like he was hitting his head against a brick wall.

"Drink this, Mr. Lute and you, too . . . what's your name?" Nurse Rooksbee looked to the other twin.

"My name is Marcellus."

"Yes, of course it is. Now drink up, gentlemen. This will relieve your pain. And don't worry about Mommy. I'll take care of her soon."

"Her eyes have closed," Marcellus said. "Oh please tell us she isn't dead."

"No, she's only sleeping. Once she gets back into a jar, she'll be her old self again."

Kilcoyn added, "Yes she will. As bright-eyed as ever."

"What about my brother?" Marcellus asked. "He needs surgery on his eyes. Can you make him see again?"

"Mr. Perry is already making arrangements for a surgeon to come down from El Paso. I'm told he can perform miracles on injured eyes and hands." Nurse Rooksbee had a fine body, voluptuous, marred only by her homely face. Her red hair was scraped back from her forehead and tied in a bun at the nape of her neck. Her brown dress, the bosom laced tight across her breasts, was adorned with a pocket watch pinned to the front. She wore red spectacles with some kind of small magnifying glass attached to the bottom of each lens and leather gloves.

Reassured by the nurse's words, Edmund took his medicine in one gulp. Marcellus, in pain but suspicious, hesitated.

She encouraged, "Down the hatch, Mr. Lute. It will make you feel better."

"I'm surprised," she said. "I thought that seventy grains of arsenic would kill them more quickly than it's doing."

The Lute twins writhed on the floor like little white slugs, dying hard and in much pain. They foamed at the mouth and made odd gibbering noises.

"How much longer?" Valentine Kilcoyn said, irritated. "I'm getting hungry."

"Let's see." She tested both dying men's chests with her tube stethoscope, listening to each for long moments "Not long now. Their hearts are faltering. There's chocolate cake and ice cream today. Did you hear that?"

"I did"—Kilcoyn nodded—"but I'll believe it when it's on my plate. All the cooks seem to know is steamed pudding and custard."

"I like that dessert," Nurse Rooksbee said.

"So do I but not every day," Kilcoyn said.

"No, not every day. Ice cream is a welcome change. I think one of them just died." She tried the stethoscope again. "Yes, this one with the damaged eyes. His brother won't be far behind."

"Mr. Perry said we had to get rid of them. The

good folks of Big Buck don't need to see this kind of thing. Questions start getting asked."

She made no answer to that. After a while, she said, "The other one is gone."

"They took their own sweet time about it."

"I still can't believe so much pain is associated with arsenic. The two of them died in considerable distress."

"A bullet would have been quicker," Kilcoyn pointed out.

"Quicker, yes, but then we wouldn't have had a chance to observe the effect of arsenic poisoning on the human body. I will make it known to the physicians of my acquaintance." She applied the stethoscope to each body. "Yes, they're gone. You can have the trolls pick them up in a while."

"A while?" Kilcoyn said.

Nurse Clementina Rooksbee began to unlace her dress. "Yes. In a while."

CHAPTER TWENTY-FIVE

"She'll be a rock steady gun platform," Garrett Mallard the mechanic said. "A city destroyer if ever I saw one."

"What about recoil?" Caleb Perry asked. "We still don't know if a full broadside will blow her across the sky."

"The prototype will be tested within a week, once the gunners are fully trained. I expect a successful trial run."

"Who's taking her up?"

"This man right here, Mr. Buck Ross."

"You're the new foreman." Perry didn't offer his hand. "Can the trolls handle the cannon?"

Jacob O'Brien nodded. "Yes. A man who served as a cannoneer in the Mexican army is instructing them. They'll be ready in a week."

"Or less," Perry insisted. "What do you think about the recoil question, Ross?"

Jacob didn't hesitate, pretending he knew more than he did. "The gondola—"

"Please. The frigate," Perry interrupted.

"Yes. The frigate is suspended by ropes and chains and it will swing when the cannons fire, but nothing too severe. The canopy will hold it in place and the steam driven propeller will act as a counterforce." His voice oozing sincerity as if he knew what the hell he was talking about, Jacob added, "Even under adverse weather conditions, I estimate my gun crews will fire two broadsides a minute."

"Very impressive, Mr. Ross," Perry said, his hard eyes searching Jacob's face. "Let's hope, for your sake, that you're right."

"I can vouch for foreman Ross," Mallard said. "His gun crews are working well together."

"We'll see." Perry looked from the gantry to where the full-sized frigate was taking shape, workmen swarming all over her. "A lovely thing, is she not, Mr. Ross?"

"Indeed she is," Jacob said, telling the truth. The half-completed flying machine had all the lethal beauty of a modern ship of the line, a weapon of wood and iron driven by the steam engines that were powering the world.

"The future of modern warfare is right here at Abaddon. We have the terror weapon that will give the strong the power to bend the backs of the weak to lives of unending labor," Perry said. "What say you, mechanic Mallard?"

"Throughout history those who beat their swords into plowshares plowed for those that didn't," Mallard said. "In these modern times, those who don't have steam-powered aerial, yes, and land weapons, will also go under the yoke."

That last statement changed Jacob O'Brien's

thinking. It was no longer merely a case of freeing Manuel Cantrell. He had to stop these men from inflicting great evil on an unsuspecting world. A fleet of aerial steam frigates could level the great cities of Europe and the United States, and bring madmen to power.

Jacob considered drawing his gun and shooting Perry, the mechanic, and the other men on the gantry, but he quickly dismissed the idea. Others would soon take their place. The only way to safeguard the future of mankind was to destroy Abaddon and let it take its secrets to the grave.

"How will you do it, Mr. Ross?"

"Huh?" Jacob realized that Perry had asked the question and turned toward him.

"Address the recoil business," the man said, slight irritation in his voice. "How will you conduct the test?"

"Fly the frigate—"

"Prototype," Perry interrupted again.

"Into the desert and cut loose." Jacob smiled. "Give the jackrabbits a broadside."

"I have a better idea. Mr. Mallard, you will instruct Egbert Killick to pilot the prototype along Big Buck's Main Street and give the buildings the port broadside. He will then turn and cut loose with the starboard battery. We will see how the airship performs under daylight battle conditions."

"But . . . but we'll kill a lot of people," Mallard objected.

"A high butcher's bill is the price we pay for progress, Mr. Mallard. Do you have any objections?"

The mechanic pushed his goggles higher on his forehead. "No. I have none."

"And you, Mr. Ross? Since you will be in command of the cannon?"

Jacob couldn't tip his hand. "Sounds like a good test to me, but we'll only be a few feet above the ground."

"Height doesn't matter. The ship will perform the same at three feet or three thousand." Perry waved a careless hand. "I've grown bored with this miscrable little town and its idiot mayor. It's high time it was blown off the face of the earth."

CHAPTER TWENTY-SIX

At the order of her Britannic Majesty Queen Victoria's government, the miserable, sweating figure of Scotland Yard Detective Inspector Adam Ready stood on the platform of the Big Buck railroad station and watched his train disappear into the desert, leaving him lost and alone at the edge of the world.

The British Legation in Washington had earlier informed Mr. Caleb Perry of his arrival and though Ready didn't expect a brass band, he thought that the Abaddon Cannon Foundry's senior executives would be on hand to meet him.

His valise at his feet in a stinging dust storm, Ready heard boots and the ringing of spurs and beheld a tall man stride toward him, a murderous revolver at his hip. His canvas pants, faded blue shirt, and battered, broad-brimmed hat were much the worse for wear. He had the look of a dangerous thug and the inspector was grateful for the reassuring weight of the .455 British Bulldog revolver in the pocket of his tweed coat.

To Ready's surprise, the big man's smile was good-humored and open and his voice was musical with the intonations of a gentleman. "Detective Inspector Ready, I presume," the man said, sticking out his hand.

"Indeed," Ready said, shaking hands. "And you are?"

"Name's Buck Ross. I'm one of the foremen at Abaddon. Mr. Perry is tied up with urgent business matters right now and he sent me to fetch you. Let me take your valise."

"My business here is of the greatest moment and equally urgent," Ready said. "I'm here because of a most singular request by Her Majesty Queen Victoria."

Jacob grinned. "How is the old lady?"

Ready's reply was frosty. "Her Royal Majesty is well."

"Glad to hear it. Now if you'll please come with me." Jacob led the way from the station and onto open ground. The Abaddon foundry came into view.

Ready was amazed. "I didn't expect it to be so huge. It looks like a manmade mountain."

"They make a lot of cannons," Jacob pointed out.

"And now airships." Ready was not an imposing figure, but a thin, smallish man with the face of an intelligent mole. His narrow eyes were black and shrewd and his motions were quick and precise, a habit that made him look like a perpetually irritated schoolmaster.

"Yes. Now Abaddon is building air frigates as well as cannon," Jacob agreed.

Blowing sand pummeling him, Ready halted in his tracks and glared at Jacob. "How many steam frigates did the Germans order?"

Jacob was surprised. "You know about the German frigates?"

"I know about many things, Mr. Ross. How many?"

"Twenty, I think."

"Then Her Majesty's government will order twenty-one. How many guns will they bear?"

"Twenty-four."

"Then Great Britain will demand twenty-five."

Jacob said, "Inspector, why did your government send a detective and not a diplomat? It seems like a job for a politician."

Ready tapped the side of his long nose. "See this? It's what Scotland Yard calls a sniffer. And I am here to sniff out chicanery. Perhaps the Germans have ordered twenty-five steam frigates each with thirty, not twenty-four guns, and wish to keep it secret. Ha! I'm used to such continental hocus-pocus, but I'll uncover the truth or my name is not Adam Ready."

"A British bobby has the authority to order a fleet of steam frigates?" Jacob asked, smiling.

"No, Mr. Ross, just one. One more than the German, French, and Russian air fleets combined."

"Inspector Ready, Caleb Perry is going to love you."

His face impassive, Detective Inspector Adam Ready stood amid a sparking inferno of molten metal, roaring blast furnaces, and hissing steam where skeletal workers toiled in stygian gloom.

Jacob O'Brien expected a horrified comment from the little man and was therefore surprised when Ready brushed blown sand from his bowler hat and

shouted above the din, "Factories are the same the
world over, aren't they, Mr. Ross? Fire and noise and
that byproduct of our industrial age, the underpaid
and overworked poor."

Jacob nodded, then yelled, "This way. I'll show you
to your quarters."

Caleb Perry kept a suite of rooms for visiting dig-
nitaries, most of them purchasers of cannon who arrived with bulging pockets. A visiting Scotland Yard
detective—who was possibly a spy—hardly moved the
dial of Perry's esteem meter and Ready's accommo-
dations reflected his lowly status. His rooms lay at
the end of a hallway with a concrete floor and were
sparsely furnished, unusual at a time when Victorian
tastes ran to the crowded and ornate.

Ready didn't seem to notice as he tossed his valise
on the iron bedstead. "When do I meet Mr. Perry?"

"I don't know," Jacob said. "Probably soon."

"How many frigates are under construction?"
Ready had eyes that probed like scalpels.

"Just one. But the bay is to be expanded so that
five can be built at a time."

"I'd like to see the craft for myself. And I mean
instanter."

Jacob shook his head. "Sorry, Inspector, but only
Perry can authorize that."

"He thinks I'm a spy?"

"I'd say he suspects you might be a spy."

Ready's amused smile surprised Jacob, like finding a diamond in a mud hole. "Maybe he's right."

"I wouldn't put that out. Perry has ways of dealing
with spies, all of them unpleasant."

"Hah! My job at Scotland Yard is to investigate murders. I was pulled off the Jack the Ripper case and sent here. What do I know about airship construction and steam engines? I'm to keep an eye on the purchases of the major European powers, that's all. Have you heard of Jack the Ripper?"

Jacob shook his head. "No."

"He kills and guts prostitutes, and is still at large. I suspect he's a clergyman of some sort who's down on those kind. When I return to London, I'll find him. Be assured of that."

"Well, good luck. I'll leave you now."

But before Jacob could go, Ready reached into the pocket of his coat and produced his revolver. "This is a British Bulldog. Have you heard of it?"

Jacob nodded. "I've seen it in use once or twice. Are you good with it?"

"No, I'm not. I have no use for firearms, but I was ordered to take this weapon with me, this being the Wild West and all."

"Get close, aim for the belly, and keep shooting until the other man falls," Jacob advised. "That's how it's done."

"I'll do no such thing. It's most unsporting. A gentleman doesn't shoot another gentleman in the belly."

"Inspector, the rannies you'll meet around here are not gentlemen. You can bet old Queen Vic's corsets on that."

CHAPTER TWENTY-SEVEN

In the latter two decades of the nineteenth century as law and order spread across the West and the telegraph shortened distances between settlements, professional gunman found themselves forced out of business and those who still lived by the shootist's code became drifters. As they had been since the end of the War Between the States, Texas saloons were clearinghouses of information where men with careful eyes and fast hands listened and learned.

One such man was Frank Tansey, a fast gun out of Decatur, Texas, who'd been many things. In between, he had practiced his true calling as a hired gunman and bounty hunter. He killed his first man at seventeen and his father, a former Confederate brigadier general, had mortgaged the family farm to hire the best lawyer in Texas to defend his son. Acquitted, young Frank had briefly served in the Texas Rangers before trailing a cattle herd to Kansas where he became a gambler and draw fighter in the wide-open cow towns. He met rustler and all-round bad man Dave Rudabaugh, followed him to the New Mexico

Territory, fell in with Billy the Kid and that hard crowd, and fought in the Lincoln County War. Sporting a thigh wound, Tansey drifted to Las Vegas and served as a peace officer there and in White Oaks and then wandered into northern Arizona and signed on with the Hash Knife outfit as a hired gun and was a major shootist in the Graham-Tewksbury feud. He drifted again and gambled, tended bar, tried his hand at gold prospecting and served for a year as a deputy U.S. marshal. By the time he rode back to Texas, he had killed thirteen men and earned a reputation as one of the deadliest gunmen on the frontier. He was nursing a beer in an El Paso saloon when he heard that down on the Pecos a man named Caleb Perry was offering a five-thousand-dollar reward for the head of the outlaw Shawn O'Brien.

The man doing the talking was a slightly built whiskey drummer by the name of Ike Crispin who said he'd heard about the reward when he was peddling his wares in the town of Big Buck.

Tansey took the man aside. "Is that the O'Brien brother they call the Town Tamer?"

"You mean there's more of them?" Crispin asked.

"Yeah. There are four brothers and the worst of them is Jake O'Brien. Was he in town?"

"I don't recollect hearing the name, so I don't think so."

Tansey wanted more information. "This Perry feller, he in Big Buck?"

"He sure is and by all accounts he wants that O'Brien ranny dead, dead, dead."

Tansey nodded. "Then I reckon I'll oblige him."

❊ ❊ ❊

Shawn O'Brien and Maria Cantrell were lovers, but they were not in love. They found solace in each other's arms and at that time and place it was all they needed.

Shawn was content to live in the ruined cabin and had even improved the roof with scrap lumber and fallen tree branches. He had not yet formulated a plan to free Manuel, but he'd killed Caleb Perry a hundred times . . . at least in his imagination.

At first light, Shawn heard Maria whimper in her sleep and her legs moved as though she was running from something. He shook her gently and she opened her beautiful eyes, still haunted by the fear of her dream.

He sat up on one elbow. "You were dreaming. You're all right now."

"I saw a man, Shawn. A man on a pale horse and he—"

"He what?"

"He carried your head on his saddle horn." She blinked, her eyelashes fluttering like black lace fans. "I ran and he came after me . . . and   and then you woke me up."

Shawn smiled. "Too much coffee before bed I reckon."

Maria shook her head. "No, it wasn't. It was real. I remember my grandmother used to put seven leaves from an ash tree under her pillow to attract prophetic dreams and she told me how to identify them. I've had a warning dream. It told me that evil is headed our way, but we still have time to change the outcome."

"Good. Then I can keep my head," Shawn said.

"It's not funny, Shawn. It's real."

Maria was so visibly upset that Shawn decided not to tease her any further and held her trembling body in his arms. "I guess we'll have to be more careful until the danger passes."

"You do believe me, Shawn, don't you?" Maria had sobs in her voice.

"Yes, yes, I believe you. And I'll be careful." Only then did he remember . . . *Behold a pale horse and he who sits on it has the name death.* "Yes, I believe you."

Suddenly, the morning air felt chill.

CHAPTER TWENTY-EIGHT

"Since my gun frigates interest only governments that can afford the cost, I'm used to dealing with diplomats, not policemen." Caleb Perry's mouth was a thin gash of irritation.

"Sir, I can assure you that her Britannic Majesty's government has given me full authority to make the necessary airship purchases," Inspector Adam Ready said.

"But I still ask myself, why send a relatively low-ranking policeman?"

"Because my detective skills will help ensure that the British Empire will have parity in the air. In other words, Mr. Perry, we must be able to match the great powers of Europe combined. I am here to see that this is the case. Of course, our immediate concern is Germany and our hereditary enemy France."

"The French have placed no orders for my steam frigates," Perry said.

"Not yet, but they will once Great Britain and Germany have them. The French are not ones to lag behind in modern weaponry. Their Lahitolle

95-millimeter breechloader cannon is the envy of the world."

"Let us not forget that the United States will not lag behind either."

"The British government entirely discounts that possibility. The United States will not let itself be embroiled in future European wars. After the slaughter of your Civil War, the American public doesn't have the belly for another fight and will always put bread before battles." Ready touched the side of his nose. "And that leads me to a question, Mr. Perry, to be answered in the strictest confidence. I have it on excellent authority that the Germans have ordered twenty frigates. Naturally, the British will require twenty-one. How do you plan to build all those air weapons?"

"I'll add more building bays to the existing foundry and increase the labor force tenfold, perhaps much more than that."

"Where will you find such numbers of workers?" Ready wondered.

"High wages will always attract professionals like engineers, mechanics, carpenters, and their ilk, Inspector. As for common laborers, I can find all I need in Mexico. Mexican peons are not real people like you and me. They are very primitive and adapt very well to hard physical labor. And they are a docile people, especially when I intend to allow them to bring their wives and children to Abaddon."

"And they work cheap, I presume. Her Majesty's government is not a spendthrift institution."

"The Mexicans work cheap and since they're small

they don't eat much," Perry said. "Be assured that every British pound sterling will be carefully spent."

"On the face of it, all seems to be well." Ready placed his cup on the saucer and switched his attention to Lizzie Skates. "You make a nice cup of tea, my dear."

"I have a lot of talents, Inspector," she said, smiling as she crossed then uncrossed her shapely legs.

That flustered Ready a little. "Mr. Perry, I would like to see the steam frigate that is currently under construction."

"Ah, the *Count Werner Von Jungen*. Why of course you can."

Ready was appalled. "That's what the frigate is named?"

"Yes," Perry said, enjoying himself. "It's the first of the German ships, named after a famous industrialist."

"Then the first British ship must be the *Queen Victoria*."

"Of course. What other name could we possibly use for such a fine vessel?"

"Indeed," the inspector said, feeling that he was being teased.

Jacob O'Brien was on the floor of the construction bay with Manuel Cantrell when Caleb Perry led Detective Inspector Ready onto the gantry. Lizzie Skates in her usual boned corset, short skirt, and boots stood with them. She wore a white top hat adorned with diamond-studded goggles and carried an ivory-handled riding crop in her hands.

While Perry pointed out the various parts of the rapidly emerging steam frigate and the work crews became suddenly busy, Jacob spoke urgently to Manuel. "You've told the others about the plan?"

The young man nodded as though the big foreman was giving him work instructions. "They will do as you tell them."

"Good. It's not going to be easy."

"Nothing at Abaddon ever is. Did you hear about the attempted escape?"

Jacob nodded as if confirming instructions. "Three men, wasn't it?"

"Five. They couldn't open a locked door and were gunned down by Breens and Kilcoyn right where they stood. One of them was sixteen years old."

"That will come to an end real soon," Jacob said, a slow-rising anger in him.

"So you say," Manuel said. "Maybe there's no escape from hell. You ever think on that?"

"There is a way to escape from this hell. And I'll help you find it."

That evening, Detective Inspector Adam Ready signed a contract for twenty-one steam frigates. The contract would later be mailed to the British Legate in Washington to be ratified.

Caleb Perry was so delighted he gifted Ready with a fine top hat and a pair of goggles to wear while he was in Big Buck. He also gave him the use of Lizzie Skates as a gesture of goodwill.

Ready chose not to remain within the smoky, noisy confines of the foundry and Perry agreed that the hotel would probably be more restful.

It would prove to be a tragic, terrible mistake, but how was Perry to know that close contact with a homicidal madman had infected Adam Ready's mind?

CHAPTER TWENTY-NINE

Lizzie Skates's death was neither quick nor pleasant. She'd tried to scream, but her vocal cords had been cut and making any sound had been impossible. Adam Ready was good with the knife. He'd studied Jack the Ripper's technique up close and modeled his own blade work on that brilliant model.

Lizzie was only his second kill, the first a nameless streetwalker in the Whitechapel district of London. His colleagues who investigated the murder said the woman's mutilations were definitely the work of Jolly Jack and Ready had been secretly pleased at the comparison.

Drenched in blood, he sat back in the easy chair that the hotel had thoughtfully provided and regarded Lizzie's body with considerable pleasure. The cutting had gone well and she was opened up like a gutted fish, her insides exposed for all the world to see. Her dead face bore an expression that intrigued him, an open-eyed look of horror, pain, and surprise all mixed together. She'd bled more than his first one, probably because that cutting had taken place outdoors in a fog shrouded alley and he'd hurried the process for fear of being discovered. But cutting and carving at his leisure, the wounds were much more extensive and, naturally, the more cuts he made, the more blood was spilled.

He lit his S-shaped pipe with scarlet hands, wishing there was someone he could tell about the difficulties he'd faced. Her boned corset, done up with straps and buckles and laces, had deflected his initial knife thrusts and for a moment he'd panicked. Subsequent stabs at her had gone home deep and he and Lizzie had become perfect friends again. He believed an onlooker would have laughed to watch his cursing struggles to divest the woman of her corset, the better to expose her large, white breasts. But in the end he'd managed . . . and as they say, all's well that ends well.

Ready consulted Lizzie's pocket watch that hung around his neck. Early yet, only eight o'clock and barely dark. He'd sit for an hour or so and enjoy the company. Ah yes, life was good, but he would kill for a nice cup of tea. *Earl Grey, please, with no milk and one lump of sugar. Thank you very much.*

Adam Ready was dozing when the grandfather clock in the lobby woke him. He opened his eyes and stretched and the thickly crusted blood on his hands and arms pulled at his skin. Lizzie Skates's body was a patchwork of gray skin and black gore. Her face was shadowed and there was no light in her eyes. She was just a corpse, stiff and cold and of no further interest to the killer.

The mess had to be cleaned up.

He rose, shrugged into his tweed overcoat, and placed his new top hat on his head. They only person he could turn to, the only man who could possibly understand his strange compulsions, was Caleb Perry.

Ready left the room, took the stairs, and once in the street, headed for the Abaddon Foundry. Guards stood at the door and looked him over, unable to see his bloodstained clothes since his coat covered them. He was allowed to enter and another guard led him to Perry's office where the man still worked at his desk, the thick ledger in front of him illuminated by an oil lamp.

When Perry looked up, Ready said, "Something terrible yet exciting has happened."

To his foremen Anstruther Breens, Blaine Keeners, and Valentine Kilcoyn, Perry said, "Bring some trolls from the foundry and get this place cleaned up, every inch of it, walls, floors, and windows. Damn it, there's blood everywhere."

"What about Lizzie?" Kilcoyn asked.

"Well, she isn't Lizzie any longer, is she?" Perry said. "Carry her back to Abaddon as though she's drunk—"

"The body will fall apart in the street, boss," Kilcoyn said.

"Then bring a box and we'll load her into it. Damn it all, do I have to tell you everything? She'll go up the chimney tonight."

Keeners glared at Adam Ready. "I liked Lizzie Skates. She was good to me."

"Yes, she was a nice lady . . . I mean, for a harlot."

"Then why did you butcher her?" Keeners's hand was on his gun butt.

"I was infected in London by a dread disease that pollutes a madman the press calls Jack the Ripper. Jack cuts up harlots for fun. An evil being he'd left at the scene of one of his murders jumped into my body and it makes me do things . . . terrible things."

"Mister, your cutting days have come to an end right here," Keeners pulled his gun.

Perry yelled, "No, you damn fool!" He saw the shock in Keeners's face and said in a more level tone, "I don't want anything to disrupt my contract with the British government. We can't gun its representative and say he disappeared. There would be an immediate investigation from Washington and London and they might even say the agreement that Ready signed is no longer valid."

"So he just walks away from this a free man?" Kilcoyn asked.

"Yeah, that's how it's going to be," Perry said. "He walks away from this."

"Don't hardly seem right, boss," Keener said. "I mean, Lizzie murdered like that . . ."

"Of course it isn't right. But it's good business. What does her life matter when a contract worth a million dollars is at stake? Now holster your gun, get the body out of here, and see that this place is cleaned up. When that's done, shoot the trolls. The fewer who know about this the better." Perry, small, stocky, and stiff with anger turned a blazing face to Ready. "You'd better come with me to Abaddon, away from the scene of your crime."

"Certainly, Mr. Perry, but could you arrange for a nice cup of tea when we get there? I have something of a headache."

CHAPTER THIRTY

Shawn O'Brien looped the reins around the saloon's hitching rail, gazed around Big Buck's main street, and lifted to his eyes to the Abaddon Foundry crouched close to town like a monstrous beast of prey. Somewhere inside that colossus was Manuel Cantrell, the man he'd pledged to save, and Caleb Perry, the man he'd vowed to kill. "Well, I'm here now, Perry, out in the open. Come and get me any time you feel like it."

Beside him, Maria Cantrell said, "Shawn, making yourself a target will solve nothing. There has to be a better way."

"If there is, I haven't been able to find it. But I'm all through hiding in the brush like a wounded animal. From now on, Perry will have to come for me gun in hand."

"He has men for that." Maria's eyes were wary, frightened.

"Then I'll kill them one by one until I finally get to Perry." Shawn smiled. "Now, can I buy you a drink? It isn't *Le Procope* in Paris, but it will have to do."

"Shawn, please don't do this," Maria begged.

"You may take my arm, madam. Shall we promenade and make a show?"

Arm in arm, they strolled along the boardwalk. Shawn lifted his hat to every woman they passed and offered a cheery good morning to the men. He was making his presence known to as many people as he could. Finally, Maria convinced him to get off the street where he was an obvious target for a rifleman.

After the glare of the late morning sun, the interior of the saloon was dark and cool—and so was bartender Ambrose Hellen's reception. "My God, O'Brien. Are you crazy?"

"Bourbon for me and a gin punch for the lady," Shawn said.

"There's a five-thousand-dollar reward for your head," Hellen said.

Shawn ignored that. "Do you have lemons for the punch? Doña Maria must have lemons."

Hellen shook his head. "Shawn, you were a dead man the moment you rode into Big Buck this morning. Don't you know that?"

"Pour my bourbon, Ambrose, and do what you can with the gin punch."

"Bourbon is fine for me," Maria said. "I think I'm going to need it before too long."

Hellen poured the drinks, casting an eye over the other patrons at the bar and tables. "Enjoy your whiskey and get out of town, O'Brien. You life isn't worth a plugged nickel in Big Buck and, Maria, neither is yours."

She nodded. "That's what I've been trying to tell him. He won't listen."

"How do I get inside Abaddon, Ambrose?" Shawn asked.

"Easy. You just go to the door, tell them you want a job, and march right in with the Mexicans. About two minutes after that, the peons will be working and you'll be dead."

Shawn absorbed that and said, "Let me have a handful of those Dutch cheroots, Ambrose."

"Big handful or small handful?"

"Call it a dozen and I need a box of lucifers."

A voice from the other end of the bar called, "Hey Ambrose, what went on at the Rest and Be Thankful last night?"

"I don't know and I don't want to know."

"They say a couple Abaddon foremen carried a heavy box out of the hotel and took it to the foundry. Carried it like a coffin they say."

"They say too much, Jeb. What goes on at Abaddon is none of my concern or yours either."

"It's strange all the same. Very strange." Jeb went back to his drink and his female companion.

"How strange was it, Ambrose?" Shawn whispered.

"Strange enough that it shouldn't concern you."

"They call me the Town Tamer and I aim to tame Big Buck. So how strange was it?"

Hellen sighed and dropped his voice to a whisper. "There was a trail of blood in the street. Charlie Elsyng the night watchman saw it. He says it led from the hotel to the foundry. Charlie said there was so much blood it was a cutting for sure."

"What did he do about it?" Shawn asked.

"Do about it? For fifty cents a night, Charlie did nothing about it. He lit a shuck and spent the rest of the night bedded down right here in the saloon, said he was scared of boogeymen."

"Shawn, whatever it was and whoever was cut up, is none of our business," Maria insisted.

"Caleb Perry was up to something last night," Shawn said. "I'd like to know what it was."

"Why?"

"I have to do something, anything, to bring Perry to me," Shawn answered. "Ambrose is right, I wouldn't last long inside the Abaddon foundry."

"In or out of the foundry you're not gonna last long." Hellen thumbed his chest. "This old crow has eaten enough field corn to know that sometimes scarecrows carry shotguns. You're in the wrong meadow, O'Brien. I suggest you get while the getting's good."

"Thanks for the advice, Ambrose. But all the same I think I'll wander over to the hotel and have a word with the desk clerk about last night. It may be preying on his mind."

Hellen suddenly looked older. "I won't come to your funeral, O'Brien, but the drinks are on me. Just make believe I'm paying for your wake."

The gloomy desk clerk opened his eyes wide when he saw Maria and wider as soon as he eyeballed Shawn O'Brien. "It's you again. Last time you was here, you shoved the barrel of a Colt's gun up my nose."

"I come in peace," Shawn said, smiling. "All I want is some information."

"That's what you wanted the last time," the clerk whined, "and I got no information to share."

Maria wore a fitted black dress split up the front over a white blouse and high boots. Her only jewelry was a skeleton pocket watch suspended on a silver chain around her neck. She wore a black top hat and goggles in the accepted Big Buck fashion. Well aware of the effect she had on men, she stepped close enough to the clerk that he felt the warmth of her body. "I do worry that perhaps some of my friends were involved. I believe several members of the Women's Temperance Guild of Texas were staying here last night."

For a few moments, the clerk seemed hypnotized by the throbbing pulse in Maria's throat, but he managed to croak, "No, ma'am. There was only an English gentleman in residence. Well, him and old Mrs. Betsy Conroy in Room Twelve. The poor old soul is our permanent resident."

"Who is the English gent?" Shawn asked. "I spent several years in England and I might know him."

The clerk looked at Shawn with obvious distaste. "Though England is not as large as the United States, I imagine that your knowing him is highly unlikely." "Besides, the gentleman in question is a Scotland Yard detective and he must be careful who he knows and does not know." The man looked Shawn up and down. "Violent roughnecks are everywhere."

Shawn O'Brien had a short fuse and it was possible the clerk would have found himself with yet another nose full of Colt had Maria not seen the danger and said, "La, la, Scotland Yard indeed, and right here in Big Buck. How perfectly exquisite! Is he here to investigate an international crime?"

The clerk smiled. "O dear no. He's a guest of

Mr. Perry. I imagine he is here to discuss the role of cannons in police work. Small cannons of course. Perhaps for controlling striking industrial workers and mobs like that."

"Did the box that was carried out of here last night come from the detective's room?" Shawn asked.

"I'm sure I don't know." Something was hidden behind the clerk's eyes.

"It could only have come from the detective's room," Shawn said. "Unless dear old permanent resident Betsy had a body stashed away under her bed."

"There was no box and no body was taken from this hotel," the clerk emphasized. "If you think otherwise, you are very much mistaken. And now I wish you good day, sir."

None of the O'Brien brothers were blushing violets. Jacob did his best to keep an explosive temper on a short leash, but since the murder of his wife, Shawn never did. It flared. His right hand shot out and he grabbed the clerk by the ear and twisted. Hard. As the man struggled and grimaced, Shawn said, "Show me the Englishman's room. Maria, do you have your derringer?"

"Yes, I have it."

"Good. If this ranny gives me any trouble, shoot him." To the clerk, he said, "Now, show me the room. What the hell is your name anyhow?"

"It's Claude Finain and Mr. Perry will hear of this."

Unaffected by the threat, Shawn led Finain to the stairs by his ear. "Rather hot out today, isn't it? But I think we can expect some rain."

The clerk said nothing. His pained expression was answer enough.

He climbed the stairs and stopped at the Englishman's room. "This room . . . this room. Now let loose of my ear."

"Open the door. Now, sonny, in you go." Shawn pushed the clerk inside, let go of the man's tormented ear, and looked around. The room had been vacated, the bed had been made up, and nothing seemed amiss.

Maria stood rooted to the spot and her beautiful face took on an expression of horror, as though she'd just seen a headless ghost. Her knees buckled and she quickly sat on the edge of the bed.

Even Finain looked concerned as Shawn said, "Maria, are you feeling ill?"

"Can't you smell it, Shawn? Blood, so much blood. And pain and fear and a terrible death."

Shawn stood baffled

Finain shook his head. and said, "There is no blood here. No death."

"Look between the floorboards." She watched Shawn get down on one knee and asked, "Do you see it?"

Shawn got out his Barlow knife and probed with the blade. He brought up some black stuff on the tip of the blade and rubbed it between finger and thumb. He sniffed the smear and studied it closely. "It's blood all right. And it's fresh." He spent the next couple minutes on his knees examining the spaces between the boards. "Maria, what do you think this is?" Between his fingers, he held up a small piece of gold-colored metal.

She looked at it closely. "It's the back of a woman's earring. It may have been lost last night or a long time ago."

"Well, there's blood everywhere between the floorboards. Somebody bled out in this room and the body was taken away in a box. The question is who?"

"And was it murder or suicide?" Maria said. "I say murder, and I think a woman may have been the victim."

"And her killer? He could only be the English detective, huh, Finain?"

"Everything you two have said is ridiculous. Inspector Adam Ready is from Scotland Yard. He wouldn't commit a crime like murder, if indeed it ever happened. Maybe somebody killed a dog."

"And maybe pigs fly," Shawn said. "Maria, what's the mayor's name again?"

"John Deakins."

"Yeah, him. Let's go talk to His Honor."

"About what?" Finain asked. "Mr. Deakins is a busy man."

Shawn shrugged. "What I have in mind won't take long."

CHAPTER THIRTY-ONE

"No, it's out of the question. I might go as far as to say that your request is as monstrous as your accusation," Mayor John Deakins blustered in his loud fashion.

"Who else could have committed murder in the Rest and Be Thankful last night?" Shawn asked.

"Mr. O'Brien, you have no proof there even was a murder."

"What about the blood?"

"Some drummer cut himself shaving weeks ago. How the hell should I know? To accuse a Scotland Yard detective inspector of such a crime is outrageous. Why, it could be a *casus belli* between the United States and Great Britain. If you know what *casus belli* means."

Shawn smirked. "Just looked it up, did you, Mayor? I think that bringing a depraved killer to justice would hardly be a cause for war."

"That is a terrible accusation, Mr. O'Brien. And who was the murdered party? Can you even guess?"

"No, I can't guess. That's why you're going to swear me in as the sheriff of Big Buck."

"Indeed I will not. Mr. Caleb Perry provides us with all the law enforcement we need. Why, thanks to him, this is the safest, most peaceful town west of the Mississippi."

"That's your the last word on the matter?" Shawn asked.

"Indeed it is. I will say no more."

"Then hear me." Shawn stepped around the mayor's desk, bent over, and whispered something in Deakins's ear.

The mayor's round face turned red. "Damn you, sir. That is most singularly unfair," the mayor said.

"You gave me no choice," Shawn said.

Angry, Deakins opened a desk drawer, searched but found nothing, and slammed it shut. He opened another and found what he was looking for, a five-pointed tin star. He passed the badge to Shawn and said, "You are now the sheriff of Big Buck with all the legal powers appertaining thereto."

Shawn glanced at the star. "Right there it says *marshal,* not *sheriff.*"

"*Marshal, sheriff,* what the hell difference does it make? For better or for worse, you're now the law in this town."

"Thank you most kindly, Mayor. We'll discuss my salary later."

After they left City Hall and regained the boardwalk, Maria snapped her parasol open and asked, "How did you get Deakins to change his mind?"

"I told him that I'd send a wire to my brother Jake and tell him that the mayor of Big Buck called him an ignorant, yellow-bellied, papist mick, and that he planned to shoot him on sight."

"A threat like that would get any man to change his mind."

"Yeah it would, especially since I mentioned that my brother has killed men for a lot less. Of course Jake would just ignore it, but Deakins doesn't know that."

"Do you think Deakins really has heard of Jacob?"

Shawn grinned, "I sure do. A man who hasn't doesn't shake like that."

"I'm shaken to the core, Mr. Perry," Mayor John Deakins said. "He threatened me with his brother, a known gunman and desperado by the name of Jake O'Brien."

Perry's eyes lifted to Valentine Kilcoyn in a question.

The big foreman said, "Last I heard, O'Brien was running with Doc Holliday up in the New Mexico Territory, but that was a couple years back. They say him and his brothers don't get along, something to do with who'll inherit their pa's ranch or some such."

"There's little chance of O'Brien showing up in Big Buck?" Perry asked.

"That would be my guess, boss. Hell, don't wet your pants, Mayor. If he does show, I'll take care of him."

Deakins's face was still troubled. "I've heard he'd

killed a score of men and he's mean enough to piss in a widow woman's kindling."

"Well dear me. I've pissed on a widow woman's kindling before and I bite so hard my mama had to feed me with a slingshot," Kilcoyn said. "So don't worry about Jake O'Brien. I've cut the suspenders of his kind before and ground their bones into dust for tooth powder."

Perry smiled. "Mr. Kilcoyn's *curriculum vita* impresses us all. I think you have little to fear, Mayor Deakins."

"What about Shawn O'Brien, our new marshal? He's no kind of bargain, either."

"We put the crawl on him before and we'll do it again," Kilcoyn said. "After the beating he took, I'm surprised he's got the gall to show his face around here."

"Let O'Brien think he's the law in Big Buck," Perry ordered. "He's harmless."

"He says the English detective murdered somebody in his hotel room. O'Brien is trying to stir up trouble."

Perry and Kilcoyn exchanged glances, then a sudden roar drowned out Perry's voice as he started speaking. After a few moments, the racket stopped and he explained. "They must be testing the new frigate's steam engine." To Deakins, he said, "Inspector Ready will leave us tomorrow on the noon train and return to Washington. So that particular mischief of O'Brien's will end." Perry smiled. "Now, I hope we've put your mind at rest, Mayor. If you encounter any other problems, feel free to come and talk to me."

Deakins replaced his top hat and goggles and rose to his feet. "Is Miss Skates available?"

"No. Lizzie will be indisposed for a few days. You understand?"

"Yes, yes perfectly. I am a married man. Well, I must be on my way. Good day to you, Mr. Perry."

"Yes, and good day to you, Mayor. Don't worry about a thing."

After Deakins left, Perry said, "I hope that fool gets decapitated in the first broadside."

"Are we worried about O'Brien snooping around the hotel, boss?"

"Of course we're worried. And we will be until Ready is safely on the train and becomes someone else's problem."

"He wants to be that Jack the Ripper ranny," Kilcoyn surmised.

"Yeah, well he can be whoever the hell he wants so long as he does his ripping in England and not here."

CHAPTER THIRTY-TWO

Detective Inspector Adam Ready strolled leisurely through a field of bloodred poppies, the summer sun warming his naked body and the air he breathed carrying the scent of distant pines. Ahead of him, the gray stone walls of a ruined gothic cathedral gleamed like ivory and from somewhere within, the laughter of a young girl fell around him as soft as a spring rain.

Ready had never felt happier . . . the poppies, the sun, the girl, and the vicious curved blade in his hand, keen as a razor, combined to assure him he'd truly found paradise.

Above his head, like a lily on the blue pool of the sky, a great sky craft clattered, its bronze cannons gleaming like gold. The canopy was as yellow as the sun and suspended underneath was a graceful Viking ship, the dragonhead at the prow snarling with painted white fangs. As the ship passed overhead, its propeller spun lazily and cast a spectrum of red, yellow, blue, and purple light on his body, making him look like a man of many colors. A rainbow man. A door opened under the ship and cascades of scarlet roses fell on his head and shoulders.

A gentle voice that was neither male nor female sang out to him, "Good luck, Adam. And good hunting."

The airship passed and became lost in distance. Ready smiled and walked through the rippling poppies like a man wading through blood and headed for the ruin where the girl was. He saw her as she stood watching him, a slender nymph with white blond hair to her waist. She wore a garland of pink wildflowers about her head and a gown as green as grass and so diaphanous it appeared to be made of spider silk. Her body was lithe and supple, white as new-fallen snow except for the coral tips of her breasts. He couldn't see the girl's face. From eyes to forehead, she wore a golden mask painted with a checkerboard pattern of tiny ebony and silver squares.

His lips wet, he increased his pace and blood drops of poppy petals fell to the ground.

The girl stood and beckoned to him with both arms and she sang in the voice of an angel, "Come to me . . . come hither to me . . . my love . . . my life . . . my death . . ."

Reaching the ruined cathedral, he walked to the girl, but she flitted away from him like a startled bird."

"Are you a harlot?" he yelled, his voice hollow as a drum. "I wish to know if you're a harlot."

The girl stopped, parted her gown so that her beautiful body was revealed, and said, "I am Kateryn, the Queen of Harlots."

"I'm down on such women, streetwalkers and the like," Ready said.

She laughed and ran into the echoing nave, roofless but with the surrounding walls still intact. Carved pillars supported pointed arches and above them, the triforiums and clerestories with their long slender windows. He followed until she stopped where the high altar once stood. A mist fell *quickly and curled through the nave like a gray serpent. Standing like a marble statue, the naked girl held chains attached to iron collars around the necks of two massive and horrific gargoyles—crouching figures of men with bat wings and grotesque, snarling faces of ravenous wolves.*

"Why do you come here, Adam Ready?" she asked.

"Because I'm down on the likes of you. I have my knife."

"I am Kateryn."

"I know who you are," Ready said. "You're the queen of all the harlots."

Her face was hidden behind her mask, her body lost in mist. "Tell me again. Why are you here?"

"I'm here to kill you, gut you like a pink hog."

"Ah, you wish to be like Jack from London town. The girls all love Jolly Jack."

"He is a master with the blade. I learned much from him."

On either side of Kateryn, the gargoyles rose to their feet. Both were eight foot tall and their savage heads and massive shoulders showed above the mist. They lifted their heads and roared like jungle beasts.

"Come closer, Adam," the girl enticed. "The gargoyles won't harm you. Jack the Jester is himself a gargoyle and so are you. Come, make your sport and let us see how well you cut."

The knife felt good in Ready's hand. He advanced on Kateryn, stepped close. The saliva from the muzzles of the towering gargoyles slicked over his head and shoulders.

"Cut," she said. "Cut . . . cut deep . . ." Her breathing was heavy. Her breath rotten, like someone long dead.

Ready placed the tip of the knife against Kateryn's belly and drew a dewdrop of blood. "Now," he said and plunged his knife into her. He must kiss her as she died in his arms. He reached up and tore off her mask . . . and recoiled in horror.

Adam Ready woke and stared at the scowling, bearded face of a man looking down at him. Something sharp and cold dug into him just under his chin. "Remember me? Blaine Keeners, Lizzie's friend. How does it feel to be her, Ready?"

He'd had a wonderful dream. It was behind him and he wanted to scream, but the sound choked in his throat as the knife went in . . . just a smidgen deeper. He tried to struggle out of his cot, but the foreman was big and strong and easily pinned him down.

"How does it feel?" Keeners's face was so close, Ready smelled his rancid, alcohol-heavy breath. "Are you scared, like Lizzie must have been?"

Ready's eyes were huge in the darkness of his room. He heard the dim roar of the foundry just beyond his wall. "She was only a harlot. My life is worth more than a hundred, a thousand of those."

"You killed her for being what she was," Keener said.

"I'm down on them, seed, breed, and generation," Ready said, his voice a whisper.

"Lizzie was the queen of harlots, and you murdered her."

Ready begged, "Don't, please don't hurt me. I'll give you money. I have it in my pocket."

"What did Lizzie say as you cut her? What did she say? Tell me what she said."

"Nothing . . . she was in shock and said nothing.

She breathed hard, gasped when the knife went in, and sobbed, but said nothing."

"Now it's time, Ready. We'll meet again in hell." Keeners pushed on the knife. The blade plunged into the detective's throat, thrust upward through the roof of his mouth, and rammed upward with terrible strength into his brain.

Adam Ready caught of a glimpse of Kateryn in the misty cathedral where the high altar once stood. The girl removed her mask, opened her mouth, and laughed . . . and then he saw nothing at all.

CHAPTER THIRTY-THREE

Just before dawn, Valentine Kilcoyn roused Jacob O'Brien from sleep. "You're on deck." He laid a cup of coffee on the side table next to Jacob's cot. "Drink that and then report to the construction bay."

Still groggy, Jacob said, "What's going on?"

"That damn fool Egbert Killick talked Mr. Perry into testing the prototype frigate with all eight gun crews. He wants fifty trolls onboard to see how she handles with that much weight."

"The cannon crews aren't ready," Jacob said, realizing that on Killick's whim his plan might be compromised.

"This trip there's no shooting involved." Kilcoyn made a face. "Killick wants to check the steering. All you're there for is to keep control of the trolls so make sure you're armed. An engineer and a few technicians will do the rest."

"How's the weather?"

Kilcoyn grinned. "Windy and raining. That's why a new man gets all the rotten jobs, Buck."

* * *

Jacob was glad to see Manuel Cantrell among the men assigned to the test flight and they exchanged a nod as the trolls were loaded into the gondola. The roof was already open, revealing a black sky, and Killick had the engineer and technicians in place so no time was lost in getting the craft airborne. The tiny frigate drifted upward, and then the propeller drove it north. From the start, high winds buffeted the airship and Killick had a difficult time keeping it on course. The rain wasn't heavy, just enough to soak everyone onboard. Miserable, the trolls huddled together, a few of them already airsick.

Jacob sat at the helm with Killick, who'd pushed his goggles back onto the crown of his top hat and was constantly glancing at the gray sky.

"A couple more miles and I'll do some maneuvering, see how she handles. When I say the word, have your gun crews stand by their cannons." Killick's wizened little face broke into a rare smile. "Despite this damn gale, so far she's handling well."

"Like a bucking pony." Jacob's lurching belly made his attempted smile twist into a grimace. He'd never in his life been seasick, but he'd never experienced anything like this. The ship was bouncing all over the sky, but Killick and the technicians didn't seem to notice.

Later, the sick, wretched gun crews at their stations, Killick forced the small frigate into a series of fast turns, climbs, and dives and soon the bottom of the gondola was rancid with vomit.

But he was ecstatic. "Wonderful!" he yelled to

Jacob, rain running from the brim of his hat. "She handles the extra weight perfectly and I predict the full-size ship will be even more stable." The little pilot grinned. "A great day, Mr. Ross! A day that will be remembered in history."

Jacob nodded. He felt as sick as a poisoned pup.

Killick helmed what, in his unbounded joy, he'd called "the dragon cub frigate" low over the Abaddon Foundry so that Mr. Perry would hear the clattering clamor of the engine. His goggles back in place, top hat pulled down to his ears, Killick looked like a demented gnome as he roared away from the foundry and lost altitude as he made a triumphal pass down Big Buck's main street, the dragon ship's gondola just six feet above the ground.

The morning crowd on the boardwalk stopped and marveled at the speeding flying machine and dear Mrs. Honoria Hatton, a nervous soul who dressed out at around three hundred pounds, fainted into the arms of her diminutive husband and flattened him like a pancake into the muddy timbers.

One of the onlookers who rushed to the groaning Mr. Hatton's help was Shawn O'Brien. As the airship roared past, parting the wind and rain, he caught a glimpse of a startled, unshaven face and a pair of icy black eyes and then Jacob was gone, his flying machine on an upward climb into the realm of the birds.

Shawn whispered, "What the hell?" and then had an awful thought. *Has Jake sold his gun to Caleb Perry?* If that was the case, he and his brother were now enemies. Shawn felt his heart sink as he fought to regain his composure. Sired by the same father, taught to live by the same code of decency and the doing of what was right, he refused to believe Jake would stoop that low. There had to be some reason for him to be in the flying contraption. *Is it his way of freeing Manuel Cantrell?* Shawn gave an imperceptible nod. That could be the only answer.

"Help me get poor Mrs. Hatton to her feet," a woman said.

He put Jake out of his mind until later. A far weightier problem needed his immediate attention.

CHAPTER THIRTY-FOUR

"Did you tell Adam Ready about the preliminary gun test?" Caleb Perry was mighty pleased with Egbert Killick and eagerly awaited his reply, but he was doomed to disappointment.

"I didn't see the inspector after I landed so I sent Buck Ross to knock on his door and rouse him," Killick said. "But he didn't wake up and after a while Ross left."

"Damn that Englishman. I want him to take a good report back to the British in Washington about the potential performance of their steam frigates." Perry shook his head. "Too much brandy last night. I'll wake him."

Accompanied by Valentine Kilcoyn, Perry pounded on Ready's door. No answer. He tried again with the same result. "Inspector Ready, open the door!" His demand was met with silence. Louder, he yelled, *"Open the damn door!"*

There was still no response and Perry cursed under his breath. "Do you have a key for this door?"

"Blaine Keeners has the keys to all the guest rooms," Kilcoyn said. "I'll go get him."

"Stay where you are," Perry ordered. "Kick the damn door down."

"But—"

"Kick it down!"

Kilcoyn shrugged, raised his booted foot, and slammed it into the thin timber paneling of the door, smashing it open in a shower of flying splinters. He followed Perry inside. Adam Ready lay on the bed, his lifeless eyes staring at the ceiling. His face was a bloody mask and had stained the entire surface of his pillow a glistening scarlet.

As a youngster, Kilcoyn had gone up the trail a couple times and had never lost the puncher's superstitious way of thinking. "Lizzie came back from the grave and done for him," he said in a stunned whisper.

"This wasn't Lizzie. It was murder. Is Blaine Keeners the only man with a key to this room?"

"As far as I know, boss." The quaver in Kilcoyn's voice revealed that he still pegged the dead woman as the killer.

Perry's face was like stone. "Go get him. Bring him here. First give me your gun belt."

The boss was in a strange mood and Kilcoyn knew better than to question him. He unbuckled his gun and passed it over.

"Bring him," Perry commanded.

"Boss, I don't think—"

"Bring him!"

* * *

Kilcoyn returned with Blaine Keeners.

Perry let the big foreman's eyes move to the dead man on the bed for a while. "You have the only key to this room?"

"It wasn't locked." Keeners looked defiant and rock steady, a man with sand.

"Did you kill him?"

"Yeah, I killed him. He had a faster death than the one he gave Lizzie."

"Keeners, do you know what you've cost me?" Perry kept his anger barely contained. "You've cost me the entire British contract for twenty-one air frigates. They won't want to do business with a company that murders their representatives."

Kilcoyn said, "Boss, maybe we can explain to—"

"Explaining leads to government investigations and government investigations take too long, sometimes years." Perry took a newspaper from his coat pocket and waved it in Keener's face. "Have you heard of the *Fontanette Falcon*? The French say it's a fifty-gun flying warship that will be ready for testing in two years. Spain, the same story, only their ten-gun prototype is currently being built. According to this paper, our own country is considering a flying platform that will carry two cannon batteries and a regiment of infantry. I read that President Cleveland is very interested in the project." Perry threw the paper into Keener's face. "Avenging your harlot could destroy me."

"She was yours, too, Mr. Perry," Keeners pointed out. "Lizzie belonged to everybody, but I loved her."

"Yes, of course you did. We all screwed Lizzie, but we all loved her," Perry agreed. "All right, I'll study on this and see if I can make things up with the British. I can tell them Ready died of a heart attack and was buried with full military honors, or whatever the hell Scotland Yard detectives are buried with." He placed a hand on Keeners's shoulder. "I understand how you feel, Blaine. In your shoes, I would have done the same thing. Now return to your duties."

"Sorry, boss. I'm sorry it happened."

Perry nodded and smiled slightly. "It's all right. No hard feelings."

Keeners turned and got as far as the shattered door before Perry fired. Three bullets slammed into the big man's back and two of them went through his body and splintered into the doorjamb.

Keeners was dead when he hit the ground.

"Burn him." Perry picked up the newspaper and tossed it onto the body. "And use that as kindling."

Kilcoyn stood where he was, like a man turned to stone, unable to move. "In the back . . ."

"Yes. I executed him. Now get the trolls to burn both bodies, but save some ashes. I need something to give the British. Talk to the undertaker. What's his name?"

"Dorian Steggles," Kilcoyn said as though he was speaking to himself.

"Yeah, Steggles. Ask him for a nice cremation urn, the best he's got, and we'll scoop Ready into it. Maybe old Queen Victoria will put it on her mantel." Perry brushed past Kilcoyn then stopped and turned back. "Send one of the harlots to my office. I always enjoy a woman after I kill a man."

CHAPTER THIRTY-FIVE

There's nothing wrong with killing a man. Everybody dies and a bullet only hastens the deceased into the grave a little early. That in a nutshell was the philosophy of Frank Tansey, probably one of the deadliest gunmen in Texas. Even the half-crazy, homicidal Dave Rudabaugh stepped lightly when Tansey was on the prod and Bill Bonney admitted that of all the pistoleros he'd known, Tansey was the fastest on the draw and shoot.

However twisted his reasoning, the tall gunman lived by a code. He drew the line at killing women and children and he never abused or ill-treated animals. For years, a little calico cat had ridden in his saddlebag and accompanied him everywhere. When the kitty died of old age, he'd never sought another.

The killing of Shawn O'Brien, the Town Tamer, was just another chore to be done. It was strictly a business proposition that would put money in his bank account.

Tansey considered Big Buck a cow town like any other and he'd seen dozens of them. The warm beer and overpriced whiskey would be the same. It would have the same creaky-floored hotel room that filled up during the day with flies and dung dust from the cattle pens and mosquitos at night. No one would be glad at his coming or sad at his leaving except the saloon girls and the bartenders.

Abaddon gave him pause. The cannon foundry thrust out of the ground like a gargantuan steel fist and dwarfed everything around it—the town, its people, and even the surrounding prairie that was the creation of God. A chimney taller than any tree erupted thick smoke and defaced the blue sky with its own black cloud. The foundry sounded like a hundred locomotives highballing on the same track, a never-ending clanking, clanging, racketing roar.

Some towns are so pleasant that they invite a man to linger. Big Buck was not one of them. Tansey decided to get his business done, collect his bounty, and ride the hell out of there and bed down under the quiet stars.

He left his horse at the livery stable and walked across the rainy street to the saloon. A bartender was the font of all knowledge and he'd know if Shawn O'Brien was in town or not. If so, it would be just a matter of calling him out and getting the job done.

Tansey gave himself an hour to get his work in, collect the bounty, and light a shuck. Looking around at the men in the street, he didn't see anyone who was likely to try and stop him.

He stepped inside and ordered a beer. "So how come everybody in town wears those spectacle things on their hat brims?" he asked Ambrose Hellen.

The bartender smiled. "They're called goggles. The workers at Abaddon wear them and it's how the folks show their support for the foundry and what it's done for the town. I got cheese and crackers. You like cheese?"

"Yeah, cheese is just fine."

"Passin' through?" Hellen set a wedge of cheddar in front of Tansey. "The cracker barrel is at the end of the bar. Help yourself."

"I'm looking for a man," Tansey said.

"Anyone in particular?"

"Feller by the name of Shawn O'Brien."

As soon as Tansey walked though the door Hellen had pegged him as a gun. He had that stillness about him that some draw fighters acquired and the ever-present aura of danger. And had no doubt that the man was dangerous.

His voice even, Hellen said, "He's the new law around here."

Tansey didn't react. "Been a lawman myself a couple times. Good employment if a man has sand and is suited to it."

"O'Brien has sand. You can depend on that."

"I know he has. And so does his brother Jake. Good cheese. Nice and sharp. Where can I find him?"

"Right here. He usually pops in around two for a bite. Well, he's done that a couple times at least."

"He eat cheese and crackers?"

"Well, his taste runs to caviar and crackers, but since I don't have any of that, yeah he eats cheese."

"Then I'll wait for him," Tansey said.

"Mister, I suggest you ride on," Hellen said. "Whatever you got in mind, it ain't worth dying for."

"I've got a job to do." Tansey took a bite. "Where does this cheese come from?"

"Wisconsin, I guess. Lot of dairy farms up that way."

"I have nothing against O'Brien. I'm just here to do business."

"You heard about the reward, huh?"

"Sure did. Man can't turn his back on five thousand dollars. Who is this Caleb Perry anyway? A rancher?"

"He owns the cannon foundry," Hellen explained.

"Judging by the size of that place, he's got to be a rich man."

"Well, I reckon he's got five thousand dollars and other money besides."

Tansey nodded. "That's good enough for me. Damn, this is tasty cheese, best I ever ate. I see you have a cat."

"Yeah, her name is Susie."

"I had a little cat once, never gave her a name though. I just called her Cat."

"What's your name, mister?" Hellen asked.

"I don't mind putting it out. Name's Frank Tansey."

"I've heard of you. As I recollect, you ran with some hard crowds."

"The Texas Rangers were the hardest. Most of them were all right, but a few were dangerous when they got to drinking."

"Like men everywhere, I guess. I can't convince you to ride on out, huh?"

Tansy shook his head. "I'm a businessman, and today my business is with Shawn O'Brien."

Hellen looked up. "Well, speak of the devil . . ."

Shawn stepped into the saloon, the star on his

faded blue shirt glinting in the gloom as though it had absorbed sunlight. His eyes traveled around the room, stopped and then dismissed the handful of patrons at the bar, but his stare lingered on Frank Tansey.

The gunman grinned. "Takes one to know one, huh, Mr. O'Brien?"

"And who are you that I should know you?"

"Name's Frank Tansey."

"I've heard of you. Finish your lunch and get out of town."

"I recommend the cheddar, Mr. O'Brien. May I buy you a piece?"

Shawn nodded. "Yes, you can. And then light a shuck."

"A nice piece of cheddar for the gentleman," Tansey said to Hellen. Then to Shawn, "Would you care for crackers?"

Shawn nodded and Tansey said, "I can't leave just yet"—his eyes moved to the star—"Marshal."

Shawn's smile was wintry. "And why is that?"

"Why, here's your lunch at last," Tansey said. "A beer?"

Shawn said nothing and the gunman sighed. "The fact of the matter is, I'm here to kill you, Mr. O'Brien. Are you sure I can't tempt you to a bottle of Bass?"

"I drank Bass in England and enjoyed it, but it doesn't travel well. I know about Perry's reward."

"Indeed? Well, as I told the bartender here, a man in my line of work doesn't turn his back on five thousand dollars. It's not good business."

"Sorry to hear that," Shawn said.

"This is just about earning money, Mr. O'Brien,"

Tansey said. "There's no ill-feeling involved and I'll see you get a funeral that befits a gentleman."

"There's only one problem with that. On your best day, you can't shade me."

"Then that matter needs to be resolved," Tansey said. "But, please, eat your lunch first."

Shawn, when a man threatens your life, don't talk the talk. Walk the walk and put a bullet into him. Shawn recalled old Luther Ironside's advice and decided to act on it. Frank Tansey was not a man to trifle with.

Shawn stepped away from the bar. "Seems like you've already spoiled my lunch, Mr. Tansey, so let's resolve it right now."

The gunman frowned. "I thought we could settle this like gentlemen. You know, after lunch and a few beers, but I can see that you're determined to get it over with. Oh well. Good-bye, Mr. O'Brien."

Tansey's right hand blurred as he went for his gun. He was good, very skilled and fast on the draw and shoot, but Shawn O'Brien had been tutored by the best and had come up against some of the fastest shootists in the West. He was more than fast. He was one of those rare men who had fully mastered the Colt and its ways. He was one in ten thousand, Luther had once told him. The old man was not given to empty praise.

Shawn pumped two shots into Tansey's chest, both bullets clipping arcs out of the tobacco tag that hung from the man's shirt pocket. Tansey had cleared leather, but was too late to get his Colt into action. He fell backwards, slammed against the wall, and stared at Shawn with wonder in his eyes. "Splendid work, Mr. O'Brien." A look of astonishment frozen on his face and as dead as he was ever going to be, Tansey slowly slid down the wall into a sitting position.

As men crowded around Tansey's body, Shawn holstered his gun and then turned to Hellen.

The bartender said, "I liked this town better when Abaddon wasn't here. One of you men get Dorian Steggles. Tell him he's got business with a dead businessman."

"Is that what he called himself?" Shawn asked. "A businessman?"

"Yeah. He surely did," Hellen said. "Drink?"

"A bottle of Bass."

CHAPTER THIRTY-SIX

"Boss, this is serious," Valentine Kilcoyn said. "Frank Tansey was the best there was. Hell, some say he was the fastest gun who ever lived."

"Second fastest," Caleb Perry said. "I think Shawn O'Brien proved that."

"He drank a bottle of Bass after he killed Tansey. Just stood there in the saloon, drinking beer as cool as you please."

"When I destroy Big Buck, I'll destroy O'Brien with the town," Perry boasted. "He doesn't scare me."

"Boss, about the town . . . do you think that's wise? I mean, there's bound to be survivors and people talk. Next thing you know, we got Rangers on the doorstep."

Perry's smile was condescending, as though he was speaking to a child. "Mr. Kilcoyn when the good folks of Big Buck look up at the steam frigate, what will they see?" He raised a hand. "No, don't tell me, I'll tell you. The answer is Mexicans at the guns. If the Rangers investigate, I'll be suitably horrified. I'll say, 'My dear sirs, the frigate was stolen by a band of renegade Mexican thugs led by some dastardly white ruffians. They bombarded the town with the intention of robbing the bank. But after the airship was disabled by their gunfire, my brave foreman and some loyal workers hunted down the miscreants and killed them to a man. Have a cigar.'"

Kilcoyn shook his head. "But, boss, why destroy the town at all? I'll willingly gun the mayor for you and make it look like he blew his own brains out."

"Why destroy the town? A very good question, Mr. Kilcoyn. The answer is—because I can. I want my invention to be the greatest terror weapon of the steam age and I must see it in action. This worthless little hamlet full of equally worthless people is not London or Paris, but it's first-rate proving ground." Perry sat back in his chair. "And what is more, the annihilation of Big Buck will take place before this month is out, say within ten days. The presence of this Shawn O'Brien person has forced my hand."

"We'll go after him again and we'll kill him," Kilcoyn said. "Now that he's wearing a star on his shirt, he's made himself an even bigger target."

"Good. I'm putting you in charge of that. But be discreet, Mr. Kilcoyn. No public display. I don't want O'Brien's death tracked back to me."

Kilcoyn's grin was not pleasant. "The blade makes no sound, boss."

"Huzzah!" Perry clapped his hands. "A capital solution to a thorny problem."

After Kilcoyn left, Flora March, Perry's new woman, asked, "Do you like killing people, Caleb? You always talk about cannons and destroying cities."

Flora was not as talented as Lizzie Skates, but

Perry gave her credit for trying. "My dear, I have a deep, abiding hatred for humanity, a vile infestation plaguing this beautiful earth. It would not bother me in the least if a great meteor came down from the heavens and destroyed all of you."

The girl pouted. "Do you hate me, Caleb?"

"Perhaps you most of all because you have something I want and need and that makes me vulnerable."

"What does that mean, Caleb . . . vurn . . . vurnib . . ."

"It means you're stupid with only one function in the world and that is to lie on your back and open your legs."

"You're cruel to me, Caleb. Why are you so cruel to me?"

Unlike Lizzie's, the girl's eyes were empty, devoid of high intelligence. She had a sweet, caring nature that Perry never cared to notice.

"Oh for God's sake, pour me a drink. I told you that you're not here to ask questions."

"You get the idea, Buck?" the foreman named Sam Shillingford asked. "We hit fast and I use the knife before O'Brien can squawk."

"Or draw," Jacob O'Brien said.

"Yeah, we don't want that. He's way too sudden. You pin his arms and I'll do the sticking. The whole thing won't take but a few seconds and we'll be in good with Mr. Perry."

"How will we know where to find him?"

"The guards told me they see him on the street just after nightfall. They say he checks every alley as a good little sheriff should. That's when we grab him. You up for it, Buck? We're on our own in this."

"Sure. I got no liking for lawmen."

"Me neither. While we're at it, I'll carve up that pretty face of his, make him an ugly corpse." Shillingford scowled. "Hey, I made a good joke and you didn't laugh."

Jacob shrugged. "Sorry. I was thinking about tonight. I'll enjoy taking down the man who killed Frank Tansey."

"He was one of the best, was Frank."

"Yeah. He'll be sorely missed."

"If you want, you can take the credit for the O'Brien kill," Shillingford offered. "I don't mind. I just want to please Mr. Perry. Hell, he'll give both of us a raise."

"That's true blue, Sam. Remind me to do you a favor one time."

"Until this evening then, Buck," Shillingford said, sticking out his hand.

Jacob nodded but ignored the proffered handshake. "Yeah. Until this evening."

CHAPTER THIRTY-SEVEN

"Shawn, I won't let you risk your life again," Maria said. "It's getting too dangerous for you in Big Buck and I want you to leave."

"What about your brother?" Shawn stood at the hotel room window looking down at the street where a dray with a broken axle blocked other wagon traffic. It seemed that an ox wagon bullwhacker had taken the dray driver to task and the two were engaged in fisticuffs, much to the delight of passersby on the boardwalk. If the situation got out of hand, he planned to break up the fight, but not much damage was being done by either party.

"Forget about my brother, Shawn. Forget you even heard the name Manuel Cantrell." She slipped into a long black dress with a high standing collar and then hung the chain of her pocket watch around her neck. "He's a lost cause."

Shawn turned from the window. "It goes deeper than that. After Hamp died, it became a personal matter between Caleb Perry and me. I'll leave after I kill him and return this insane town back to sanity."

"That is where the danger lies. You're right. This town is afflicted by madness. Abaddon has taken over its people mind, body, and soul."

"And as I told you, it's now my job to set it free." He turned back to the window. "Ah, good straight right, sir. I think the bullwhacker has this fight won."

Maria's high-heeled boots thudded on the thread-bare rug as she stepped beside Shawn.

He put his arm around her slender waist. "Yup, the dray driver has had enough. He's staying down."

"They're all mad." She grimaced.

Shawn smiled. "Wagon drivers fight all the time, even in the big cities. I think New York and Boston are the worst, but Rome is not far behind."

"Will you take me to Rome one day, Shawn?"

"I'd love to. My father is a close personal friend of Pope Leo the Thirteenth. They exchanged rosaries, but His Holiness got the better of that bargain. The colonel's was gold and he got pewter in return."

"Did the Pope Leo bless the rosary he gave to your father?"

"Yes, several times."

"Then it was Colonel O'Brien who got the better of that bargain."

"Spoken like a gal who was educated at a mission run by nuns." Shawn smiled.

"French nuns to be exact," Maria pointed out. "Were you ever taught by nuns? They're very strict."

"No, I was taught by a man named Luther Ironside. And he was very strict."

"You often talk of Luther Ironside, Shawn. I'd like to meet him and your family. I'll go with you now, on the next train. We'll leave this terrible place together."

Shawn shook his head. "Maria, if I did that, I'd be pissing on the memory of Hank Sedley. I'll leave when Caleb Perry is rotting in hell and not before."

"Then you're a fool." Tears welled in her eyes as she shook her head. "No, no, Shawn, you're not a fool. You're an honorable man and I'm not used to dealing with honorable men. Do what you have to do, but don't expect me to be a part of it. I'll come back later for my things."

"You're leaving me?"

"Yes I am. I won't stay around and watch you die in the street, Shawn."

"Maria, I won't die that easily."

"No you won't. But in the end, you'll do the honorable thing and you'll be killed. I don't want to talk about it anymore. I can't bear to have terrible pictures in my mind." She stepped to the door and left.

Shawn stood and watched her go, wondering if she'd walked out of his life forever. He looked into the street where the dray was being repaired and the driver was nursing a black eye. He felt that a part of him, maybe the best part of him, was gone and there was not a damn thing he could do about it.

Later that night, the weather turned unseasonably cool and it started to rain just a little, drifting up from the south as fine as a mist. Three men dressed in slickers left the Abaddon building and walked into the street. The black man in front angled toward the boardwalk and the others followed. There was still a while to go before dark, but the saloon windows glowed yellow, all the lamps inside lit against the gloom. He motioned to the others to follow him. He stepped into the shadow of a storefront and nodded in the direction of a man who'd just walked out of the saloon. "Once that gentleman gets out of the way, we'll move."

The man was short and had a potbelly. He peeled the band off a cigar and dropped it onto the boardwalk. A match flared, temporarily illuminating the plumpness of the man's face, and then he stepped back inside.

"Now." The black man and the others walked through the fragrance of rose water as they passed the saloon and stopped at the entrance to an alley.

"This one for sho'," the black man said, "I seen the sheriff go in here this past two, three nights, me. Always around this time."

"He carry a lantern?" Sam Shillingford asked.

The black man shook his head. "No. He got good eyes, I guess."

"Shotgun?"

"No, sir, Mr. Shillingford. Just the Colt on his hip."

Shillingford nodded. "All right, Jules, you can head back to the foundry. Me and Mr. Ross will handle it from here."

"Yes sir, Mr. Shillingford." The black man glanced at a blacker sky. "Rainy night though, sho' enough."

Shillingford watched the man go. Light from the saloon windows gleamed briefly on the shoulders of Jules's slicker and then he lost himself in darkness. "You ever see one of these, Buck?" Shillingford pulled a massive bowie knife from the sheath on his left side. "This is the twelve inches of good Abaddon steel I'll ram into O'Brien's guts."

Jacob nodded his approval. "That's a real mean Texas toothpick if ever I saw one."

"Damn right." Shillingford was a big man with mean blue eyes and his spade-shaped beard fell to the second button of his slicker. "Now into the alley with us and let's get it done." His teeth flashed in the darkness, revealing incisors like a wolf. "I'm looking forward to this killing. Are you?"

"You bet," Jacob said. "I've always enjoyed a pig-sticking."

CHAPTER THIRTY-EIGHT

The *clink* of a bottle, the *thud* of a big man's body as he stumbled against the wall of the hardware store that formed one side of the alley, and then a string of curses that raised the surrounding air temperature at least twenty degrees were heard in the alley.

Jacob O'Brien smiled to himself. Yup, that was Shawn all right. Shillingford's slicker rustled softly as the foreman tensed and turned to him, warning that he should get ready to make his move soon.

Jacob nodded but couldn't tell if Shillingford saw him or not.

The sound of clinking glasses and a woman's strident laugh carried from the saloon to the alley. Somewhere a feral cat wailed its hunting song and an outraged dog barked.

Shawn stopped. Jacob heard the *snick* of his brother's Colt leaving the leather.

Shawn had the instincts of an Apache. "Is anyone there?"

The hiss of Shillingford's labored breathing

seemed loud. Rats scuttled and squeaked at the end of the alley.

"Who's there? Show yourself."

From the saloon drifted the solemn *dong . . . dong . . . dong . . .* of a grandfather clock striking midnight.

Shawn moved forward slowly, sensing danger. "Who's there?" Closer, one small step at a time . . . closer . . .

Jacob's Colt was in his hand. Across from him, Shillingford was a hulking black shadow. Only the huge blade of the bowie glinted. The big man's mouth was stretched wide in a savage grimace and his breath slid softly in and out between his back teeth, a deadly, predatory animal steeling himself for the kill.

To Jacob's surprise, he heard Shawn's Colt drop back into the holster.

"Damn rats." Shawn turned his back . . .

And Shillingford yelled, "Get him!"

The darkness shifted as the huge foreman got to his feet and charged, the knife ready in his hand. His turned to Jacob, expecting help.

Jacob fired into the middle of the hazy white oval of Shillingford's face and the man screeched as lead smashed into the bridge of his nose. The shot ringing in his ears, Jacob was aware that Shawn's revolver was coming up fast. Panicked, he yelled, "It's Jake!"

"Jake?" Shawn questioned.

"Yeah, it's me and be damned to ye for a useless, trigger-happy lawman."

"I could have killed you," Shawn said.

"Damn right you could." Jacob stepped close to

his brother and shoved a folded paper into the pocket of his shirt. "Read that later. Listen up. Two men came at you in the alley. You shot one of them and the other scampered. Got that?"

Shawn made no reply.

As men's voices were raised in the street, Jacob said, "Damn it, Shawn. You got that?"

"I got it."

"Good, then I'm out of here." Jacob turned, walked quickly to the end of the alley, and was gone into the gloom.

"What happened here?" Ambrose Hellen stepped into the alley, a scattergun in his hands. "O'Brien, it's you. Are you hurt?"

Behind him several men craned their necks to see what was going on.

"No." Shawn repeated what Jake had said. "Two men came at me in the alley. I shot one, but the other feller ran."

"Lantern," Hellen said.

One of the onlookers passed the lantern to the bartender, who adjusted the flame higher and then stepped to the dark mound of the fallen man. "This is Sam Shillingford. He's one of Caleb Perry's foremen."

Shawn stepped beside him. "Is he dead?"

"As dead as a bullet between the eyes can make a man." Hellen raised the lantern, the better to see Shawn's face. "Damn good shooting and a damn big mistake. Now Perry will really keep trying until you're dead."

"Maybe. Unless I get to him first." Shawn felt angry with Hellen and didn't quite know why.

The bartender sighed. "I'll send for Dorian Steggles.

I guess Perry will want to bury his dead." He shook his head. "Right between the eyes in almost pitch darkness. Could be you're right, O'Brien. If I was Perry I'd be damn worried."

When Shawn returned to the hotel, Maria's clothes and other things were gone. He stood in the middle of the floor and looked around him. He saw Maria's shadow everywhere, gliding around the dark, dingy room like a candle flame. He didn't love her, but her presence pleased him and made him feel whole again after the death of his wife had shattered him into so many sharp pieces that cut him daily.

He lit the lamp, sat on the edge of the bed, and opened the note Jake had stuck into his pocket. He smiled as he saw the familiar block letters, awful spelling, and hit-and-miss punctuation. Jacob was arguably one of the most brilliant pianists of the age, yet he'd had so much trouble with reading, writing, and arithmetic that after hiring tutor after tutor who threw up their hands and quit in defeat, the Colonel had despaired of him.

Shawn read the note.

DERE SHAWN. I HOPE THIS NOTE FINDS YEW WELL. LIE LO SHAWN AND DONT LET PERRY GIT TO YEW. I HAVE A GUD PLAN IN MIND AND YULE NO WHEN IT HAPPENS. LISSEN FOR THE BANGS AN KUM A-RUNNIN.

YURE VERY AFECTONATE BRUTHER,
JACOB O'BRIEN, ESQ.

PS. IF I AM KILT YEW CAN HAVE MY HOSS

Shawn folded the note and stuck it back into his pocket before he thought its contents through. Jake had a plan to release Manuel Cantrell and it involved bangs and bangs meant shooting. Was he about to grab Cantrell and then shoot his way out of the foundry? It seemed unlikely. Jake's scholastic skills were sadly lacking, but he was a very smart man. Depending on revolver fighting to save Manuel didn't make sense. He must have something else in mind. But what?

Shawn took off his gun belt, hat, and boots and lay on the bed, staring at the ceiling. The woman smell of Maria was still on her pillow. Her drowsy morning smile, so sweet with invitation, was the last thing he remembered before he let sleep take him.

CHAPTER THIRTY-NINE

"Sam Shillingford should be asleep in his bed right now, not lying in a dirty alley like a slaughtered hog," Caleb Perry said. "Why did you leave him, Ross?"

Jacob played the role of confused, not-too-smart gunman. "There were too many of them, boss."

"Shawn O'Brien is only one man!" Perry was livid. "You cut a hole in the wind running from one man."

"He had others with him, deputies maybe. It could've been one of them that shot Sam. It all happened so quick."

"Damn you, Ross, for a yellow-bellied dog. I'll have you shot for this."

Jacob took that standing, unwilling to show his hand. He let his head hang in pretended remorse and shuffled his feet. In the distance, a locomotive bell clanged as it neared the loading dock and the guard outside Perry's door walked back and forth, his boots thudding.

Anstruther Breens was one of three foremen present, all of them named gunmen. He leaned over

Perry's desk and said something so quickly and quietly Jacob couldn't hear him.

Perry looked up at the man. "Is that the case?"

Breens nodded. "He whipped them into shape."

Perry's cold blue eyes fell on Jacob again. "Mr. Breens tells me that you're making a good job of training the gun crews on the prototype frigate."

Jacob nodded. "I whip the trolls into shape and take no sass." He tried to look tough, which wasn't a stretch.

"Then go back to the construction bay, damn you. Get out of my sight, Ross, before I change my mind and order you shot."

Jacob beat a hasty retreat, relieved he'd had no need to draw and kill Perry. After that shot, his life would have been measured in seconds.

On his way to the construction bay, he stopped and watched a dozen new employees being pushed into a bewildered line. Deafened by noise, blinded by scarlet furnaces and the white-hot dazzle of cascading molten iron, the new men stood openmouthed and looked around them. Apart from one black man, all were Mexicans, ragged and skinny refugees from the two-year drought and famine devastating central and northern Mexico. Foremen pushed and pummeled the peons into a shambling walk and led them to what Jacob had come to regard as the slave quarters.

The black man, in better shape than the Mexicans, understood what was happening and made a break for the door. He never made it. A foreman Jacob didn't recognize pumped three shots into the fugitive's back and then stepped beside the writhing body and fired a fourth into the man's head. The terrified faces of the Mexicans who'd watched the whole thing got the message loud and clear—attempted escapes from Abaddon would not be tolerated.

It was yet another atrocity Jacob witnessed, but he did nothing, his face empty. He had to consider the greater good and could only silently regret the killing of yet another human being Caleb Perry considered expendable.

Egbert Killick and the engineer Garrett Mallard sought out Jacob as soon as he walked into the hammering clamor of the construction bay. His mouth close to Jacob's ear, Mallard pushed back his cap and goggles and yelled, "Egbert and I have something to show you, Mr. Ross. Please come this way."

Jacob followed Mallard to a small corner office and stepped inside. The interior was furnished with a desk, chair, and an easel with a chalkboard that was covered by a rectangle of canvas.

"What is that thing?" Jacob pointed to a cylindrical metal object about the size and shape of a Jamaican rum keg supported by a wooden beam on top of a pair of sawhorses.

"That thing is a wonder of the modern age," Mallard said. He smiled at Killick. "Will you do the honors, Egbert?"

Killick smiled back. "Indeed I will, Garrett. This, Mr. Ross, is an aerial bomb. Once dropped from a steam frigate, it will detonate when it comes in contact with any solid object. It looks harmless just sitting there on a board, but it's packed with nitroglycerine and has the explosive power of five hundred sticks of dynamite."

Wary, Jacob stepped back from the bomb and opened his mouth to object.

Mallard smiled at Jake's reaction, explaining, "The nitro is combined with diatomite earth and is perfectly stable. It needs a blasting cap to detonate the explosive."

Killick said, "When the bomb hits a solid object, the cap goes off and detonates the nitro and then *boom*!"

That last was so loud, accompanied by a handclap, that Jacob nearly jumped out of his skin. When he'd recovered his composure, he asked, "And why are you telling me this?"

"Good question." Killick was a little gnome with crazy eyes. "By God sir, an excellent question. Mr. Mallard and I have had several conferences about your role in this project. But let me say this first. It is our considered opinion that the frigate's broadsides will destroy Big Buck and most of its population."

"After all, we're talking about two batteries of cannon," Mallard put in.

"That is indeed the case, Mr. Mallard, and succinctly stated," Killick said. "After the destruction is complete, Mr. Ross, you will then drop the bomb in the middle of Main Street. Mr. Mallard and I believe that the ruins of the town and the wounded and dead humans appertaining thereto will be blown off the face of the earth."

"Oh dear lord yes," Mallard said, shaking his head. "The destruction will be . . . if I may use the word . . . *epic*!"

"A fine choice of words yet again, Mr. Mallard." Killick consulted his pocket watch. "Before I go, I applaud you, Mr. Ross. You are a pioneer on the very cutting edge of modern weaponry and warfare, After the bomb is tested and shown to work, your services as an instructor will be eagerly sought by governments around the world."

Mallard smiled. "As Egbert says, the world will be your oyster, Mr. Ross. A man who has the ability to destroy great cities will be much honored and revered."

"Well, and what do you have to say for yourself, Mr. Ross?" Killick said.

"I don't know what to say." Hating himself for mouthing words as vile any he'd ever spoken, Jacob offered, "I guess all I can say is thank you for this wonderful opportunity."

CHAPTER FORTY

Ah, but it was grand to be on a horse again with a vast land stretching out before him and a blue sky overhead. Shawn O'Brien wasn't going anywhere specific. He had no destination in mind. His intention was to get out of Big Buck for a while, away from the stink of the Abaddon Cannon Foundry and the soot and dust of the town. Jake had told him to lie low. Out in the empty brush, cactus, and mesquite country was about as lie-low as a man could get.

After an hour's ride toward a far horizon that rippled constantly in the heat haze, Shawn thought he saw something move, heading north toward the piney woods. A black bear, he figured—one already thinking about finding a cozy berth for winter. The movement stopped as though the creature, whatever it was, had fallen. Intrigued and having nothing better to do at that particular moment, Shawn kneed his horse into a canter, intent on solving the mystery. Besides, it served to take his mind off Maria Cantrell and the sense of hopelessness and loss that accompanied his thoughts of her.

As he rode closer, he made out what looked like a human figure lying facedown on the ground. Three doglike creatures slunk out of the brush and nipped and snarled at the body—coyotes determining how much fight was left in their potential prey.

Hooting and hollering, Shawn galloped straight at the animals and they quickly decided to seek an easier dinner someplace else. He drew rein in a cloud of dust, swung out of the saddle, and stepped to the . . . woman. He shook his head. "What is a slip of a girl doing out here alone in the wilderness?"

The manner of her dress, short skirt, knee-high boots, and laced blouse added to the mystery. Beside her lay a blue top hat, goggles on the brim.

"So she is from Big Buck." Shawn looked around him but saw no sign of a horse and the only tracks he saw were the girl's. He grabbed his canteen, took a knee beside her, and cradled her head and shoulders in his arm. She seemed unhurt, but her lips were swollen and cracked. He uncorked the canteen and put it to her mouth.

She drank a little and then her eyes fluttered open. She looked at Shawn, let out a little shriek, and promptly fainted.

"Not the usual effect I have on women. I must be slipping." He eased the girl back onto the ground and retrieved his slicker from behind the saddle. He made a pillow of it and put it under the girl's head. That done, he sat, built a cigarette, and waited.

Clouds passed the bright face of the sun and their shadows raced across the open ground. In the distance, he watched a small herd of white-faced cattle graze on a patch of sparse grass and then move slowly west into the rippling haze. Bees droned in the undergrowth and a green lizard did pushups on a flat rock.

The girl stirred and sat up, her head in her hands.

"Glad you're back with us. You had me worried for a spell." Shawn handed her the canteen. "Drink."

She poised the canteen at her mouth. "I seem to remember coyotes."

"Uh-huh. They figured you were on the lunch menu."

The girl shuddered. "You chased them away?"

"Sure did. I have no regard for them."

She drank deep.

She's rather plain, Shawn thought, *although she's dressed in an outfit that puts a lot of her on show. But that doesn't suit her. Her eyes—golden brown laced with green—are her one redeeming feature.*

She interrupted his musing. "Well, aren't you going to ask me, cowboy?"

Shawn smiled. "That 'ask me' covers a whole lot of territory."

"Only a man would say something like that. I meant along the lines of, 'What's a nice girl like you doing in a place like this?'"

"I could say that, but reckon I'll ask your name first. It's much more polite than saying, 'Hey you.'"

"My name is Flora March. You don't talk like a cowboy, more like a swell. What's your handle, Professor?"

"Shawn O'Brien."

Flora was shocked. "You're the one Caleb Perry wants dead."

"There's no doubt about that. Do you know Perry?"

"I am . . . I was his kept woman." The girl smiled slightly. "That's putting it politely, Professor. I was his harlot, but only for a while."

"So why did you leave him?"

"Because he'd kill me one day. I gave him what he wanted and he used me for convenience's sake. As soon as he found someone prettier, he'd put a bullet in my head."

"That's one way to end an affair," Shawn muttered.

"It's Caleb Perry's way."

"How did you escape Abaddon? It couldn't have been easy."

"It was easy. It was real easy. I told the guards at the gate that I was going into town because Perry wanted me to buy garters. They laughed and let me go. I just kept walking and found myself here, weak from thirst and fright. I thought Perry might come after me."

"He still might," Shawn said.

"Oh please don't say that. I'm scared enough as it is." Flora glanced at Shawn's shirtfront. "Does the star mean anything?"

"Not a damn thing."

"It says Marshal."

"I know what it says. Where did you think you were going?"

"I thought I'd head for the piney woods."

"And do what?"

"I don't know. Hide, I guess."

"If Perry didn't find you, the wolves, bears, coyotes, and snakes certainly would."

"Are you going to leave me here?" Flora looked

frightened. "Please don't tell me you're leaving me with the wolves and stuff."

Shawn shook his head. "No, I guess you'd better come with me."

"Not back to Big Buck?"

"No. I know a place where you can hide out for a while."

"And then?"

He shrugged. "And then I'll think of something."

"What's that noise?" Startled, she looked around her.

"I think that's the sound of some mighty big trouble."

CHAPTER FORTY-ONE

Shawn O'Brien shaded his eyes with a hand and studied the sky to the east. The small steam frigate that had first appeared as a black dot rapidly grew in size. Sunlight flashed on its spinning propeller and gleamed on rifle barrels. He grabbed Flora March's hand and pulled her to her feet.

"What is it?" she asked.

"I reckon it's Perry coming after you. In his flying machine." He dragged her to his horse, mounted, and pulled her up behind him.

"What are we going to do?"

"Find some cover," Shawn answered.

"There is none. Shawn, I'm scared."

"I know. But hang on and let me be scared for the both of us, huh?"

Around them lay mile after mile of barren open ground. Shawn knew his only hope was to head back in the direction of town where scattered wild oaks and the occasional cottonwood would provide cover of a sort. He kneed his horse into a gallop and behind him he heard Flora yelp in fear as a bullet split the air above their heads. He drew his Colt and charged straight for the flying machine. If he could get under the craft, the half dozen riflemen onboard would have a problem bringing their rifles to bear.

But someone, probably Perry himself, was as smart as Shawn was.

The little frigate made a sharp turn to port and suddenly Shawn found himself galloping into the fire of six rifles. Bullets ripped past him and a few kicked up dirt in front of his running horse. He thumbed off shot after shot at the gondola, but as far as he could tell, he scored no hits. It seemed that the flying machine was not a steady gun platform because the riflemen were not scoring hits, either.

Then Flora cried out in sudden pain and put the lie to that statement.

"Hang on!" Shawn yelled. He holstered his revolver and pulled the Winchester from the boot under his knee. Again, he rode directly for the machine as a couple gunmen stood to get into a better firing position.

The reins trailing, he fired from the shoulder and levered a couple shots at the standing riflemen. Hit, one of them threw up his hands, pitched over the side, and screamed all the way down until he thudded onto the ground.

Shawn didn't wait to see what effect his fire had on the other gunmen. He galloped under the keel of the gondola, firing into its bottom as he went. "Hold on!" he yelled to Flora.

Instead of riding straight out from under the steam frigate, he cut a fast left turn. His mount, trained as a cow pony, could turn on a dime and swung so fast Shawn was at the stern of the gondola. A man wearing goggles and a top hat peered down at him. Shawn snapped off a fast shot and sent the man's hat soaring into the air. The flying machine, momentarily out of control, veered to port, the dragonhead on its prow pointed east. The riflemen onboard seemed confused and there was no more fire from the gondola.

Shawn took advantage of the lull and hammered shot after shot into the steam frigate's woodwork and canopy. He heard a yelp as another man took a bullet . . . and suddenly it was over. Belching smoke from its chimney, the airship headed back the way it had come, rapidly gaining height to get out of range of the deadly rifle fire.

Anyone but an O'Brien brother would have let it go. But the Colonel, recalling the lessons the War Between the States had taught him, had raised his sons to believe that the best defense was attack and hard old Luther Ironside had shown them how to put that dogma into practice.

Shawn gently let the wounded girl down from his horse and then swung away, galloping to attack again. Keeping to the stern of the gondola, he levered his Winchester dry, slamming shots into the flying machine before it gained sufficient altitude and picked up the speed to finally leave him behind. He was the only one grinning as the frigate scudded away, trailing smoke and leaking steam, smearing soot across the blue sky like a dirty thumbprint.

It seemed that Caleb Perry had anticipated a pleasant hunting expedition that would bag him a fine trophy—the head of a frightened girl—but he and his sportsmen had come up against a trained fighting man who didn't know the meaning of cut and run and had sand enough for a dozen others just like him.

Shawn smiled to himself as the steam frigate was lost in the distance. He had certainly spoiled Perry's day and he felt good about that.

Remembering Flora's cry of pain as she was hit, he swung his horse around and rode back to her. She stood and watched him come, her left arm hanging loosely by her side. The shoulder of her white blouse was stained with blood.

"You hit bad?" he asked.

"What does it look like, Professor?"

"Let me take a look." He pulled down the shoulder of her blouse. "I beg your indulgence, ma'am."

"It's all right," Flora said. "You've seen it all before, I reckon."

"The bullet is still in there. I'd better get you to a doctor."

"Can't you dig it out with a knife?"

"If I was Daniel Boone, maybe. But all I'd do is make the wound worse."

"If Caleb Perry sees me in Big Buck, I'll be dead," Flora said.

"He'll have to kill me first, and so far he hasn't done a good job of that," Shawn said. "I'll help you onto my horse."

Once she was in the saddle, he led the horse to the body of the man who'd fallen from the flying machine. The dead man lay on his belly and Shawn used his boot to lever him onto his back.

Touching the still vivid bruises on his face, he said,

"I never forget a face. He's one of the Abaddon men who gave me this."

Flora had no pity for the man. "His name is Anstruther Breens. He was mean and arrogant, but Perry set store by him so now we're dead for sure."

Shawn smiled at her. "Nothing is ever sure, lady. Don't count us out just yet."

CHAPTER FORTY-TWO

It's a pretty sure bet that a man who foams at the mouth and chews on the leather of his desk blotter while snarling like a wild animal is somewhat irritated. The group of foremen assembled in Caleb Perry's office watched the man with expressions ranging from horror to, in Jacob O'Brien's case, suppressed amusement.

Finally exhausted, Perry tossed the blotter away from him and wiped his mouth with the back of his hand. "I want him dead. You hear me? I want him *dead, dead, dead!*" He jumped to his feet and pointed to the picnic basket in the corner. It was covered with a blue and white checked cloth and smelled of fried chicken. "It was to be a fun little hunt, a pleasure jaunt for my best foremen and technicians. But no, Shawn O'Brien had to go and spoil it. Anstruther Breens is dead. Val Kilcoyn took a bullet up the ass, and the prototype frigate is all shot to pieces."

"Ah, just minor damage." Egbert Killick looked shrunken and timid.

"You shut the hell up!" Perry cried. He swung on

the foremen. "I want O'Brien's head. Bring it to me in a sack so I can piss on it. Have I made myself clear?"

That last was met with a murmur of agreement.

"And the girl . . . what's her name?"

"Flora March," a man said.

"Hang her," Perry barked. "Wherever you find her, don't waste any time. Just string her up. Now is that also clear?"

"Sure is, boss," a man said.

"I'll pay a thousand dollar bonus to the man who brings me O'Brien's head in a sack and his eyes on a plate," Perry offered.

That brought a cheer that he cut short, much to Jacob's relief. He didn't want to be the only sourpuss at the party.

"All right. You men be about your business," Perry said. "Be advised, I want only two searchers at any given time. We must leave enough guards on the foundry floor to keep the trolls in check. Mr. Ross, you will remain in the construction bay and Mr. Killick so will you. You two men stay. The rest of you may go."

After the foremen filed out of the office, Perry asked, "How long to repair the damage to the prototype ship, Mr. Killick?"

"I have men working on it right now," the little man said. "She'll be ready to go by this time tomorrow, evening at the latest."

Perry looked at Jacob. "Mr. Ross, how are your gun crews?"

"Trained and ready," Jacob said. That was true. Under Manuel Cantrell's tutelage, the Mexicans were a quick study.

Perry nodded. "Very well. The bombardment of Big Buck will take place the day after tomorrow. And you have been informed about the bomb?"

"Sure have. It will blow what's left of the town and its people to smithereens."

Perry allowed himself a smile. "I'm warming up to you, Mr. Ross. We're both on the same page of the book." He picked a small piece of blotting paper from the corner of his mouth and stared at it a moment. "Despite my anger over yesterday's spoiled outing, this O'Brien business is in fact a trivial matter. My men will find him and kill him. It's as simple as that. Count Von Jungen will return soon and I want to show him a destroyed town and say, 'Look. This was done by a small air weapon, *mein lieber Graf.* Imagine what a full-sized, twenty-four gun steam frigate will do.'" Perry smiled. "Are you catching my drift, Mr. Ross?"

Jacob nodded. "The count will be suitably impressed."

"Excellent! Now I'm in a good mood again." Perry reached into a desk drawer and pulled out a Colt. "I'll take a stroll around the foundry and shoot the first troll I see slacking. It doesn't compare to a hunt for a harlot, but it does relieve my anxiety." He stared at Jacob. "Keep uppermost in your mind that the frigates are everything. Millions of dollars are at stake, Mr. Ross. Oh dear, yes, many, many millions."

"So this Shawn O'Brien feller played hob, huh?" Jacob asked Killick as they walked back to the construction bay.

"The man's not human. Damn him, he became the aggressor. He went at us like a starving wolf after a lamb."

Jacob felt a surge of brotherly pride. Nobody ever considered the Town Tamer a pushover and he'd proved it yesterday out there in the scrub country.

Killick was talking again. "Poor Mr. Breens was struck by one of O'Brien's bullets and then fell to his death. And I don't even want to talk about Mr. Kilcoyn. His left buttock hurts terribly, I'm told."

Jacob decided to play the loyal employee. "Well, now Shawn O'Brien's reign of terror will come to an end. Mr. Perry has seen to that."

Killick shook his head. "No, Mr. Ross, I'm not too sure it will. I'm not too sure it will at all."

CHAPTER FORTY-THREE

Shawn O'Brien stared into the hotel room mirror and did not like what he saw. His face still showed the purple and yellow legacy of the kicking he'd taken and his eyes had an odd, haunted expression. He looked . . . vulnerable . . . and that was death to an O'Brien.

Flora March lay on her back in the bed, her arm over her eyes hiding tears. She had no confidence that he could protect her from Caleb Perry. She'd refused a room of her own, clinging to whatever slender protection Shawn represented.

Turning his attention to the mirror again, he searched for any lingering trace of the Town Tamer. He thought he'd rediscovered that young man yesterday during his battle with the flying machine, but whatever he'd found was gone, holed up in a hotel room with a terrified girl who barely spoke to him. Unable to bear the sight of the man in the mirror, he turned away and stepped to the window. Nothing had changed. The street was still thronged with wagons and people crowded the boardwalks—mostly plump matrons with shopping baskets over their arms and a few young belles wearing impossibly small top hats above their swept-up hair, bustles of the largest size, and layers of petticoats that made their high-heeled ankle boots look like they were wading through snow. Big-bellied businessman sporting gold watch chains as thick as shackles tipped their hats to the matrons and smiled at the belles, who fluttered the black fans of their eyelashes in appreciation.

Big Buck hadn't changed. Only Shawn O'Brien had changed.

Flora lifted her forearm from her eyes. "What do you see?"

Without turning, Shawn said, "The street. Every time I look out this window, I see the street."

"Is there coffee in this hotel?"

"Yes. There's an urn downstairs. Do you want a cup?"

"I could sure use it." Tears reddened her eyes. "You can leave me for that long. I'm not going to walk out on you, Professor."

Shawn smiled. "A woman has already done that to me. I'm getting used to it."

"Who was she?"

"Someone you don't know. I'll get your coffee."

"I'd like a bathtub."

"I'll talk with the clerk. I'm sure that could be arranged."

"And soap."

"Normally that goes with the tub and so does a towel. Even in Big Buck." He put on his hat, buckled on his gun belt, and stepped out the door . . . into hell.

* * *

Nine times out of ten a few hard words precede a gunfight. Only when the talking is done does the fight commence and the conflict is then summed up in two or three seconds. But Bonzo Hones and Gus Orlo, Abaddon foremen both, were not, by nature, talking men.

It was Hones who uttered the only words spoken that morning when he saw Shawn on the stair landing . . . "That's him!"

Hones's gun came up pretty fast. Orlo, surprised by the suddenness of the confrontation, was a tad slower.

Shawn O'Brien was faster on the draw and shoot than either of them.

The moment he heard, "That's him!" and saw Hones go for his gun, Shawn drew and fired. Orlo drew, but Shawn ignored him and pumped a second bullet into Hones. The man roared, threw up his hands and as his Colt clattered onto the stairs, he toppled backward onto Orlo. Both men fell but Orlo got off a shot that thudded into the stair riser just under Shawn's boots. In a tangle of arms and legs, the Abaddon gunmen clattered down the entire staircase and landed in a heap at the bottom. Orlo, thin and wiry, pushed the large, dead bulk of Hones off him and quickly scrambled to his feet. He looked around for his fallen Colt and an expression of horror flashed across his face when he saw that it was on a stair halfway between him and Shawn.

Orlo's long, narrow face grew longer as he stared up at Shawn. "Hell, I'm a dead man."

Shawn nodded to the blue Colt on the stair. "Pick it up and get to your work."

For a moment, Orlo hesitated, then he made a dash for the revolver, taking the stairs two at a time. Shawn let the man pick up the Colt before he shot him.

Hit hard, the gunman leaned against the balustrade and his gun slipped from his hand. "You didn't give me an even break, damn you."

"I live longer that way. What's your name?"

"Gus Orlo."

"Good night, Gus." Shawn fired and the man crashed through the flimsy bannister and thudded onto the floor . . . at the feet of Claude Finain, the nervous desk clerk.

Finain's horrified gaze lifted from the dead men to Shawn on the landing. He didn't say a word, just stared, his mouth agape.

"They wanted a fight," Shawn said as he thumbed fresh shells into his Colt. "They got one."

Like a man waking from a bad dream, Finain said. "Both these boys work for Abaddon."

"Not any longer. I just retired them."

The shooting had attracted a crowd that gathered outside the hotel door, but it parted to let Mayor John Deakins through. "What's going on here?"

"You see it, Mayor," Finain said. "O'Brien shot them both."

Shawn's boots and spurs sounded on the stairs and then he stepped into the lobby. "They drew down on me, Mayor. I didn't get time to pass the time of day."

Deakins looked ill. "That's Bonzo Hones and Gus

Orlo, Abaddon men. Mr. Perry is not going to like this."

"I don't suppose he will." Shawn looked at the bodies. "They were surefire killers and didn't amount to much."

"Two against one," Deakins said. "I suppose it's a clear case of self-defense, Sheriff."

Shawn nodded. "I suppose."

"Then that's it," the mayor said. "One of you men out there, get the undertaker."

"No," Shawn disagreed. "I want Caleb Perry to take care of them. They're his."

Deakins was stunned. "I can't ask Mr. Perry to do a thing like that."

"No, but I can." Shawn pushed past Deakins and the gawkers and stepped into the street. After a few moments, he saw what he was looking for—a brewery dray drawn by two Percherons stood outside the saloon. He crossed the street.

Ambrose Hellen met him at the door. "All right. What happened, O'Brien?"

"Two of Perry's men drew down on me."

"Their mistake."

"Seems like."

The driver of the dray, a small, wiry man named Winter Quale, came out from the gloom behind the bar. "Just in time, Sheriff. A new load of Milwaukee's finest right off the train, guaranteed fresh and ready to bust heads."

"Glad to hear it," Shawn said. "I'm commandeering your wagon for police work."

The little man shook his head. "That won't do,

Sheriff. I still got deliveries to make and I'm always on time. Quale by name, Quale by nature, folks always say."

"I'll bring it back soon." Shawn looked at Hellen. "Shotgun?"

The bartender nodded, stepped inside, came back with the Greener, and handed it to Shawn. "It's loaded. Double-aught buck."

"I'm obliged." Shawn turned and yelled across the street, "You men, carry those bodies over here."

"Now see here, Sheriff . . ." Quale said.

"Mister, don't give me problems when I've got a scattergun in my hands," Shawn said. "I get all nervous and twitchy."

Winter Quale read the writing on that wall clear enough and he beat a hasty retreat. "Just don't damage my beer."

Shawn grinned. "I wouldn't dream of it."

The two dead men were loaded onto the back of the dray where there was space.

One of the makeshift pallbearers asked, "Where are you talking these boys, Sheriff?"

"Back to the feller who sent them."

"I sure hope you know what you're doing," the man said.

"So do I."

CHAPTER FORTY-FOUR

The Percheron team handled well but would not be hurried as befits horses that haul a precious commodity like beer. The trouble was that their slow pace gave Shawn O'Brien time to think, the last thing he wanted. Too much thinking made a man build obstacles on a bridge he hadn't crossed yet and could weaken his resolve . . . but not for a moment did Shawn consider turning back. He was about to toss the dice and he'd live or die by how they rolled.

To the north, the sky had a strange amber tint as though a dust storm was kicking somewhere. A single buzzard rode the upper level winds, a black shape gliding as effortlessly as a fallen angel. Abaddon loomed in the middle distance, more fortress than foundry. Three men stood outside the main door, their backs against its iron panels. They saw Shawn coming but didn't stir. To their mind, a brewery dray was a welcome sight that did not offer any kind of threat.

That changed when one of the Abaddon gunmen

recognized him and whispered a warning to the others. The three became alert, their rifles at the ready.

Shawn saw no friendly faces in the group as he halted the team. "Howdy boys." The butt plate of the Greener rested on his right thigh and its hammers were back.

"What the hell do you want?" The guard had a thick black mustache and heavy eyebrows.

"Got a couple of your friends in the back," Shawn said.

"They drunk?" Eyebrows asked.

"If they were, I'd say they were dead drunk, but since they were sober when I shot them, I'll just call them dead. Tell Perry to get out here and collect what's his."

After studying on that for a spell, Eyebrows motioned to a younger companion. "Ellis, go back there and see what the hell he's raving about."

Shawn let the fore end of the shotgun slap into his left hand. "Shuck the rifle and belt gun first, Ellis. I'm not what you'd call a trusting man."

Ellis looked at Eyebrows for guidance.

"Do as he says."

Ellis laid his Winchester on the ground and placed his Colt beside it.

"Step easy now, Ellis," Shawn said. "Like you were in church."

The man walked to the back of the wagon and after a few moments sang out, "Esau, it's Bonzo Hones and Gus Orlo."

"They dead?"

"Yup."

"You sure?"

"I've never seen two rannies deader."

Esau glared at Shawn. "Well?"

"They drew down on me."

"Bonzo and Gus were good men. Fast on the draw."

"Not fast enough, apparently." Shawn kept his eyes on Esau as he yelled, "Ellis, get them down from there. I don't want them two souring the beer."

"Mister," Esau said, "don't you know that you're already a dead man?"

"I've reckoned that a time or two before now, but I'm still here. Now get Perry and tell him to come outside and claim his dead. Tell him the Town Tamer is here and that he's himself again."

Esau nodded to the third man who took a massive iron key from his belt, unlocked the door, and stepped into the inferno.

Shawn smiled at Esau.

The man tried to ignore him but said finally, "You got nothing to smile about, O'Brien."

Shawn's smile stayed in place. "As long as I'm holding this here scattergun, neither have you." He glanced at the sky. "Funny kind of day, huh? Overcast sky but real hot. Makes a man wish he was up north somewhere, Montana way maybe."

"Texas is good enough for me," Esau said.

"I'd say you'd a pretty rough upbringing, Esau, but you had a good mother, huh?"

"You keep my mother out of it. Just shut your trap."

"I had a good mother, but she died when I was

still young. That's hard on a boy, having no mother. I have a fine pa though. How was your pa, Esau?"

"I don't want to talk to you."

"Why not, Esau?"

"You're the devil."

"Nah. I'm a living saint."

"You're a damned mick. Every mick I ever met was the devil. My pa told me it's all that damn popery that turns people into devils."

"Ah, he must have been a fine man, your father," Shawn said.

"The hell he was. I was ten years old when he was hung fer a hog thief."

"I'm right sorry to hear that, Esau. Ellis, just you let them guns lay right where they're at."

The man looked defiant, but Esau said, "Let them be, Ellis. He'll kill you if you don't."

"Listen to Esau, boy," Shawn said. "He gives good advice like his pa taught him before he was hung for stealing a hog."

"Don't talk to him, Ellis," Esau said. "He's a devil."

How that conversation might have ended Shawn would never know because the door opened and Jacob O'Brien stepped outside, followed by two gunmen and finally Caleb Perry.

Shawn was surprised by how short Perry was, but the man was very muscular and his rugged face looked as though it had been chipped from granite. He reminded Shawn of the hard-bitten ranchers he'd known as a boy.

Like them Perry wore a holstered Colt. "You got something to say to me, O'Brien?"

"Yeah, I have. Bury your dead." He glared at Jacob.

"And you, the one with the shifty eyes, keep your hand away from your gun."

"Do it, Mr. Ross," Perry said. "The scoundrel has the shotgun aimed right at my belly and he's liable to use it."

Shawn nodded. "Wise words. Double-aught buck can scramble a man's guts. I said keep your hand away from the iron, mister. I won't tell you again."

Suppressing a grin, Jacob let his hand drop. "You scare me, O'Brien."

"I should. I'm the Town Tamer, a title I don't take lightly."

"Is 'bury your dead' all you have to say to me, O'Brien?" Perry snarled.

"Yes, Perry, that and a warning: The more men you send against me, the more of them I'll kill. Soon, you'll be the only one left and then I'll kill you.

"Oh, there's one more thing. You're a lowdown piece of human vermin, walking, talking filth, and I look forward to the day I put a bullet in you and rid the world of a monster."

"O'Brien, you won't live beyond tomorrow," Perry threatened, his face black with anger. "Count on it."

Jacob offered advice. "O'Brien, after making a threat like that, I suggest you lie low. Understand me? Just lie real low."

"No need for that, Mr. Ross. O'Brien is aware that he's a dead man." Perry stepped to the door and one of his gunmen opened it. "If he makes any kind of fancy move with the shotgun, kill him. Otherwise let him go."

Jacob looked at his brother with amused eyes. "*Ta tu fear dusachtach.*"

"*Ta a fhios agam,*" Shawn answered.

After Shawn turned the team and drove away, Ellis said, "What the hell was that all about, Buck?"

"I used the old Irish tongue to tell him he was a crazy man."

"And what did he say?"

"He said, 'I know.'"

CHAPTER FORTY-FIVE

Maria Cantrell had been walking since the young cowboy driving the buckboard had dropped her off and pointed the way to the stage station.

"It's a ways, Miss, maybe a five mile," he'd said. "I wish you'd change your mind and come back to the ranch. Mr. and Mrs. Cornton will make you right welcome, especially Miz Flossie. She don't get many lady visitors at the Rafter-C and none as pretty as you."

But Maria was determined to put as much git between her and Big Buck as she could. She politely declined the puncher's request but did kiss his freckled cheek, a tender gesture he would recount and embellish for the rest of his life.

She walked steadily north across the brush flats in the general direction of the distant piney woods. The day was hot and cactus snagged at her skirt and sweat trickled down her back and between her breasts. She had enough money left to take a stage to the back of beyond and figured she'd end up in some mining town where she might prosper as a saloon singer and dancer, entertaining horny tin pans willing to overlook her lack of talent for her more obvious charms. Of course, she had to reach the stage station first and the walk seemed endless, especially in knee-high boots and a corset.

After an hour, Maria saw two towheaded children riding bareback on a massive draft horse. She could make out a boy with a mop of unruly hair and a girl in pigtails. They looked like twins no older than seven or eight. The boy kicked the horse into motion and the huge animal plodded slowly toward her.

"Hi," Maria said. "I'm looking for the stage station."

The boy pointed. "That way just over the rise."

"My daddy runs the station." The girl had wide brown eyes.

"I bet he runs it very well," Maria said.

The girl nodded. "My name is Arabella. What's yours?"

"Maria."

"Mine is Byron, Byron Holding," the boy said. "My pa said he named me for a poet. Would you like to ride with us on Hercules?"

Maria shook her head. "I don't think I could get onto him. He's very tall."

"Then I'll take your bag. It's not a far walk to the station."

In fact, it was another half mile, but relieved of her heavy carpetbag, she covered the distance without difficulty.

Comanche Station was a long, adobe building with a shingle roof. It had three doors but only a single window illuminated the passengers' dining room. That room, the largest, also had a stone fireplace and a couple rough-cut tables and benches. A curtained-off sitting area at the rear was provided for ladies who sought privacy. A pole corral held a spare team of rawboned Missouri mules and close by was a two-holer outhouse, a rare luxury.

The man who welcomed Maria and introduced himself as Cooley Holding was a tall, rangy young man with thick brown hair and hazel eyes. He had wide shoulders, big, work-worn hands and the sensitive face of a scholar. "I'm real sorry, ma'am, but it will be three days before the next stage gets here. The schedules have been cut because of competition from the railroad." He smiled. "We live in a steam-powered age.

"I'm sorry to hear about the stage," Maria said. "Does that mean I have to impose upon your hospitality for three days?"

"Not if you got somewhere else to go."

"I don't."

"Then I guess you're stuck with me and my young-uns." He hesitated as though thinking over his next words, then said, "I fixed up a parlor for my wife, but she died before she could use it. I recently put a bed in there for guests and I'll get you clean sheets." He shifted his feet. "You'll be comfortable in the parlor and you can eat there. And I have books. Do you like to read?"

Maria shrugged. "I've never had time before. Can I read a book in three days?"

"Well, probably not, but I have works by Lord

Byron and Sir Walter Scott. I'm sure you can find something to interest you."

"I'm sure I will. I'd like to have my meals with the family. That is, if you don't mind."

"Not at all. The children and me would like that." His smile was shy. "Byron and Arabella don't remember the other pretty woman who used to sit with them at table." He again was hesitant, like a man about to take a giant leap into the void. "I . . . I bought Ellie, my wife, a dress for wearing to dances and the like. She never got to wear it. If you'd like—"

"I'm sure it will be more comfortable than what I'm wearing. Boned corsets and high boots are for show, not for relaxing in."

He was suddenly embarrassed. "I didn't mean . . . I mean you look real nice . . . I just . . ." He shook his head. "Hell, ma'am, I don't know what I mean. When I look at you, I get kinda tongue-tied and . . . talk silly."

Maria smiled. "Well, after you get used to me being here that will pass. Now I think I'll lie down for a while and take a nap. The walking I've done has tired me."

"I'll show you to your room."

The children brought Maria's bag and Byron said in a loud, boy's voice, "Pa says we're having fried chicken for dinner. He only does that for special folks. That means he really likes you."

Maria smiled, shooed Byron outside, and gently closed the door on Cooley Holding's blushes.

For a while, she lay on her back and stared at the wood ceiling. It had been a long time since a woman had lived in the house and it had an empty, lonely feeling as though it awaited Ellie Holding's return to come to life again. Spiderwebs hung in the corners and the room itself was dank and dreary though outside the sun shone brightly and birds sang and chirped in the trees.

Maria blinked her drooping eyelids awake. She thought about Cooley Holding. The tall man had no claim to handsomeness. He had none of Shawn O'Brien's masculine beauty and flashing vitality, none of his well-traveled sophistication and confidence that comes from being born a rich man's son. Cooley might have first seen his first light of day in the stage station and had never left it since. In every sense of the word, he was a rube, a bumpkin tongue-tied in the presence of a woman who fully understood her sexual attraction and the effect it had on males. Men like Shawn who'd slept with many beautiful women could handle it. Poor, bumbling Cooley could not.

Yet she sensed a serene stillness in the man, an inward beauty like a lake in moonlight. He was gentle with the children and seemed caring. When he'd first looked at her, he did not undress her with his eyes but seemed to stare into her soul as though trying to uncover her essential being and solve the mystery of the woman named Maria Cantrell.

Could she love such a man?

Maria fell asleep before she could answer that question.

When Cooley Holding tapped on Maria's door to tell her dinner was about to be put on the table, she was already wearing Ellie's dress. She looked at herself in the mirror and shook her head in wonder. Instead of a laced and buckled corset and split skirt that revealed more than it covered, she wore a demure black gown buttoned to the neck with white collar and cuffs and no bustle. She had forsaken her high-heeled boots and was barefoot. Along with her corsets, the boots lay at the bottom of a planed timber armoire. She had kept only her skeleton watch that hung around her neck. Her transformation from Spanish lady was complete and Maria thought she looked like a schoolmarm . . . or a prairie wife.

Her arrival at the table was greeted by *oohs* and *ahs* from the children and Cooley's wide-eyed admiration.

She dropped a little curtsey. "Well, do I pass muster?"

"You look like a princess," Arabella said.

"Indeed you do, ma'am," Cooley agreed. "That dress suits you very well."

"Please call me Maria."

"Then Maria it is." He pulled out the chair and Maria sat at the rough wood table.

"My word, that's a lot of chicken and biscuits," she said.

"And there's plenty of buttermilk too," Byron said.

"Before we say grace, I'd like to ask you a question, Maria," Cooley said.

"Is it about the stage when it comes or about my past?"

"No. Just about the stage."

"I can't answer that question right now, Cooley. Maybe tomorrow or the next day."

"That's good enough for me."

The family bowed their heads as Cooley said grace. When it was over he looked up and said, "Please pass the biscuits, Maria."

For the first time in her life, Doña María Elena Cantrell felt that she'd found a home.

CHAPTER FORTY-SIX

The fire ax crashed into the foreman's skull with tremendous force and spit him open to the chin. The troll, a stocky Mexican peon, levered the weapon free and looked around for another victim. Behind him six other men, all similarly armed, fanned out across the foundry floor and began killing. Blood-maddened, they murdered their own kind, anyone who got in their way. Already two furnace stokers lay sprawled on the ground. One of them, missing an arm, shrieked in pain, but the axmen ignored him and shuffled toward the foundry door.

A foreman wearing a bowler hat and goggles came at a fast run, a Colt in his hand. Disoriented by the terrible cries of the wounded man and blinded by the sudden roar and dazzling scarlet light of a blast furnace disgorging molten steel, he ran headlong into the trolls . . . and paid the price.

Before Jacob O'Brien's horrified eyes the man was chopped to the ground and his writhing body was hacked to pieces. Blood formed a pool under him and spread across the floor.

Up on the gantry, a man fired. Above the constant roar of the machines, Jacob heard men yell and boots pound on concrete.

The trolls, driven wild by their violent rage and urge to destroy their slave masters, saw Jacob and advanced on him slowly. Eyes burned with hatred in swarthy faces and blood, red as a danger signal, tricked from the honed blades of the axes.

"No!" Jacob yelled. "Throw down your weapons and get back." But he talked to the wind.

The trolls came at him in a rush and instantly, his Colt bucked in his hand. One . . . two . . . three trolls went down, but the rest came on, showing their teeth, growling like wolves.

Sudden as a lightning strike the thought flashed through Jacob's head that he could drop two more and then was a dead man. He steeled himself for what was to come.

Bam! Bam! Bam!

The shots came from behind the trolls. A group of foremen opened up on the four Mexicans who were still standing. Their axes clanged to the bloody concrete as the trolls dropped together in a heap.

Valentine Kilcoyn, his butt strangely bulky from the bandage under his pants, stepped around the dead and dying men without a glance. "Buck, are you all right? Damn savages."

"Yeah, I'm fine." But he wasn't fine, not by a long shot. He'd killed three men driven to the edge of madness by the inhuman conditions under which they slaved. They were not savages, they were martyrs, and Jacob grieved that he'd had a hand in their martyrdom.

"Damn good shooting, Buck," Kilcoyn said as a foremen finished off the wounded Mexicans. "You did good. Stood your ground like a man."

"You came just in time, Val. Thanks." Jacob played his role to the hilt because he needed time. He needed tomorrow.

Caleb Perry conducted the witch hunt that followed and appointed himself lord high executioner. Three guilty parties who'd joined the revolt but had found no weapon and thus held back from the attack on the foremen were to die by the ax, a method he described as, "a sharp example of poetic justice."

Because of the recruitment of extra workers for the steam frigate venture, around a hundred and fifty men, armed foremen as well as trolls, gathered on the foundry floor to witness the heavy hand of Perry's retribution. Jacob, dying a little inside with every passing moment, was posted with Kilcoyn to guard the surly trolls from the construction bay. Later, when he thought about it, Jacob remembered that the atmosphere was tense, but the overriding emotion was fear, that and an air of helplessness. Naked, unarmed trolls were no match for Colts, Winchesters, and Greener scatterguns in the hands of hard-eyed men who knew how to use them.

Perry made a speech from the steel gantry where the executions were to take place. He went on at some length about treachery, lack of loyalty, and the murderous ways of the brown and black races. The man was an orator of great power and despite his reservations, Jacob found himself listening to Perry's hate-filled talk. His message was wrapped up in rhetoric designed to make the white men present feel good about themselves and reinforce their notions concerning the superiority of the white race and its rightful place in the world. The trolls stood sullen and silent. Perry's speech was not intended to make them feel good but to terrify and remind them that they were subhuman slaves, obedient to his will.

During the Middle Ages, the headsman's trade was passed on from father to son and apprentices learned the executioner's art by chopping off the heads of pigs. Cleanly decapitating the condemned—the ax was reserved only for those of noble birth—took years to learn and like any other trade it had its closely guarded secrets.

Caleb Perry had no such training. The block was a blacksmith's anvil and he took so many swipes at the necks of his victims, he blunted three axes that, slippery with blood, clanged metal on metal.

By Jacob's horrified accounting, it took Perry eleven strokes of the ax to behead three men. The faces of the heads that bounced on the steel gantry floor were openmouthed from the sudden shock of the pain they'd suffered. Hidden in his pocket, Jacob's rosary beads slipped through his fingers as he prayed for the deceased Mexicans. Each time Perry grabbed a head by its shock of black hair, the foremen below cheered. But Val Kilcoyn did not and neither did Jacob.

CHAPTER FORTY-SEVEN

"I'm very impressed by the way you handled yourself this morning," Caleb Perry said. "Three of the damn rogues fell to your gun, Mr. Ross. I couldn't have done much better myself."

"Thank you," Jacob O'Brien said.

"Coffee? Something stronger?"

"Not at the moment."

"I insist. You're a hero, Mr. Ross, and a hero deserves a drink." Perry stepped from behind his desk and lifted a crystal decanter from the drinks table. "I think you'll enjoy this. It's a champagne cognac from the Frapin distillery in France, fruity and very smooth. Quite acceptable for even the most discerning palate."

Jacob declined again. "I don't care for any."

Perry's eyes hardened. "I said, *I insist.*"

The thought of drinking with this monster curdled Jacob's stomach, but Perry would not be denied in anything, even something as trivial as a drink, and Jacob was forced to step back. He smiled. "Well, I guess it's not too early in the day."

Perry accepted that and returned Jacob's smile.

"Mr. Ross, it's never too early for a good cognac." He sat behind his desk and watched intently until Jacob tried his drink. "Well?"

"Excellent. It's fruity and smooth, just as you said."

"A little too fruity, perhaps?" Perry said.

Jacob shook his head. "Not for my taste."

Perry sat back in his chair and beamed. "Then we agree on that." He offered a cigar box. "Cuban."

Jacob didn't make the same mistake twice. He took a cigar, forced a smile, and said, "Thank you."

"So how did you enjoy the show, Mr. Ross?" Perry said after he'd lit Jacob's cigar. "The greasers surely squealed when the ax hit them, did they not?"

"They most certainly did," Jacob said. *Dear God, just let me get through this day. I'll kill this crazy evil man for you tomorrow.*

Perry kept at it. "I'd say they paid for their crime, wouldn't you?"

Jacob nodded. "They paid all right. They were long in the dying."

"Why do you never call me Mr. Perry?"

"I wasn't raised right, I guess." Hating himself, Jacob added, "I'll make sure I call you that in the future."

"It's a small thing, but a mark of respect, you understand?"

"Yes, Mr. Perry, of course it is."

Perry spoke from behind a blue haze of cigar smoke. "I have a job for you, Mr. Ross. I want you to seek out Shawn O'Brien, the self-appointed sheriff of this town, and kill him. And I want you to kill anyone you find with him. It will probably be a harlot, so don't hesitate."

Jacob tried to keep his face impassive. It wasn't easy. "When do you want this done, Mr. Perry?"

"Why, the day is still young. If O'Brien is dead by nightfall, I'll be quite satisfied. And of course the reward will be yours. Normally, I would have given this job to Mr. Kilcoyn, but I don't think he can handle the rogue. And besides, Mr. Kilcoyn's shot-up ass is slowing him. You can't give a shootist like O'Brien that much of an edge."

"No you can't. He's fast on the draw." Hurriedly, Jacob added, "Or so I've been told."

"Well, will you do it?"

Jacob crawled out on a limb. "Of course, Mr. Perry. Shawn O'Brien will be dead by tonight."

"Good, I'll take your word on that. Now, one last thing. We must discuss the test of the small frigate's guns tomorrow. Egbert Killick assures me the weather will be ideal with bright sunshine and little or no breeze. How he knows these things I have no idea, but he does generally get it right. More brandy?"

Jacob really did need a drink and held out his glass.

Perry poured from the decanter. "Remember, you will head south along Main Street at treetop level, deliver a broadside, turn and cut loose with the other."

"And then drop the bomb. Or so Killick told me."

"Yes. I want the complete destruction of Big Buck. The vile town is a stench in my nostrils. Besides, I need all the land around Abaddon for future testing and I don't need prying eyes."

"I'm looking forward to it." That at least was honest.

"I'll have all my foremen gathered inside the foundry. The trolls will be locked up in their mess hall. After the bombardment is completed, I'll unleash my men on the ruined town with orders to kill anyone who might have survived, man, woman, or child. By then, you will have returned to Abaddon, Mr. Ross, having earned further laurels."

"It sounds like an excellent plan, Mr. Perry."

"I will observe the attack on Big Buck unfold from a high vantage point and oh, how I will enjoy it." Perry's eyes took on a demonic glint. "It is my intention to travel to Europe after the frigates are delivered. I want to see great buildings fall, people crushed and burned and blown to pieces. Do you understand? That is the fate most of humanity deserves, especially the racial trash, the stinking, diseased poor, and the mentally insane. I will ensure that a white elite survives to steer the world on a new course toward peace and prosperity, their boots on the necks of a servile population." Perry smiled. "I do go on about my future Utopia, don't I, Mr. Ross? But I'm sure you share my vision."

Jacob nodded. "Yes, I do, Mr. Perry. I can close my eyes and see the future you plan."

"Good man, Mr. Ross. By God, sir, once I intended to execute you, but I'm glad my mercy prevailed. You're true blue." Perry stretched in his chair. "Now I grow weary from my exertions of the morning. When I next see you, I hope you'll be carrying Shawn O'Brien's head under your arm."

"Yes, sir. You can depend on it, Mr. Perry."

CHAPTER FORTY-EIGHT

The afternoon sun dropped lower in the sky and shadows lengthened along Main Street. Above City Hall, the flag hung listless in the breathless heat and over at the Abaddon loading platform, a locomotive vented steam.

Shawn O'Brien had the window of his hotel room open to catch whatever coolness was available but succeeded only in attracting rising dust and flies. Across the street at the saloon, a bored customer picked out the first few notes of "Rosie Lee" and then stopped.

"I'm hungry, Professor," Flora March said.

"I'll get you something later." Shawn glanced at the soaked rug in front of the fireplace. "I see you had your bath."

"Yeah, I had a bath, but I'm still wearing the same clothes," Flora complained.

"When it gets dark, I'll take you over to the New York Dress and Hat Shop. You can find what you need over there."

"Except money," Flora whined.

"I'll give you some," Shawn offered.

She smiled. "You know, Professor, you're not a bad sort. I'm slowly cottoning to you."

Shawn wasn't listening to her. The sound of heavy footsteps in the hallway grabbed all his attention and he drew his Colt. "Get over there into the corner, out of the line of fire."

"Who the hell is it?" Flora looked scared.

A loud, aggressive knock rattled the door.

"I guess we're about to find out." Shawn walked to the door and stepped to the side, wary of shots though the thin timber. "Who is it? I can drill ya."

"For God's sake, open the door, Shawn. You sound like a frightened old lady." Jake's voice was low and as rough as a cob.

Shawn unlocked the door and stepped back.

Jake stood in the doorway wearing his usual threadbare pants, suspenders pulled over a washed-out blue shirt, a ragged bandana that had once been red, battered hat, scuffed boots, and a worn blue Colt shoved into a holster and cartridge belt that must have cost at least a dollar. "Helluva way to greet your long-lost brother." He set down a bulging burlap sack.

He and Shawn hugged.

Jake said, grinning, "Damn, it's good to see you still above ground."

Shawn closed the door. "What brings you here?"

"Well, I'm here to kill you . . . on Mr. Perry's orders."

"Nice of him."

"You don't seem scared of my fast draw."

"Not on your best day, Jacob O'Brien."

Jacob smiled. "I recollect Luther Ironside telling me that very thing about you."

"And now you mention Luther, how are the Colonel and Patrick and Sam'l?"

"Doing real well. Right after he gets back from Rome, Pa's talking about buying an interest in the El Paso and Southwestern Railroad. He's got a private audience with the Pope Leo, you know."

"I know. Luther must be loving that."

"Well, Luther is going along and he says he's taking his gun. He reckons papists are not to be trusted. Patrick wants to go. You know how his head is always full of strange notions, but the colonel says he needs to stay home and help Sam run the ranch."

"And Sam and his wife and younguns?" Shawn said, feeling suddenly homesick.

"They're just fine. Sam is as serious as ever and he's not one for gallivanting all over. His home is Dromore and he never wants to leave it."

"And you, Jake. How are you?" Shawn finally asked.

"All right, I guess. But I've seen and heard things at Abaddon that a man should never see. I think Caleb Perry is as evil a man as ever lived and when I kill him, I'll be doing the world a favor." Jake shook his head. "Shawn, I don't like where the world is headed. Imagine a future where steam-powered flying machines can level entire cities and kill thousands of people in a single afternoon. Bombs in the hands of madmen like Perry more powerful and destructive than any that have gone before. People penned up and destroyed because of their race . . . the list goes on and on."

"None of that will ever happen, Jake. Flying machines are like horseless carriages, just a passing fad. The United States is a peace-loving nation and Europe is more civilized than ever before in its history. Wise heads in government will always prevail. Countries like Britain, Germany, and France will never go to war again so all that death and destruction Perry talks about will never come to pass."

Jake shook his head. "Well, I just hope you're right, Shawn. Hey, you haven't introduced me to the young lady."

"Oh, I'm sorry. Jacob O'Brien, this is Miss Flora March."

To Shawn's surprise Flora dropped a little curtsey "Pleased to meet you, Mr. O'Brien, I'm sure."

"Obviously you're a well brought-up young lady, Miss March," Jacob said, bowing. "It's an honor."

Shawn angled Flora a look but said nothing then turned his attention to Jacob "Well, where do we go from here?"

"Once it gets dark, you have to get out of town, Shawn, but just until tomorrow. The steamship's flight is scheduled for noon. I want you back in town before then." Jacob looked uncertain. "Do you have a place to go? You can't take your horse. That would be too obvious."

"There's a place on the other side of the graveyard where we can hole up, but we need grub."

"I'm hungry," Flora whined again.

"Food in the sack," Jacob said. "No coffee, but I shoved a bottle of wine in there."

"Tell me what's going on," Shawn said. "What's your plan, Jake?"

"It's a good one, Shawn. Just crackerjack."

"I'm listening."

Flora raided the sack and chewed on a beef sandwich. With her little finger, she pushed a breadcrumb into her mouth and said, "Me too."

"It's great," Jacob said. "I mean, it's brilliant."

"We're listening, Jake," Shawn said, his impatience showing.

"Well, listen up, here it is . . ."

After Jacob finished talking, Shawn and Flora stared at him in stunned, slack-jawed silence.

"What do you think?" Jacob asked.

Shawn recovered first. "Jake, that's the most crazy, hare-brained scheme I've ever heard. You'll break your neck in that damn flying machine thing. Do you even know how to drive it?"

"Fly it," Jacob corrected.

"Whatever the hell you call it. I always knew you were loco, Jake, but this plan of yours hits a new height of craziness. It's . . . it's . . .

"Preposterous?" Jacob offered.

"Yeah, that's it, *preposterous* . . . insane, demented, mad . . . and downright dangerous."

"But it will work. Shawn, if I don't stop Perry, by this time tomorrow Big Buck will be a smoking ruin and every man, woman, and child who calls the place home will be dead. Sure my plan is mad, but it's the only one I've got that has a hope in hell of working."

Shawn absorbed that. "Then at least let me come with you."

Jacob shook his head. "No, brother, you'd be recognized in Abaddon and spoil the whole plan. Just be here tomorrow before noon. That's when I'll need your help most."

"Jake, do you think you're going to live through tomorrow?"

"I don't know. A man can't predict the time and manner of his death. I promise you that I'll do my best to stay alive."

"Is the cause worth that much risk?"

"It's not about Manuel Cantrell any longer. It's about stopping the spread of evil." Jacob smiled. "Hell, I sound like a preacher."

"If what you've been telling me about bombs and flying machines is really true, you can't stop what's to come. You can delay it maybe, but you can't stop it."

"I'm content to cause a delay," Jacob said. "And if I survive, I'll use the colonel's influence in Washington to spread the word that the United States can't stand idly by and let monsters like Caleb Perry plunge the world into barbarism."

"You think they'll listen?" Shawn asked.

"Sure, they'll listen, because the alternative is too terrible to contemplate."

"I can't talk you out of it?" Shawn asked.

"Not a chance. It's my plan and I'll stick to it. Besides, it's a good way to kill Caleb Perry and a bunch of others just like him."

"Can the Mexicans really escape like you say?"

"I can't say for sure all of them, but most will."

Shawn smiled. "Well, maybe the politicians in

Washington will listen to you about flying machines and bombs because you speak so well. You can't spell worth a damn, but you can talk the talk."

"I've always had a problem reading too, yet I can read music just fine," Jake said. "Strange that, isn't it?"

"Seems like." Shawn hugged his brother close. "Whatever happens tomorrow, know this, Jake. I'm damn proud of you."

"And so am I." Flora popped a last piece of crust into her mouth.

CHAPTER FORTY-NINE

Moonlight gleamed on the graveyard and turned the marble and granite headstones into slabs of polished iron. To the west, the sky above the Abaddon foundry glowed red and even at a distance its constant clamor scarred the beauty of the night.

"Not far now," Shawn O'Brien said. "How are you holding up?"

"My feet hurt," Flora March complained. "My boots are for show, not walking."

"Our camping spot is just beyond the cemetery fence. Not far."

"You've said that since we left Big Buck. Wait just a minute. I want to show you something. And I need a rest."

Shawn stopped. Looking at her, he thought she looked quite pretty in the moonlight, not as hard around the mouth and eyes. "Show me."

She reached into the pocket of her skirt and produced a small paper bag. "Look what your brother put in the grub sack. Motto hearts."

"What's that?"

"It's a kind of candy with stuff written on it." She poked a finger into the bag, came up with something small, pink, and heart-shaped, and looked at it closely. "It says, *I Love You*. Ha." She popped the candy into her mouth and then extended the bag to Shawn. "Want to try one, Professor?"

He shook his head. "I reckon not. I'm not much of a hand for candy."

"Oh go on. Don't be such a spoilsport."

Shawn sighed and took a candy.

"What does it say?"

"It says, *I Miss You*."

She frowned. "Well, that's not very exciting, is it?"

"I guess not." He dropped the heart into his shirt pocket. "I'll save it for later."

"Why would Jacob put heart candy in the grub sack?"

Shawn smiled. "Because he's a very strange and wonderful person. Now let's get going."

"How far is it?" Flora asked.

"Not far," Shawn said again.

"Then you'll have to carry me. I can't walk another step in these boots."

"I don't think—"

"Carry me," she insisted. "I'm all used up and I need to be carried, Professor."

Shawn shook his head, let out another long-suffering sigh, and picked up the girl effortlessly. He held her with one arm, grabbed the grub sack, and dumped it on her lap. "I carry you and you carry the grub. That's the deal."

Flora smiled and snuggled into Shawn's shoulder. "You're so big and strong, Professor."

"That's because you're only the size of a nubbin'," Shawn said, but he enjoyed the compliment.

With the resilience of the very young, Flora snored softly in Crop Hermon's old lean-to while Shawn sat outside beside a hatful of fire. He was not drunk, but the wine had dulled his worry over what tomorrow would bring. At least a little.

He reached into his shirt pocket and brought out the heart-shaped candy. *I Miss You.* Yes, he missed Maria, her vivid beauty and the closeness they'd enjoyed during their exile from Big Buck.

Where is she now? Back home in Mexico probably. He didn't want to think that there could be any other, perhaps crueler, answer, . . .

Maria Cantrell sat in a rocker opposite Cooley Holding, bonded by the fire that flickered scarlet in the hearth. His head was bent over a volume of Dickens and the collected works of Edgar Allan Poe lay closed on her lap. She felt uneasy, as though something terrible, something awful, was going to happen. Or was it Poe's raven gently rapping, rapping at her chamber door? She listened into silence. No, it was the prairie wind and nothing more.

"Maria, are you feeling quite well?" Cooley asked.

She managed a smile. "Yes, I'm fine. Just a little tired."

"Can I get you a shawl?"

"No thank you, Cooley. I think I'll just take a short stroll and catch some fresh air."

The man closed his book. "I'll come with you."

"No," she said a little too quickly. She smiled. "Sorry, Cooley, but I just want to be alone for a few minutes."

"Are you sure? There are coyotes out there. Listen to them."

"I'll be quite all right." She rose, walked to the door, and stepped outside into a rising south wind. Small black clouds edged with tarnished silver raced across the face of the moon and the air smelled of the pine woods to the north where the brown-eyed deer slept. She walked directly away from the house into darkness of the brush.

Behind her, mules stomped in the corral, made uneasy by the yips of hunting coyotes. Like a dark cloak, the sense of impending doom hung heavily on her. But for whom? *Is it Cooley, the children, or me? Or could it be Manuel? No, my brother is dead. Jacob O'Brien then, or Shawn?* Maria shivered in the coolness of the night, suddenly very afraid.

Then came the flying thing.

It flew so close that she felt the death-scented breath of its passing and the bat flap of its wings and then it was gone, a dark shape soaring upward, blacking out the stars. She knew instantly what the creature was, the dreadful *Santa Muerte*, the Angel of Death.

Maria cried out in fear and turned to run. Immediately, strong arms encircled her and she cried out again in her terror and tried to struggle free.

"Maria! Maria! It's me! It's Cooley!"

She looked up into the man's concerned face. He held her close, an immobile pillar of iron that nothing on earth could prevail against, not even Santa Muerte.

"I think it was the Angel of Death . . . I was so afraid," she said, her face buried in his chest.

"I'm here now," he said, "Maria, as long as there's breath in my body, I'll let no man, beast, or demon ever harm you."

Suddenly Maria Cantrell was no longer afraid. She was safe in the strong arms of her man . . . and she knew with glorious certainty that nothing could ever hurt her again.

CHAPTER FIFTY

"I expected O'Brien's head, not excuses," Caleb Perry said to Jacob then. looked up at a gauge—big around as a dinner plate—attached to the steam pipe running across the ceiling of his office. "That damn pressure is too high." He shouted, *"Somebody!"*

A moment later, a foreman in a bowler and goggles opened the door.

"Get a mechanic to check this pipe," Perry said. "The pressure is way too high."

"Sure will, boss."

After the man left, Perry stared at Jacob without enthusiasm. "What happened?"

"He made a run for it, Mr. Perry. He didn't even take time to get his horse."

"Was there a woman with him?"

"Yes. I believe so."

"Good. I want to kill O'Brien and use his woman."

"I'll hunt for him again tomorrow," Jacob promised.

"No, you have bigger and better things to do tomorrow. After the cannons and munitions are tested and Big Buck is destroyed, we'll mount a search for him. He won't get far without a horse and his woman will slow him down."

"The steam frigate is ready to go, Mr. Perry," Jacob said.

"And the crew?"

"They'll do their job."

"Talk to Egbert Killick and ask him if he plans to make any last-minute changes. And I want the mechanics to be on their toes."

"Yes, sir." The word *sir* scalded his tongue like acid.

"Right, Mr. Ross. Be on your way. You'll make history tomorrow, the worst mass murderer since Genghis Khan. How does it feel?"

"It feels just fine."

"Good man." Perry beamed.

"There are no changes to the standing arrangements." Egbert Killick wore his top hat, goggles, and leather gauntlets and hopped around the small frigate like a rather scraggly bird. "We will go at noon, Mr. Ross, and the day promises to be fair and bright."

Killick adjusted a boiler dial and then stepped back to the stern where he sat down beside Jacob and put his hand on the tiller. "Mr. Ross, I did suffer a little disappointment when it came to munitions. As you no doubt are aware, when cannons are loaded with canister, the grapeshot does great execution among the enemy. Is that not so?"

"I guess the artillery in the War Between the States proved that many times over," Jacob said. "My father talked about the effect of cannon fire on attacking infantry."

"Yes, indeed, Mr. Ross. You corroborate my case and I admire your sagacity. Now, I approached Mr. Perry no later than yesterday evening and asked in a most respectful fashion if I may load the starboard battery with canister. I said, 'I wish to determine the effect of grapeshot on a fleeing civilian population when delivered from the air.' But said he, 'Not this time, Mr. Killick. My customers are interested in building-busters, not taking potshots at peasants. If in the future we can find an Indian village or a collection of hovels the Mexicans call a town, then by all means go ahead and shoot it up with canister. But until then, I want only ball.'"

Killick looked peevish, like a man who'd been wronged. "Soldiers obligingly stand in line and defy grapeshot to do its worst. But what about civilians? That is my question, Mr. Ross. Under an air attack, mommy and daddy and the kids will panic and run, so how effective will canister be against such fleeing targets? That is the question I need answered." The little pilot shook his head. "We can only find out what the ratio of number of rounds fired to human units killed is through trial and error. It's all pluses and minuses, cost effectiveness, et cetera. You can readily see my problem."

"It's a puzzle to perplex any man." Jacob was really looking forward to putting a bullet into the little gnome, an accountant who considered the lives of men, women, and children only as statistics penned in a profit-and-loss ledger.

"It is indeed a mystery, and thank you, Mr. Ross, for your kind understanding." Killick smiled. "Now I must be about Mr. Perry's business and what he calls the dawn of a glorious new age that will last for a thousand years."

CHAPTER FIFTY-ONE

By the low standards of Abaddon, the hard work in the construction bay and extra food had put weight on Manuel Cantrell though he was still more living skeleton than man.

Jacob O'Brien sought the young man out. "Are you ready for tomorrow?"

Manuel nodded. "As I'll ever be, me and a group of starved Mexican scarecrows."

"Can your men handle the guns efficiently? Fire and reload in reasonable time?"

"You can depend on that. It's about all you can depend on."

Jacob stepped closer and dropped his voice to a whisper. "Remember, escape through the construction bay. The roof will be open and every man in the place should be able to climb the wall over there by the workbenches and make a run for it."

"The men are very weak and we could lose a lot of them," Manuel pointed out. "When they start climbing the wall, they'll be sitting ducks."

"Defend yourselves. Grab whatever kind of club

you can find. Surprise is your best weapon and when everything comes down, the foremen will be busy trying to save their own miserable skins and may not try to stop the escape."

"Do you think all this is going to work? It sounds thin."

"Let me put it this way . . . it's got to work. There will be no second chance." Jacob's face was bleak. "Yeah, you'll lose some of your people, but there's no way around it."

Manuel nodded. "A quick death is better than slowly rotting away in this hell." From out of the blue, he asked, "What news of my sister?"

"I believe she's gone back to Mexico."

"You believe?"

Jacob shrugged. "I can't say it any surer than that."

"Maria deserves some happiness. She's had a hard life."

"If it's any consolation, I liked her a lot."

Manuel's eyebrows lifted. "You didn't love her?"

"I don't know. I don't know what love is supposed to feel like."

"Then you didn't love her, Jacob. If you had, you'd know what it feels like all right." Manuel removed his goggles from his face and pushed them up to the brim of his hat, leaving two white circles in his blackened face. "Have you ever heard of Santa Muerte?"

"Yes. I've felt his closeness a few times."

"He came to me a few hours ago. I felt his wings flutter past me."

Jacob smiled. "Sometimes a bullet will do that."

Manuel shook his head. "It was the Angel of Death.

He left his mark on me." He pulled up the sleeve of his ragged shirt and revealed an angry red welt on his right forearm. "Look there."

"It's a burn, Manuel. A burn and nothing more."

"It's the mark of Santa Muerte. Tomorrow night the moon will come out and he will look for me, but he won't find me. I will be gone."

"Damn it, Manuel. I'll be on that damn flying contraption," Jacob said. "I'll make sure you don't get hurt."

Manuel pulled his sleeve down. "Look, the cannonballs are being loaded. They look so small, no bigger than an apple."

Glad to change the subject, Jacob said. "The cannons are small because the guns had to be light. But they'll get the job done."

"I better get back to work and supervise the loading of the ordnance." To Jacob's surprise, Manuel managed a smile. "Now I sound like the raving lunatic Killick."

"Maybe the Angel of Death came for Killick and just brushed past you. "

Jacob left the floor and again climbed the ladder into the steam frigate. The billowing canopy had been painted on each of its sides with a black bat on a red background. The dragon's head on the prow was the same shade of red, its fangs bright silver. Though small and armed with only eight cannons, the airship was a fearsome weapon of war. He felt like David in the presence of Goliath.

Egbert Killick found him again, clutched him by the arm, and took him aside away from the ears of the laboring trolls. "I'll load the bomb last, since we don't really know how stable it is." He took a brass key attached to a thin iron chain from his pocket. "The bomb's firing mechanism is clockwork. Once it's wound up with this key, you will hear the device start to tick. You will have thirty seconds to get rid of it. I will be totally involved steering the ship so it will be up to you to activate the bomb and drop it on the ruins of Big Buck." He hung the key around Jacob's neck. "It's an important job, Mr. Ross, but I think you're up to it."

"Thanks for your confidence in me."

The little man smiled. "Do you feel it, Mr. Ross? Tell me, do you feel it all around you?"

Jacob frowned. "Feel what?"

"A sense of history . . . that and the excitement of course. Tomorrow will be a splendid day, Mr. Ross. Mark my words."

CHAPTER FIFTY-TWO

Shawn O'Brien had no desire for sleep. The events of tomorrow preyed on his mind and gave him no rest. The coyotes drew closer, yipping their hunting cries, and he was startled when the fire flamed and sparked by a sudden gust of wind that flapped like bat wings. Uneasy, he rose to his feet, adjusted the lie of his holster and stared into the darkness.

From somewhere hidden came the creak of a wagon and the footfalls of a walking horse. The sounds stopped and a voice cried out, "Hello the camp."

"State your intentions," Shawn said. "I'm not a trusting man."

The man's voice was not unpleasant. "Coffee, if you got it. Companionship on a dark night if you don't."

"Come on ahead like you're visiting Grandma."

"My grandma is with the Lord," the man said.

"Then good for her," Shawn said.

"Walk on," the man instructed to his horse, and a

moment later, a wagon materialized from the gloom. When he was a few feet from Shawn, the driver drew rein on his bony nag. "Don't smell no coffee."

"Don't have any."

The unexpected visitor was a pleasant-faced man wearing a threadbare black suit, a round-brimmed hat with a low crown much favored by country parsons, and a clerical collar. Over his left eye, he wore a black leather patch decorated with a silver spider and to Shawn's surprise, the man carried a bone-handled Colt in a shoulder holster.

"I have coffee," the man of the cloth said, for that's what Shawn deemed him to be. "And a seedcake made by a lady of this parish. Do you like seedcake? Ah, I see you have a young lady with you." The parson doffed his hat. "It's a pleasure to meet you, ma'am."

Flora pulled her blouse up over a naked shoulder. "Likewise, I'm sure."

As though he was extremely pleased by this exchange, the clergyman smiled. "My name is the Very Reverend Matthew Mark Luke John Lombard-Fullbourne the Third. But you can call me Matt." He looked at Shawn. "And you, sir, if I may be so bold?"

"Name's Shawn O'Brien. The lady's name is Flora March."

"Not to pry," the reverend said, "but are you one of the Dromore O'Briens out of the New Mexico territory?"

"Yes. My father owns the Dromore ranch."

"And how is Jake? I assume he's your brother."

"He is."

"One time, Jake helped me survive a shooting

scrape up Albuquerque way. It was three against one until he took a hand and then it was just one against one. So, what news of your brother?"

"Mister—"

"Call me Matt, please. Any brother of Jake O'Brien is a friend of mine."

"I think you'd better ride on. You don't want to be around Big Buck tomorrow."

"Do I sense evil?" the reverend asked.

"You do."

"But evil is my business. My dear sir, I am death on evil. I smite the lawless wherever I find them. As the Good Book says, "If the wicked will not change their ways and heed holy scripture then let them heed the thunder of Sammy's Colt."

Shawn frowned. "I never read that in the Bible."

The reverend grinned. "It's not in the Bible. I just made it up."

"I think you should ride, mister," Shawn said.

"Coffee? Seedcake? No interest?"

Flora said, "I'm interested in coffee and seedcake, Reverend . . . um . . ."

"Lombard-Fullbourne, ma'am. But please call me Matt."

"Shawn, I'm hungry," Flora said.

"You're always hungry." To the reverend, Shawn said, "I guess you'd better light and set, mister. Miss March is hungry."

The seedcake was good, the coffee better, and the Reverend Matt Lombard-Fullbourne basked in Flora's effusive thanks.

For his part, Shawn was suspicious of anyone who came near Big Buck without a valid reason. He voiced his reservations to the preacher. "What exactly do you do, Reverend?"

"Matt."

"Right, Matt. Are you a circuit preacher of some kind?"

"You could say that, since I go where I'm needed. I received a wire . . . well, let me ask you, Shawn. Have you ever heard tell of a town by the name of Falcon Haven down in the Glass Mountains country?"

"Can't say as I have."

"Neither has anybody else, it seems. It's an outlaw town, run by a lady gambler called Drusilla McQuillen."

"A woman?" Flora asked. "That doesn't seem right."

"Right or not, it's true and she rules the roost in Falcon Haven, mostly thanks to her right-hand man, a killer by the name of Morgan Ashmore, and his fast gun."

It was Shawn's turn to be surprised. "Morg Ashmore out of Killeen? Ran with Cole Younger and them back in the day?"

"That's him," Matt said. "He never could get along with Frank James and quit the gang. He became a lawman in the Arizona Territory for a spell and then took to selling his gun. For sure, he killed Johnny Kirivan and Hiram Coin, reckoned to be two of the fastest guns in Texas, and they say he gunned a draw-fighting Ranger named Burns or Bourne in El Paso back in the spring of 1884. I don't know if that's true or not, but a month later Ashmore was hired by

Drusilla McQuillen, so she must have given him credit for the Ranger killing."

"Reverend, Morg Ashmore is bad news," Shawn said. "My advice is that you steer clear of him. He did kill Frankie Burns but at a saloon in Fort Griffin not El Paso. Burns was a hardcase and mighty sudden on the draw and shoot. Stepping away from a fight never entered his thinking. He was wounded three times in the line of duty and after the smoke cleared, buried three men."

"You knew him?" Matt asked.

"I met him once. Frankie Burns was something, a man to step around."

"Well, here's my thinking on Morgan Ashmore." The preacher held up a long-fingered, muscular left hand. "This is the hand I use to hold the Holy Bible when I read it to bad men. I will do so again when I confront Ashmore and do my best to turn him from the ways of violence, drunkenness, and harlotry." He raised his hat. "If you will excuse the expression Miss March."

Flora had her hand cupped under her chin to catch seedcake crumbs. Chewing, she shrugged. "Doesn't bother me none, Reverend."

"Now to this hand," Matt said, holding up his right. "This is a terrible, avenging weapon of the Lord. When the wicked and the lawless persist in their iniquities, I use this hand to smite them down. The Colt you see on my breast has destroyed seven such men and there will be more ere I am done with the Lord's work."

"Preacher," Shawn said. "Do you know you're crazy?"

"Yes, as a bedbug. But it's the price I pay to be the sword of the Almighty."

"Being nuts doesn't make him a bad person, Professor," Flora remarked.

"Professor?" Matt asked.

Shawn smiled. "She calls me that."

"He looks and talks like a professor," Flora explained.

Matt shook his head. "No, dear lady. Our friend Shawn O'Brien has the look of a warrior angel. Will you accompany me to Falcon Haven, Shawn?"

"To tame a bunch of outlaws? I don't think so."

"There are some decent, hardworking people in the town, but without help, I fear they are doomed. The wire I received was from their pastor, Deacon Galahad Smolley. He says his flock live in terror of Drusilla McQuillen and her hired gunmen." Matt stared hard at Shawn. "Helping those poor folks is a Christian duty."

"If I'm alive this time tomorrow, talk to me again," Shawn said.

"You are facing danger? Do you wish to tell me about it?"

"Sure. But it might be long in the telling."

The reverend smiled. "I have cigars and something in a bottle to keep out the night chill. I'll go get them and then you can recount your story."

CHAPTER FIFTY-THREE

"So all you know of Jake's plan is that he's staging the equivalent of a mass jailbreak?" Matt Lombard-Fullbourne asked.

"That's about the size of it. He wants me on the street with my guns at noon."

"I've listened intently to what you've told me, Shawn, and I agree that the Abaddon Cannon Foundry is a place of evil. Slavery, cannons, and flying machines are indeed the devil's work."

With his little finger, Shawn O'Brien knocked ash off his cigar. "It's no concern of yours, Reverend. Heed my advice and head on out of here."

Matt disagreed. "Ah, but it is my concern. Very much so. My covenant with God is to confront evil wherever I find it. And in that regard, I've come up with my own plan."

Flora March grinned. "This is going to be good."

"I don't want to hear your plan, Reverend," Shawn said. "Jake has a plan and we'll go with that."

As though he hadn't heard, Matt continued. "To-morrow morning, I will take my Bible and demand admittance to the foundry. I will tell whoever is in charge that my business is with Caleb Perry and him alone. When I meet him, I will introduce my left and right hands and demand he make a choice—Bible or Colt. And then I'll say, 'Perry, you are the baddest man in Texas. Listen to the Word and repent of your ways or face the righteous wrath of my pistol.'" The man smiled. "That will make him sit up and take notice, I'll be bound."

"That will make him sit up and put a bullet in your belly," Shawn said.

Matt shook his head. "No, such will not be the way of it. 'Let my people go,' I'll say. And with the power of God behind me, Perry will see the light and do as I say." The man shrugged. "And if he doesn't, I'll raise my Colt like a fiery sword and blow his brains out."

Despite his irritation, that last made Shawn smile. "We'll stick with Jake's plan and so will you. I don't want you to go putting Abaddon on guard and spoiling everything."

"Is that your considered opinion?" Matt asked.

"That is my *order.*"

"Then I'll stand beside you in the street. You might be glad of my gun at your side."

"Yes, do that. I want you where I can keep an eye on you, Matthew Mark Luke John. You're a few bricks shy of a full load and that concerns me."

"Well, perhaps I misled you, Shawn. I'm just a little bit crazy."

"That's like being just a little bit pregnant," Flora said. "Any of the cake left?"

* * *

Disquieting and terrifying thoughts cartwheeled through Jacob O'Brien's mind as he lay on his cot and stared at the ceiling. He closed his eyes and breathed hard. *My God, will morning never come?*

He wanted to get this thing over with. Count the dead and then see if his conscience can cope with the slaughter. He was keenly aware that it would take only a tiny flaw in his plan—a locked door, a closed window, a stampede across the construction bay that turned to disaster after men fell and others piled on top of them—to make everything go wrong and his mistake would be measured in dead Mexicans. He envisioned Perry's grinning gunmen slaughtering scores, hundreds, at their leisure. . . .

Jacob was conscious of one certainty. It all depended on him. If the plan failed, the fault was his and the tears of widows and mothers would fall, salty and hot, on his head. If Caleb Perry survived tomorrow and lived to continue his reign of terror, better Jacob O'Brien tie a millstone around his neck and jump into the deepest ocean.

He groaned and the rosary beads on his hand stilled. He'd lost the will to pray for a victory that might well be impossible, beyond the reach of even heavenly intervention. There were too many *maybes* in his plan, too many variables . . . too many ways it could end in disaster. As a man who lived with depression, the black dog that crouched in a corner waiting to spring, he knew there were also too many ways that could force him to take his own life.

That thought disturbed him and he rolled out of his cot, hurriedly dressed and buckled on his Colt. A glance at his watch told him it was almost two in the morning, but the blasting thunder of cannon forging went on where trolls served the machines, moving like naked automatons in a bloodred glare.

Jacob walked through an empty corridor to the foremen's canteen. The place was empty but for a few cooks. He ordered a whiskey from the bar and sat at the piano. He forsook his beloved Chopin and began to play the hauntingly sad First Movement of Beethoven's "Moonlight" Sonata that so perfectly fit his mood.

A few moments after Jacob began playing, the door opened and Valentine Kilcoyn stepped inside, wearing his gun. He drew up a chair and then soundlessly stared at Jacob for the entire seven-and-a-half-minute duration of the movement. When the last notes faded, Kilcoyn rose to his feet and applauded. "Bravo. You play well, Buck."

Jacob turned from the keyboard and said his thanks.

"Big morning coming, huh? Lot of exciting things happening."

"Seems like," Jacob said.

"But I've been thinking. When a man soars into the air, free as a bird, he might take on strange notions. I mean, from up that high, he might start to see things from a different point of view. It could happen."

Jacob nodded. "I guess it could at that."

"But if a man is wise, he'll keep his feet planted firmly on the ground. If he flies too close to the sun, he might burn up and that would be the end of him."

"You got a man in mind, Val?"

"Can't say as I do just yet. I got a strange feeling

though, Buck. I'm descended from a great Irishman, King Niall of the Nine Hostages, and all Irish have the gift of second sight, do they not?"

"Not all, but most," Jacob corrected.

"Do you?"

"Yes. I often dream about events before they happen. Maybe I'll see you in one of my dreams, Val."

"And you in mine, Buck. Just to let you know, I'll be on the air frigate come morning."

"Glad to have you onboard, if that's the correct expression."

"No, you're not glad I'll be onboard, Buck. I don't need a dream to see the what-the-hell expression in your eyes as you sit there. You don't want me anywhere near the airship." Kilcoyn touched his gun. "And this is one cannon you don't want onboard, either."

"A man does what his inner voices tell him, Val," Jacob pointed out.

"Then you tell me . . . am I welcome?"

"Of course you're welcome. Why would I say otherwise?"

"I don't know, but I'll be there to make certain you play honest poker, Buck. Deal from the bottom of the deck and I'll take it hard."

Jacob rolled his shoulders and stretched his neck. "Will this night ever end?"

"Long, isn't it?" Kilcoyn said. "I couldn't sleep, kept tossing and turning. I put it down to wondering about what the morning will bring. Then I heard a flapping and thought a bat or a big bird had flown into my room. Of course, nothing was there. That's when I decided to get up."

"Maybe you should voice your concerns about tomorrow to Caleb Perry."

"No, I don't want to do that. He'd take it as a sign of weakness. I'll handle it myself."

"Handle what, Val?"

"I don't know, but I can guess. There will be a lot of trolls onboard, a mutiny maybe? Yeah, it could be mutiny."

"Then you should be wary, Val."

"That's what I intend to be, Buck," Kilcoyn said. "Will you play again?"

"The Second movement of Beethoven's *Moonlight Sonata* is a scherzo in D flat major. It's more light-hearted than the First and might cheer us up, huh?"

"Yeah, I think we need some cheering up, Buck. Let's hear it and leave morning until morning comes."

CHAPTER FIFTY-FOUR

Shawn O'Brien refilled the coffeepot at the stream. When he returned to the campsite, Matt had a fire going and was slicing bacon into a fry pan. He asked the reverend, "Is there anything you don't have in your wagon?"

"Well, I don't have a woman and I don't have a dog, but I aim to get both pretty soon. Nothing makes a nicer pair than a pretty, yellow-haired woman and a yellow dog. At least, that's my thinking anyway." He glanced at the lean-to where Flora March was asleep. "I'm always willing to compromise."

As Shawn grabbed the sack of Arbuckles' that lay close to the fire, Matt added, "Throw a good fistful of coffee in the pot and then get it on the bile. Bacon's gonna be fried before the coffee's ready."

A morning mist cleared over the graveyard and the night shadows melted like black snow. The morning promised a hot, sunny day with no breeze. Shawn stretched a kink out of his back. "You all loaded up, Matt?"

"Wagon or guns?"

"I'm only interested in your guns today."

"Sure am. Got all six chambers of my Colt loaded and two loads of buck in the Greener. Now it's up to you to point out a target."

Shawn grimaced. "I have a feeling there will be plenty of those."

"Then I'm ready to smite the unrighteous."

"Those seven men you killed, were any of them named guns?"

Matt hesitated. "Well, they all had names. Boy, this is going to be tasty bacon, I can tell. The smell is delicious. Making my mouth water."

His suspicions roused, Shawn said, "Tell me about the shooting scrape and the time my brother Jake saved your life."

"Just between us? I don't want Miss March to hear."

"I won't tell her if you don't. Now what about all those bad men you've killed."

"You want the truth, don't you?"

Shawn nodded. "I can tell a professional shootist by the way he conducts himself and talks. I don't think you've ever been in a gunfight, Reverend."

"All right then." The man sighed. "Jake saved me from being hung by vigilantes for horse theft. Even though he notified them, those boys didn't want to be cheated out of their fun and it came down to gunplay. The hemp party left two of their number dead on the ground and the rest lit a shuck. See, they'd never had to deal with the like of Jake O'Brien before." Matt looked miserable. "Here's the truth . . . I didn't shoot anybody."

"What about all that left hand, right hand stuff?" Shawn asked.

"That's not how it was, but how it's going to be. I'm just getting started in the salvation or slaughter business. I had a vision you see after I overheard some Texas Rangers talking about Falcon Haven and how it was a bandit town. It was to the Rangers that Deacon Galahad Smolley had sent a wire, not me. However that night my vision told me to journey—"

"I don't give a damn what your vision told you," Shawn interrupted. "Since you got here, all you've done is tell one big windy after another. Hell, I have a good mind to put a bullet into you myself."

"What's all the bellering about?" Flora March had her skirt hiked up and scratched a mosquito bite on her thigh.

"The draw fighting reverend has never shot anybody in his life," Shawn explained. "He's not going to be of any help in the street. Just a liability."

Matt tried to make himself small. "I'm not a reverend and my real name isn't Matthew Mark Luke John Lombard-Fullbourne, it's Archibald Lark. Before this, I worked as a clerk at a clothing and women's sundries store in El Paso."

Flora shook her finger. "You're a bad boy, Archie."

"But I am headed for the Glass Mountain country and Falcon Haven, Miss March. Honest I am. And as far as the Good Lord is concerned, I'm a reverend."

"Can you even shoot?" Shawn asked.

Lark brightened and seemed to grow in size. "When I bought a Colt's gun in El Paso, the store owner took me out back and I hit a peach can. Mr. Foster said I was a natural."

Not yet convinced, Shawn asked, "How far away was the can?"

"At the end of an empty beer barrel. I shot into the barrel, you see."

"Go home to El Paso and sell woman's fixin's, Archibald. You don't want to be in the street with me come noon."

"I think Archie's got sand, Professor," Flora said, studying the man's face. "He's not going to run away. And he did shoot a peach can in El Paso."

Shawn shook his head. "Let's get breakfast started. Flora, you're as loco as he is."

The sun climbed higher in a blue sky as Shawn made his way through the graveyard in the direction of town. Trailing behind him, Lark and Flora walked hand in hand. Archie was there because he dearly wanted to prove himself and Flora was there because she did whatever the hell she wanted.

Cemeteries can be quiet shady places well suited to deep contemplation. Shawn, raised by punchers who had passed on to him all their many superstitions, felt uneasy walking through the headstones. It was the baddest kind of luck to visit Boot Hill before a gunfight, or so old Luther Ironside had told him.

"Hold on there, Professor," Flora said. "You're walking too fast."

"I'm supposed to be on the street by noon," Shawn argued.

"Plenty of time." She reached beneath her blouse to let out the side buckles of her corset and loosened the laces between her breasts. That done, she lifted her dress to mid-thigh and tucked the hem into the waistband. "Ah, that's better. You can carry on now, Professor."

Irritated, Shawn frowned. "You should have done that fixing before we left camp."

"I wasn't hot before we left camp," Flora pointed out.

"It is getting hot," Lark said.

"Don't encourage her, Archibald."

The word that an Abaddon aerial steam frigate was making a test run had been broadcast around town by Caleb Perry's men, and an added attraction was that the foundry would supply beer and cake and ice cream for the ladies and little ones. Thus was Perry's plan—to attract as many people as possible to his killing ground.

Shawn was surprised to see that the noisy street and boardwalks were crowded with people in a holiday mood, as though it was Independence Day. The six-piece Big Buck brass band was in attendance and played renditions of "How Sweet the Roses" and "Where the Woodbine Twineth" to considerable applause.

Jake had told Shawn to be on the street at noon and according to the fliers posted around town that was when the airship would lift from the foundry's construction bay. The clock above City Hall claimed it was as yet only eleven-thirty and Flora and Lark went in search of ice cream. Shawn found himself a rocker on the hotel porch and settled down to wait. Amid laughing, bright-eyed people, he was the only one who dreaded what the noon hour would bring.

CHAPTER FIFTY-FIVE

The frigate was already crowded when Jacob O'Brien clambered onboard. The gun crews under the watchful eye of Manuel Cantrell were clustered around their cannons and technicians made last-minute checks on the ship's furnace, boiler, and the tangle of brass pipes, levers, handles, and dials that were the veins and arteries of the craft.

Valentine Kilcoyn, wearing two guns in crossed cartridge belts, had stationed himself at the prow, the painted dragonhead looming over him. Egbert Killick would not arrive with the bomb until just before launch, but he stood on the gantry with Caleb Perry anxiously watching the preparations.

The roof, raised by steam power, lifted slowly, its massive gearwheels and greased pistons smoothly taking the strain of the enormous weight. The black bats painted on the balloon bobbed up and down as though they were ready to take off and fly at any moment.

Kilcoyn made his way through the gun trolls

gathered in the ship's waist and stood beside Jacob at the stern. "We've got an audience, Buck."

"Yeah, I see him."

"Mr. Perry is expecting great things of us today. This will be the first aerial bombing attack in history. You have the key?"

Jacob showed the key on the chain around his neck. "A clockwork bomb. It sounds so harmless."

"You won't think that when you see it wipe Big Buck off the map," Kilcoyn said. "What an experiment this going to be, the future of modern warfare."

"We're going to kill a lot of innocent people," Jacob pointed out.

"Why would you care, Buck? They mean nothing to you."

Jacob nodded. "No they don't."

"When fleets of steamships like this one drop bombs on cities, do you think the men who fly them will fret over the numbers of people they're killing? No, of course not. They'll be bombing bridges, roads, factories, and seats of government, not people. Mr. Perry calls dead civilians *collateral damage*. That's how you need to think of the Big Buck dead, just incidental casualties. Understand me?"

"Yeah, I get it," Jacob said. "You've clearly stated the case, Val."

Kilcoyn slapped Jacob on the shoulder. "I had my doubts about you, Buck, but no longer. By God, you're a white man through and through." He glanced at his watch. "Fifteen minutes to launch. Are you ready?"

Jacob forced a smile. "There ain't a bump in the road ahead of me that I can see. Yeah, Val, I'm ready."

"You're true blue, Buck," Kilcoyn grinned before he went back to the prow again.

Five minutes later, Egbert Killick approached the frigate. Behind him, two nervous trolls lugged the bomb in a specially made rack with two handles at each end. The Mexicans looked as though they were carrying a large Christmas pudding on a stretcher.

"Mr. Ross, are you ready to receive ordnance?" Killick called up.

"Bring it onboard, Mr. Killick. Take the loading ramp."

"You didn't forget the key, did you?" Killick hollered.

Jacob dangled the key so that the little man could see it.

Killick turned to his helpers. "Right, up the ramp with you two." He brandished a bulldog revolver. "I'll kill the man who drops it."

Without the clockwork firing mechanism being wound, the bomb was relatively stable and was loaded onboard without much difficulty.

Killick followed, mopped his brow with a red bandana, and took his seat at the helm. "I must confess, Mr. Ross, I was worried about the bomb. Had one of those fools dropped it . . . well, I don't know what would have happened."

"Something mighty unpleasant, I guess."

"Mr. Ross, you are a master of understatement."

As the time for launch drew close, the brass band had moved closer to the foundry and was playing selections from *The Pirates of Penzance*, including "A Rollicking Band of Pirates, We."

Jacob thought it apt.

All over the foundry at a minute before noon by the clock on a construction bay wall, steam whistles shrieked to herald the coming event. Up on the gantry, Caleb Perry raised fists above his head and pumped them in the air, then he and his entourage of gunmen left to climb to his aerie on top of the roof where he would have a grandstand seat to watch the proceedings.

The clock on the wall chimed twelve followed by roaring orders.

"Cast off fore and aft!"

"Cast off amidships!"

"All hands to stations!"

"Steady as she goes . . ."

The steam frigate rose majestically as the balloon soared through the roof and for a moment, held itself motionless against the backdrop of the blue sky. People cheered themselves hoarse in the street as they watched the great airship gain altitude and then come under the power of the steam engine. The propeller at the rear of the craft sputtered a few times and then roared into life, spinning in a glittering circle like a steel saw. Under power, the frigate, its eight cannons bristling, headed north away from town. Moans of disappointment rose from the crowds of onlookers as they wondered if the beautiful airship was leaving them.

* * *

"Mr. Perry ordered me to fire a test broadside before we level the town," Kilcoyn said to Jacob and Killick. "He doesn't want this ship to go down the first time we try to fire the guns."

"Embarrassing." The breeze at an altitude of a hundred feet tugged at Jacob's clothing.

"Worse than that if we lose the British and German contracts. Heads will roll and us three will be the first." Kilcoyn tapped Killick on the shoulder and shouted above the din of the steam engine. "Take her down fifty feet, find an open spot, and we'll cut loose."

Killick nodded and swung the tiller. The airship turned to the west toward open brush flats. Jacob watched how the little pilot handled the unwieldy craft and was aware that Kilcoyn was watching him. Manuel Cantrell seemed to feel the growing tension. He stood on the swaying deck among his gunners, his face set and concerned.

Killick looked over the side and found a spot that suited him. "Roll out the guns," he shouted. Then after a few seconds, "Fire!"

The four starboard cannons crashed in unison and belched sheets of flame and smoke. The frigate rolled slightly and threatened to yaw, but Killick had her firmly in hand and kept her to a straight and level course. A cheer went up from the gun crews the moment they realized that the ship had remained steady under recoil and they were still alive. Kilcoyn grinned and looked relieved.

"Reload, you damn scum!" Killick roared. "There will be time enough for cheering when the job is done."

Kilcoyn yelled down the length of the ship to Jacob, "What do you think, Buck?"

Jacob let go of his white-knuckled grip on the gunwale and yelled back, "Surprised the hell out of me. I thought she'd go loco on us, roll over, and we'd all be dead by this time."

Kilcoyn grinned wider and gave Jacob a wave. For a moment, Jacob thought he might even like the man, but that thought was quickly banished from his mind as the big foreman yelled, "Go about, Mr. Killick. Now let's go kill a town."

CHAPTER FIFTY-SIX

Shawn O'Brien watched the airship vanish to the northwest, a mechanical thing of great beauty despite its sinister purpose.

Flora March and Archibald Lark joined him on the hotel porch. She had an ice cream stain on her front.

"Looks like it's headed away from us," Lark said, stating the obvious. "What are we doing here?"

"It will be back."

Like the sound of a distant battle, cannons roared in the badlands.

More to himself, Shawn said, "They're testing the guns."

"When it comes back, what do we do?" Lark asked.

Shawn smiled. "I wish I knew. Jake told me to be here. That's all."

"Maybe he wants you to shoot it down," Flora said.

"There's always that," Shawn agreed. "I tried it before, but it didn't work."

Flora nodded. "I remember. You saved my life that day, Professor."

He remembered, too. "And my own."

"A great day, Sheriff O'Brien." Mayor John Deakins stepped onto the porch, his round face shiny from beer and pride. "That there flying contraption will put Big Buck on the map."

"I believe the Abaddon Cannon Foundry has done that already," Shawn said.

Deakins waved a pudgy hand. "My dear sir, cannons are the past. The flying machine is the future. Why, I heard one of Mr. Perry's engineers say that the time will come when an airship will fly faster than a highballing locomotive and higher than a hawk." The mayor beamed. "Glory days, sir! Glory days are right around the corner and our fair city will be part of them." He raised his goggled top hat. "Well, good day to all of you. Don't forget the cake and ice cream."

After the man left, Flora said, "I didn't forget. Abaddon should quit making cannons and sell ice cream."

"The ice cream is very good, Mr. Perry." Nurse Clementina Rooksbee sat back in a chair and showed a great deal of smooth long leg and swelling bosom

Caleb Perry was considering the woman as an interim mistress and was prepared to be agreeable. "I'm so glad you like it, my dear. One of my chefs whipped it up for this momentous occasion."

"I do so enjoy treats," Clementina said. "Don't you, Mr. Perry?"

The man's knowing smile told the nurse that he did.

The observation post was a teetering timber rookery

at the highest peak of the Abaddon building. Round in shape, it looked like an ancient castle tower open to the air and was outfitted with benches and tables and several large brass telescopes. A waiter in a white jacket served drinks and ice cream and a couple hard-faced foremen stood silent guard.

"Ah, hear that? The frigate has fired a broadside." Perry rose quickly, swung a telescope to the north, and stared into the eyepiece. "It's still flying!" he yelled. "It survived the recoil."

The two foremen applauded politely and with just the right amount of enthusiasm, but Nurse Rooksbee said, "Oh please let me see, Mr. Perry."

"Of course, my dear." Perry stepped aside and Clementina bent to the eyepiece, revealing a wider expanse of hip than was strictly necessary.

"Do you see it?"

"Yes. And I think it's turning," she said.

"Good. In a few minutes, the real fun will start."

Clementina giggled like a schoolgirl. "I declare, this is just too, too exquisite."

CHAPTER FIFTY-SEVEN

Valentine Kilcoyn ordered Egbert Killick to reduce speed so that the clanking of the steam engine was reduced and he could hear himself talk. "Take her down to just a few feet above the ground, That will bring people out to watch from the boardwalks. Give them a port and starboard broadside, reload, and give them another. You will then turn and do the same again. You got that, Killick?"

Killick nodded. "Civilian casualties and damage to structures will be extensive. What about the bomb?"

"We'll judge the damage done and may have to repeat the process a few times before we drop the bomb," Kilcoyn said. "Buck, on my word, you'll wind the clockwork mechanism and drop the bomb where you figure it will do the most damage. Do you understand?"

"I understand, Val, but it's not going to happen that way." Jacob took a wide stance on the deck, his gun hand hanging loose but ready.

"You have a better plan, Buck?"

"Yeah, I plan to take over this . . . whatever the hell

you call it. Drop your gun belt, Val. I don't want to kill you. And the name isn't Buck. It's Jacob, Jacob O'Brien."

"That figures. I always thought there was something strange about you. It goes against my grain to kill a man who plays the piano as well as you do . . . Jacob."

"Then just unbuckle your gun belt and let it drop, Val," Jacob said. "Caleb Perry isn't a man worth dying for."

Kilcoyn smiled. "He pays my wages, Jacob. I ride for the brand."

The man's face changed to stone and he drew and fired. Jacob matched his speed, shooting as his gun came to bear. Kilcoyn took the hit dead center and it killed him instantly. He fell back and was stone dead when his back hit the deck.

Jacob knew he should have been shot. A gun like Kilcoyn didn't miss at a distance of a few feet, even in a pitching gondola. Then why was he still alive?

An engineer supplied the reason. He ran past Jacob to the stern and turned the man at the tiller. "He's dead."

Egbert Killick slumped in the seat, a bullet hole in the middle of his forehead. He still had a .32 Smith & Wesson army revolver clutched in his lifeless hand and a snarl was frozen on his wizened face.

As the airship drifted across the sky now that Killick was no longer steering her, the engineer yanked the little man from the seat, grabbed the tiller, steadying the frigate. He looked up at Jacob. "I saw how it all came down. Killick was going to gun you in the back and Val shot him. I guess he couldn't let it happen."

Jacob nodded. "No, he couldn't let that happen. He had the makings of a noble soul but was corrupted by an evil man. May God rest him."

Every face was turned to Jacob and the engineer voiced the question that the others were silently asking. "What do we do now?"

"You tend to your engine." Jacob turned to Manuel Cantrell. "Are all the cannons loaded?"

"Ready to go," the young man said. "Jacob, can you steer this thing?"

"I watched Killick. I reckon I can make a pretty fair go of it."

The engineer, an earnest young man wearing a bowler hat and goggles, said, "I think we should land and let Mr. Perry decide what to do next. Killick's death changes everything."

"I know what he wants to do. He wants to destroy the town of Big Buck and all the people in it," Jacob said. A crow flapped in front of his face and then cawed loudly as it soared up and then over the balloon. He didn't know if it was a good omen or bad.

"I didn't hear about that," the engineer said. "I swear I didn't."

"Kilcoyn didn't tell you?"

"No. And at Abaddon, it's dangerous to ask too many questions."

"Don't you want to see the steam frigate in action?"

"I already did," the engineer said. "It remained stable all right, but we still don't know how a full-size ship will perform with heavier cannons and more recoil."

"What's your name, engineer?" Jacob asked.

"Mathias Lane. I was hired three weeks ago to work on frigate engines and furnaces."

"Well, Mr. Lane do you want to see Big Buck destroyed by cannon fire?"

"No sir, I do not."

"I plan to attack the Abaddon foundry and raze it to the ground. How do you feel about that?" And then, because Jacob was the kind of man he was, he added, "Give me the wrong answer, Mr. Lane, and I'll scatter your damn brains all over the gun crews."

Lane was silent for a few moments, then said, "If that's your plan, I suggest you attack right away. Our wood supply for the furnace was limited, and it's already running low."

Jacob smiled. "I think I'm going to like you, Mr. Lane."

"I don't think I could ever grow to like you, Mr. O'Brien."

Jacob thought that last so funny that he was still laughing as he turned the airship and readied her for war.

Caleb Perry stepped back from the telescope and said to his foremen, "I saw gun smoke. I'm sure I saw gun smoke." He pointed to one of them, a tall man with a huge dragoon mustache. "Mr. Budd, take a look."

The big foremen bent to the eyepiece for a few moments and then he straightened up and said,

"There's black smoke from the chimney aft, Mr. Perry, but I don't see gun smoke."

"Let me take another look." Perry tried the telescope again. "You're right. I don't see gun smoke. But why is the ship drifting? Oh, wait . . . wait . . . it's turning. She's coming back on course for Big Buck." He stepped back from the telescope, clapped his hands, and grinned. "Good. For a moment there I thought we might be in trouble."

Perry sat beside Nurse Rooksbee again and pulled a bottle of champagne from the ice bucket next to him. "I believe the bubbly is chilled enough. May I pour you a glass, Clementina? The curtain will soon be raised."

The woman cooed like a dove and nodded yes as the man called Budd said with worry in his voice, "Boss . . . where the hell is that thing headed?"

Perry stood and followed the foreman's stare. "It's headed straight toward us." He waved his arms and yelled, "Back! Back!"

Slowly, ominous as a stalking hawk, the airship drew closer. Sunlight gleamed on her cannon barrels and smoke from the chimney trailed behind her like a black plume. The dreadful, jagged-winged bats on the canopy looked like hellish heraldry as the sound of the brass band could be heard playing "The Bonnie Blue Flag."

Panic-stricken, Caleb Perry screamed, "What the hell is happening?"

He was soon to find out.

CHAPTER FIFTY-EIGHT

"Lane, drop her ten feet!" Jacob O'Brien ordered. "Gun crews ready?"

"Ready," Manuel Cantrell answered.

"Fire only on my command," Jacob warned.

The steam frigate dropped lower. Looming ahead, Jacob saw the immense corrugated iron bulk of Abaddon grow closer. The smoke from its main chimney, black as mortal sin, rose straight into the air. People teemed on the street of Big Buck, eating cake and ice cream, thinking it was all part of the show.

A bullet slammed into the seat beside him, splintering wood. A couple foremen stood in a tower-shaped dias above the roof. They had a two-handed hold on their revolvers and were taking pots at the ship. Jacob thought he caught sight of Caleb Perry with them, but he couldn't be sure.

Fifty yards and closing . . .

The gun crews stood by their cannons, their swarthy Mexican faces intent. Mathias Lane and another man fed wood into the furnace. The ship's

propeller spun faster, cutting through the air like a
buzz saw.

Thirty yards . . .

The tiller bounced in Jacob's clenched fists as the
frigate bucked. Sensing a rising breeze, she demanded
her own head.

"Steady, boys," he yelled. "Steady as she goes." He
grinned, showing his teeth, realizing that he sounded
like a third-rate John Paul Jones.

Twenty yards

The foundry looked like a red mountain, a
demon's lair.

Ten . . .

"Fire!" Jacob roared.

Four cannons crashed in unison and punched
great holes into the side of the building just under
the projecting eaves.

With open mouths, Shawn O'Brien and the entire
town of Big Buck watched the destruction of the
Abaddon Cannon Foundry. The town's festive mood
turned to one of horror as the gigantic factory was
shot full of holes.

Certain it was Caleb Perry he'd seen on the dias,
Jacob watched him push a woman in a nurse's uniform away from him and then trample her underfoot
as he made a dash for the stairwell. Jacob saw no
more. The airship was a hundred feet beyond the
building and he fought the tiller to skid her into a

tight right turn so the starboard battery could be brought to bear.

He heard people screaming in fear and the brass band squawked into silence as the musicians dropped their instruments and ran for the hills. A few drunken roosters stood in the middle of the street, raised their revolvers, and took pots at the ship. Bullets *ping*ed in the rigging.

The steamship yawed badly as Jacob fought to straighten her up for another attack. Lane left his overheated engine and helped him battle the kicking tiller.

Once the frigate was flying level, Lane yelled into Jacob's ear, "She's overheating. Carrying too much of a load."

"What's the worst that can happen?"

"She'll explode and blow us all into smithereens."

Jacob nodded. "I'll make a note of that. Keep her nice and level, Mr. Lane. We're going in for another attack. Manuel, stand by your guns."

Smoke poured out of the holes in the side of the building as the frigate began her second attack run. As the bottom of the facing wall hove into view, Jacob was relieved to see men scrambling out of the loading bay. He heard some shooting, but the trolls were escaping in droves.

After the first explosions, Mayor John Deakins sought out Shawn and demanded, "Sheriff, do your duty and put a stop to that vandalism."

"Sure." Shawn looked at the men clustered in the street. "I need a posse to help me save the foundry. Volunteers step forward."

Not a man moved, including a few of the town's harder element.

Shawn turned to the mayor. "Seems like there's only you, Deakins. Grab yourself a broom."

He was incensed. His eyes blazing, he yelled, "You men, get your rifles. We'll put an end to this."

Men stared up at the flying machine with its roaring cannons.

One big fellow, Ezra Mander the blacksmith, voiced the opinion of the others when he said, "I want no truck with flying machines, Deakins. If you want to bring that thing down, you do it yourself."

The mayor puffed up and blustered, but he knew he was up against a stacked deck. He retreated into self-pity and a speech. "Citizens, this is a terrible day in the history of our fair town of Big Buck. Let us hope that Mr. Perry, our beloved benefactor, has survived this dastardly attack."

There were a few muted "Hear-hears" but everyone's attention was riveted on a new and greater horror. A host of living skeletons, at least two hundred strong, streamed from the direction of the foundry and descended on the town.

Again Deakins turned to Shawn. "Sheriff, what is this? Who are those people?"

"Mayor, you called the tune and now you pay the piper. Those are the slaves who worked for your beloved benefactor."

Surprised, Jacob felt a twinge of disappointment. He'd expected greater destruction from the cannon fire, but he fervently hoped the second attack would do the trick. Once again, the wall was in range and

Jacob gave the order to fire. Four more jagged holes were added to the first, like poking an open wound with a stick. It seemed that time stood still and there was no apparent result from the cannon fire.

Situated in a corner of the Abaddon building close to the railroad loading area, the gas-making plant was well away from the factory floor and usually posed no danger. A cannonball ricocheted off the beveled side of an iron furnace, caromed across the entire floor, and slammed into a tangled complex of brass and copper pipes that carried gas to an underground main. Sparks were always flying through the air at Abaddon, the reason everyone wore goggles, but the cannonades had burst pipes, shattered boilers, and caused white-hot cascades of molten iron to leak from the furnaces. When sparks from this conflagration met the escaping, hissing gas the result was inevitable . . .

Boom!

The gas exploded in a circular direction and as a result, the wall between the blast and the railroad loading bay was blown outward and the foundry roof went straight up into the air to a height of a hundred feet. A locomotive sitting at the loading bay was hit by the blast of the detonation and reared up like a bucking horse, its yellow cowcatcher the apex of a forty-five degree angle formed by the engine and the track. It remained in that position for a long moment and then crashed onto its side, hissing like a wounded dragon. As the engineer and fireman fled for their lives, the locomotive exploded, flying chunks of jagged metal adding further damage to the Abaddon building.

In a matter of moments, it looked like the entire state of Texas had gone up in smoke and flame.

Hit by the force of the explosion, the frigate bounced fifty feet higher into the air in an instant and became uncontrollable, refusing to answer the helm. A moment later, the Abaddon foundry collapsed in on itself with a terrible grinding crash, crushed like a tin can that had been stepped on by a giant. A series of further explosions shook the ruin to its foundations and a massive, churning dirt and soot cloud rose into the air

Surprised by the ferocity of the gas blast, Jacob let the steamship have its head and it staggered on an erratic course north and then began to make a slow turn to the east.

Finally getting the frigate to answer the helm, he yelled to Lane, "Take us down to ground level and let the gunners leave then fly me over the foundry. I'll drop the bomb on Mr. Perry."

"You're crazy!" the engineer yelled, his eyes frantic. "You'll kill us all."

Jacob held onto the tiller with his left hand and drew his Colt with his right. "I'll kill you right now if you don't do what you're told, Mr. Lane."

Grumbling, Lane went back to his post as Jacob steered the frigate back toward what was left of Abaddon.

When the keel touched ground, he yelled, "Manuel, abandon ship." He pointed the Colt at the engineer. "Mr. Lane, you stay put."

Manuel Cantrell and his gun crew needed no further urging. For abused, half-starved men they showed surprising agility as they leaped over the side and put distance between themselves and the frigate.

"You may take us up again, Mr. Lane," Jacob ordered. "And then over the Abaddon building with our colors flying, if you please."

Lane's assistant, a thin, bookish-looking youngster, became scared as the engineer said, "The upward force of a large explosion could deflate the balloon. If that happens, we're dead men."

"At most, a broken bone or two when we hit the ground, Mr. Lane. You're quite safe." Jacob turned to the trembling assistant who was about eighteen years old. "What's your name, lad?"

"Barnabas Pym, sir. Texas born and raised."

"All right, Barney, grab a-holt of the bomb and bring it here. And don't drop it."

That was exactly what the nervous youth did. Round and greasy, it slipped from Pym's hand, trundled across the deck, and bounced against the side of the ship. Lane shrieked. As though it was going to help, he shut his eyes and stuck his fingers in his ears. Pym was frozen in place, motionless and pale.

Jacob, keeping his voice level, said, "Pick it up, Barney."

"It's ticking!" Lane yelled. "Oh my God, it's ticking."

"It can't tick unless I wind up the clockwork firing thing," Jacob explained.

"By God, man, it's ticking!" Lane yelled. He was bug-eyed and looked as though he was ready to jump over the side."

"By God, man, you're right! Quick, Mr. Lane, take the tiller. Now, steady as she goes over the foundry."

"It's going to blow!" Lane cried.

Jacob stood on the deck, his leg wide apart, the bomb in his hand.

Tick . . . tick . . . tick . . .

"Keep her on course, Mr. Lane. We're almost there."

"Oh my God! I'm dead," Lane yelled.

The airship glided into thick smoke belching from the factory and the searing upward draft of heat was almost unbearable.

Tick . . . tick . . . tick . . .

"Let it go!" Pym howled. "Let the damn thing go!"

"Tick . . . tick.

"It's stopped ticking," Pym screamed. "Drop it!"

His belly doing somersaults, Jacob peered through the curtain of black smoke and figured he was close enough. He tossed the bomb away from him . . . and an instant later it exploded.

It was a tremendous air blast. The huge lethal ball of scarlet and yellow flame and greasy gray smoke collapsed what remained of the Abaddon building. The ragged walls fell with a tremendous cacophony of shrieking corrugated iron, clanging steel beams, and the *dong . . . dong . . . dong* of heavy chunks of cast iron. Blast after blast ripped the foundry apart.

Jacob saw a headless, armless body soar into the air, tumbling over and over.

For a moment, all eyes in town were on Abaddon as a massive explosion rocked the already ruined building and metal debris reined down in the street and sent people scrambling for shelter.

"We're hit!" Lane yelled. "Look at the canopy."

A great hunk of flying iron had ripped through the balloon and the torn and tattered bats flapped around as though mortally wounded. Still driven by its propeller, the ship was dangerously out of control. Jacob and the others held on to anything they could find as the frigate cartwheeled across the brush flat like a dog chasing its tail and then dived bow first into the ground. The cloud of dust that rose around the wreck suddenly glowed pink and then red as flames from the furnace spread to the wooden hull.

Two columns of smoke marred the blue Texas sky. The one above the shattered hulk of Abaddon drifted high in a great, billowing mushroom shape. The one that marked the crash site of the steam frigate was slighter and soon blew away in the prairie wind.

CHAPTER FIFTY-NINE

Shawn O'Brien saw the airship hit and start to descend, spinning to the ground out of control. *Is Jake onboard? Or is he with the escaping workers?* He had no time to ponder that question as the sound of breaking glass and screaming women broke into his concentration. The escaped Mexicans were looting the town, smashing down doors and windows. Scores of skinny men with ferocious faces forced food down their throats as they wandered from store to store. Shawn had seen riots before. Once the vengeful Mexicans looted the saloon and got among the whiskey, the real trouble would begin.

Reading the mayor's face, he saw that Deakins knew it, too. He realized that it was only a matter of time before his town was ravaged by an orgy of wholesale rape and murder.

Deakins, his top hat askew on his head, raised his hands and advanced on the mob. "Now see here, you men. You will gather at the far end of town in an orderly fashion and your needs will be attended to."

Very few of the Mexicans spoke any English and

they ignored the big man. It was unfortunate that Deakins, in his frustration, grabbed the thin shoulders of a young Mexican and shook him hard. "Do you understand me?" he yelled. "Do you damn fools underst—"

Deakins went down under a pile of punching, clawing arms and the man's dying shrieks stirred Shawn into action. To the men around him, he yelled, "Get the women and children into City Hall and guard them there. If you're not armed, arm yourselves." He turned to Flora March. "You go with the womenfolk."

"The hell I will. I'm staying right here." She hiked up her skirt and pulled a derringer from a lacy black thigh garter. "I can take care of myself, Professor."

"And so can I." Archibald Lark reached his arm around Flora's waist. "We stay together."

Shawn shrugged. "Let's hope you don't die together."

A rioting mob is a savage creature with many heads and one mind, it's single thought—*get even.*

The last thing Shawn wanted to do was to shoot into the ranks of men who'd been held as slaves and suffered unthinkable atrocities, but they had to be stopped before the slaughter and destruction started in earnest and gave a savage voice to the voiceless. Across the street, the men of the town herded women and children into City Hall, a partially brick-built building that was the strongest structure in town. Most of them were armed and they wouldn't hesitate to shoot to protect their loved ones.

Ambrose Hellen stood guard outside his saloon, a shotgun in his hands. The bartender was grim-faced.

The situation was bad and getting worse and Shawn saw his duty clear—he would join the defenders of the women and children. No matter where his sympathies lay, he had no other choice.

A small miracle happened . . . or a large miracle if one based it on the imposing size of Jacob O'Brien. He appeared at the end of the street with one man thrown over his shoulder and supporting another, a weak-kneed youngster with auburn hair and a pained expression.

A young Mexican broke from the crowd, called out to the men with him, and pointed to Jacob. He said something very fast in Spanish that Shawn didn't understand and his words drew cheers. Mexicans stepped out of the few stores that had already been looted, one of them wearing a woman's poke bonnet, and joined in the revelry.

Shawn walked to the edge of the mob, ignoring the surly or threatening glances thrown his way. "Jake, what the hell is happening?"

"Didn't you see me up there playing hob in the flying machine? That's why they're cheering. The Mexicans reckon they're free because of me. Here . . . you men, help me with this feller. His name is Mathias Lane and both his legs are broke."

None of the Mexicans moved and a growl of anger rose from the crowd.

The man in the poke bonnet said, "We kill him. He's Perry's hombre."

Jacob shook his head. "No. He's an engineer and he had no part in Perry's killings or his plan to destroy this town."

A few white men carrying rifles had moved closer

and one of them said, "Destroy Big Buck? What the hell are you talking about, mister?"

At some considerable length, Jacob told them.

The townsmen stood in stunned disbelief and then anger. "Are you telling us the truth?" a man said. "All that jabber about testing cannons and a bomb on people sounds like a big windy to me."

That last brought nods of agreement and Shawn was aware that Jake's temper was on a hair trigger.

"Look at the damn foundry," Jacob yelled. "That was what Big Buck was supposed to look like, you damn fool."

"He's telling the truth!" Manuel Cantrell stepped out of the crowd of angry Mexicans. "Caleb Perry planned to destroy the town and kill everyone in it."

"Why would he do a thing like that?" a white man asked.

"Because he could. That's all. Damn him to hell, because he could."

Manuel still sensed doubt. He ripped off his ragged shirt and revealed his shrunken, emaciated chest, his ribs standing out like a picket fence. "Look at me. Look at the rest of us. What do you see? Skeletons, not men! We were Perry's slaves—starved, beaten, and murdered. And why? To produce cheaper cannons and flying machines. Slaves like us don't need to lie. The truth itself is terrible enough, don't you think?"

A couple Mexicans helped Jacob place the groaning Mathias Lane on the ground.

Jacob turned to the crowd. "Listen up, all of you— Mexicans and Americans alike—Perry believed that steam-powered flying machines could destroy great cities and to prove it he planned to wipe out Big Buck. If he'd succeeded, there wouldn't be a single man, women or child, alive in this town. You damn lunkheads, open your eyes."

Ambrose Hellen stepped forward. "I believe there's truth in what you say, O'Brien, but our town is under threat again. The Mexicans have already committed one murder and they plan to loot and destroy the town. Our womenfolk and the children are forted up in the town hall and by God, we'll fight to save them."

From the white men came shouts of "Damn right," and "Let 'em try it."

Shawn was on edge, his hand close to his gun. The situation could get out of hand almighty sudden and there would be dead men on the ground. It was time to do some town taming.

The Colt in his fist spoke louder than words, but the words he spoke were loud enough. "Ambrose Hellen, if you want to end this threat to your town, it's got to come from you and the rest of the men and women of Big Buck. One way or another, you all profited from Abaddon and the railroad it brought with it. Did it ever occur to any of you that many men—mostly Mexicans, but there were others—stepped through the foundry gates and never reappeared. Didn't you even once think that strange?"

"Hell, O'Brien, we lived in the town. We'd no call to go anywhere near the cannon factory," Hellen said. "Isn't that right, men?"

Shawn ended the murmurs of agreement when he said, "Behind those corrugated iron walls, men were being starved, beaten, and murdered on a daily basis, yet you knew nothing."

"We heard rumors . . ." Hellen offered.

"But did nothing?" Shawn asked.

Hellen shrugged. "The mayor went up there from time to time. . . ."

"The mayor is dead and can't talk for himself. I want to hear you talk, Ambrose, you and the rest of the people in this town."

"You go to hell," a man in the crowd shouted. "We didn't know."

"The next man who interrupts my brother, I'll kill him." The look on Jacob's face convinced everyone present that he meant what he said.

"You heard rumors but did nothing," Shawn said again. "Ambrose, is that the way of it?"

The big bartender nodded. "I guess you could say that."

Shawn took the skeletal arm of a young Mexican who was no more than a boy and gently pushed him toward Hellen. "Then you're just as responsible for this as Caleb Perry."

Hugo Long, the owner of the hotel, cast a worried look at the grim Jacob O'Brien then asked Shawn, "Hell, what do you want us to do?"

"Do? Take care of these men, feed, clothe, and house them until they recover their strength and health. I can't do that. Only the people of this town can do that. It's not up to me. It's up to all of you."

All the time Shawn had been speaking, Manuel Cantrell had been translating and some of the tension had left the bright afternoon. The Mexicans seemed expectant, as though waiting to see how it all turned out. The man in the poke bonnet had taken it from his head and dropped it onto the ground and stared at Hellen.

In the end it was Ambrose Hellen who saved the day and the town. "Well, boys, what do we do?" he asked the white men present.

Hugo Long said, "I guess after what they've gone through we owe them Mexicans that much." It seemed that he spoke for the rest of them because no one voiced an objection.

Hellen said, "Our first task is to feed those men and later we'll form committees and . . ."

Shawn stepped away while the bartender was still talking. He'd let Hellen and his committees work out the details.

"What's the reaction from your men?" Shawn asked Manuel Cantrell.

"They'll wait and see. Starved, scrawny men are not much inclined to riot when a breath of wind could blow them away."

Archibald Lark nodded to the couple looted stores. "You could have fooled me."

"After their anger passed, reality set in," Cantrell said. "The men will give this town no further trouble. And once they are ready to leave, I will lead them back to Mexico."

"I think your sister is already there," Shawn said.

Manuel nodded. "I will search for Doña Maria Elena and hope to find her well and happy."

Jacob had Mathias Lane carried to the doctor's office and dispatched Barnabas Pym to the saloon, ordering him to drink a brandy and maybe two. "Good for your nerves, boy."

"I don't think my nerves will ever be the same again." Pym cast Jacob an accusing look. "Mr. O'Brien, you're a wild man."

"Damn right."

CHAPTER SIXTY

Jacob O'Brien stood at Shawn's hotel window and glanced outside. "I see some Mexicans wearing new shirts and pants. The town seems to be doing all right by them."

Ambrose Hellen spoke from a chair beside the fireplace. "Maybe so, but Mayor Deakins is dead and some of those boys are murderers."

Jacob turned from the window. "You might have a problem identifying them."

"That's the sheriff's job," Hellen said.

Shawn smiled. "Nice try, Ambrose, but I'm no longer the sheriff. My job ended when Jake blew up the foundry."

"And a train waiting on the tracks," Hellen pointed out. "Now that Abaddon is gone there's no reason for the railroad to keep the branch line open."

"So what happens then?" Jacob asked.

"Then? The town of Big Buck dies and blows away in the prairie wind," Hellen said.

Jacob said, "Maybe some towns don't deserve to survive."

"It's doing all right by the Mexicans," Hellen agreed. "You said that yourself."

"Only because I shamed the good citizens into it," Shawn said. "The ruins of Abaddon will be a constant reminder of their failure and they will move on."

Hellen shook his head. "Hard talk, O'Brien, mighty hard."

"Abaddon is a scar on the face of this town," Shawn said. "Man or woman, every time he or she looks into a mirror, they'll see the scar on their own faces."

"I don't have a scar on my face," Hellen said.

"But it's there all the same," Shawn said.

Jacob was tired of the conversation. "Shawn, I think it's time. Hellen, will you organize a search party?"

"Yeah. It will take me time to round one up, though." The angled a look at Shawn. "They're all taking care of their scars."

"Then get it done, Hellen," Jacob said. "Shawn and me will go on ahead."

"I'll come with you," Archibald Lark said. "Perhaps there are some poor souls still alive who need a prayer."

"I can almost guarantee it." Jacob turned to Flora. "You stay here."

"Why do men keep telling me to stay where I am? I'm going with Archie."

"Maybe you won't like what you see," Jacob said.

"In my business, I've seen worse."

* * *

The street was almost deserted as people stayed home to care for the Mexicans. A concerned middle-aged matron who met Shawn and Jacob on the boardwalk told him that two of the older men had already died from neglect and malnutrition. "And too much excitement. Doctor McKearns said their poor hearts were weakened and just gave out."

"Where is Dr. McKearns now?" Jacob asked.

"I believe he's still at Mrs. Afton's place," the woman said.

"Tell him to meet us at the foundry," Jacob said. "We believe the wreckage has cooled enough that we can look for survivors."

"I'll tell him." She hurried away.

When Shawn and Jacob stopped to talk to the matron, Flora and Lark had gone on ahead. They strolled slowly so the O'Brien brothers could catch up, but then halted in their tracks as a threatening roar filled the air. Caleb Perry's steam car skidded onto the street and accelerated, trailing a cloud of dust and smoke.

Jacob yelled, "It's Perry!" and then disaster struck very fast.

Lark raised his Bible and called out, "Stop in the name of the Lord!"

Grinning, Perry swung the massive vehicle right at him. The thud of steel ramming into flesh was sickening. Hit hard, Lark was thrown high into the air. Neither Shawn nor Jacob waited to see him land. They both drew. Jacob was fast but Shawn was faster. He slammed three shots into Perry. The impact of the big .45 slugs jolted the man in the driver's seat and he lost control. Shawn and Jacob dived for the dirt as the yellow car rumbled past them. Shawn rolled and then looked up in time to see the last act of the drama.

The steam car, swerving wildly, kept accelerating all the way along the street, kicking up dust and gravel from its spinning wheels. Perry was still alive, bending over the steering wheel as he tried to straighten his careening vehicle. He slammed into the solitary oak standing at the end of the street, just beyond Lem Grater's rod and gun store, The resulting crash sounded like a shelf full of crockery and pans hitting a marble floor. For long moments, the mangled car, a single wheel spinning, *tick . . . tick*ed . . . in the sudden stillness, then a sheet of flame erupted as the furnace and boiler exploded, engulfing the vehicle in fire.

Horror piled on horror . . .

Although Parry had taken three bullets, he was a stocky, muscular man and hard to kill, but he was no match for roaring flames and white-hot heat. His shrieks and screams were heard for a long time before his body was charred into a column of cinders so black that only the white of his teeth showed.

It was, as Shawn would say later, a terrible death for any man, but one richly deserved.

Flora stained Archibald Lark's face with her tears as she bent over his recumbent body. When she saw Shawn and Jacob walk toward her she wailed, "He's dead. My Archie is dead."

Shawn kneeled beside the fallen man and placed his hand on Lark's chest. "He's still breathing. We'll get him to the doctor."

"Both legs broken. I can see that," Jacob said. "He's not going to be walking around for a spell."

"I'll take care of him," Flora said. "I won't let him out of my sight."

Shawn asked the men who'd gathered around to carry Lark to Dr. McKearns. "And be careful, he's got broken legs and maybe other injuries."

The wounded man was carried away, Flora walking beside him, his hand in hers.

Jacob stared down the street. "Well, look at that."

"Now that's what I call mighty strange." Shawn said.

About fifty Mexicans had gathered around the wrecked steam car, gazing in silent vigil at Caleb Perry's charred body. The peons stood perfectly still, like meditating monks, and their quietness was made even more profound by the dreadful clamor of a croaking crow that fluttered back and forth above the wild oak.

"Seems like the devil's come to take his own," Jacob said.

"And the Mexicans know it," Shawn said.

CHAPTER SIXTY-ONE

The bodies in the Abaddon wreckage were burned beyond recognition, but Dr. McKearns managed to identify one of them as female. There were seven survivors, including a white man who died three days later. The rest were Mexicans. All were found in the construction bay along with thirty-four dead.

Archibald Lark's legs were splinted and he was moved to the hotel where Flora March divested herself of boned corset and high boots and bought herself a used but serviceable brown dress and sensible shoes.

"He's feeling much better, Professor," she told Shawn, "and wants to talk to you."

His spurs chiming, Shawn stepped across the hotel room's pine floor to the bed. "How are you feeling, Archibald?"

"Getting better, thank you," Lark said. "Flora is taking good care of me and my horse and wagon. Takes a big load off my mind."

"You just concentrate on getting well," Shawn said. "How are you fixed for money?"

"I had some saved and have enough, Shawn. But thank you for asking."

"If you need—"

"I'm fine, honestly." With Flora's help, Lark managed to sit up in bed a little. He was very pale and his eyes looked too big for his thin face. "I really thought I could convince Caleb Perry about the evil of his ways. But it didn't work."

"Three rounds from a forty-five convinced him just fine," Shawn said.

"I heard. Flora told me he's dead."

"Uh-huh. Now he's a rug in front of the devil's fireplace," Shawn said.

Lark managed a smile. "Shawn, can I ask a favor?"

"Given your present condition, Archibald, I can hardly refuse."

"You remember that town I told you about down in the Glass Mountains country? A settlement they call Falcon Haven."

Wary, Shawn said, "Yeah . . . I remember."

"The people in the town need your help, Shawn. Drusilla McQuillen and her gunmen won't rest until the respectable folks are all dead or forced to leave. She is a bandit queen and rules like one."

Shawn said, "This town tamer thing came about by chance, Archibald. I don't intend to make it my life's work."

"I understand," Lark said. "I should not have asked such a favor of you."

"Maybe you can find someone else, Archie," Flora said. "Mr. O'Brien is a very important man and he doesn't have time for little people like us."

"All right, Flora, you don't need to lay guilt on

me," Shawn said. "I tell you what I'll do, Archibald. I'll ride down that way and if things are as bad as you say, I'll see what I can do. I'm not making any promises, mind. It's my intention to visit England for a while and pay respects at my wife's grave."

Lark said, "That's all I ask, Shawn. Just take a look."

"As I said, no promises. Some towns are not worth saving. Falcon Haven may be one of them."

Someone banged on the door and when Flora answered it, Jacob stepped inside. He nodded to Shawn and then said to Lark, "So, how is the invalid?"

"Feeling much better, thank you."

Jacob laid a tin container with a wire handle on the bedside table. "Got this made up at the restaurant for you. It's sumbitch stew like my pa's Chinese cook makes for the ailing. There's heart, liver, sweetbreads, tongue, beef tenderloin, marrow-gut, onion, and plenty of hot sauce in there. Get you back on your feet in no time, Archie."

"If it doesn't kill him first," Flora muttered.

Jacob shook his head. "Nah, it will make a man of him." He turned to Shawn. "I'm moving on, brother. Manuel Cantrell is a free man and I've done what I came to do."

"Where are you headed, Jake?" Shawn asked.

"Well, when I was home, the Colonel told me that he bought shares in a diamond mine in the Cape Colony in South Africa. He asked me to head over there and look after his interests for a year or two."

"And you're going to do it?"

"I've never been in Africa before so I reckon I will. There's good big game hunting at the Cape, buffalo and lions and the like, or so I was told. Seems like as good a place as any. You?"

"I figure I'll spend some time in England, visit Judith's grave and get reacquainted with her family." Shawn saw Lark staring at him, disappointment on his face, and said, "But first I'll ride down to the Glass Mountains. I hear it's real pretty country down that way."

Jacob nodded. "A while back, a feller by the name of Morgan Ashmore was raising hob in that country. You heard of him?"

"I might have heard the name."

"Morg and me found ourselves on opposite sides a time or two and went around. But nothing ever came of it," Jacob said. "Probably just as well, He's fast on the draw. But he isn't one to stay in a place long. Probably moved on by now."

Shawn nodded. "I'll keep that in mind."

"Flora, you make sure Archibald eats the stew now, you hear? Put hair on his chest." Jacob turned to Shawn and hugged him close. "I'm riding on now, brother. If you're ever in darkest Africa . . ."

"I'll surely look you up, Jake."

Then Jacob was gone and as always, when he parted from his brother, Shawn wondered if it was the last time he'd ever see him.

Shawn O'Brien rode out of the livery and then swung toward the burned-out shell of the Abaddon foundry. He sat his horse and stared at the wreckage that marked the end of one man's mad dream. The overturned locomotive still blocked the railroad track and a couple workmen stood looking at it, scratching their heads, trying to figure how to salvage a steel and iron monster. One of the workmen turned and saw Shawn and gazed at him with open curiosity. Shawn raised a hand and waved. The man didn't wave back.

Shawn's horse was eager for the trail and shook his head in irritation at the inactivity, the bit chiming like a bell. After patting the big stud's neck, Shawn swung around and headed down the street, oddly busy at that time of day when the sun was high. He rode at a walk and people watched him as he rode by, but no one smiled or waved or said so long.

He reached the end of street and open ground stretched ahead of him, shimmering in the heat. A single Mexican, ragged and skinny, stood at the edge of town and as Shawn passed he removed his straw hat and gave a little bow.

Shawn O'Brien smiled. For the Town Tamer that was thanks enough.

Turn the page for an exciting preview!

USA Today and *New York Times* **Bestselling Authors**
WILLIAM W. JOHNSTONE
with J. A. Johnstone

*A train full of killers. Two passengers marked for death.
And one legendary mountain man. Matt Jensen is in for
the ride of his life. And it may be his last . . .*

RICH MAN, DEAD MAN

After surviving a brilliantly plotted murder attempt,
the richest man in San Francisco is looking to hire
the best protection that money can buy. Enter Matt
Jensen, who, for the princely sum of $5,000, agrees
to escort millionaire John Gillespie and his very
fetching daughter on a railway journey from Frisco
to Chicago. There's just one catch: the world's
deadliest killers are coming along for the ride . . .

In Provo, Utah, a knife-wielding assassin leads
Jensen on a life-or-death chase across the roof of
the train. In Cheyenne, Wyoming, a ruthless pair
of hired guns climb onboard, ready to kill anyone
who gets in their way. And in Omaha, Nebraska,
three more cutthroats join the party. It doesn't take
Matt Jensen long to realize this is no ordinary job.
It's a one-way ticket to hell . . .

MATT JENSEN, THE LAST MOUNTAIN MAN
THE GREAT TRAIN MASSACRE

On sale now, wherever Pinnacle Books are sold.

CHAPTER ONE

Onboard the Western Flyer

The train was heading south on the Denver and Rio Grande Railroad. It was a little past four in the morning, and from Spruce Mountain the train was a symphony of sight and sound. Red and orange sparks glittered from within the billowing plume of smoke that was darker than the moonlit sky. Clouds of steam escaped from the drive cylinders, then drifted back in iridescent tendrils to dissipate before they reached the rear of the engine. The passenger cars were marked by a long line of candescent windows, glowing like a string of diamonds.

There were ninety-three passengers on the train, counting Matt Jensen. Matt was more than just a passenger, because he had been hired by the Denver and Rio Grande Railroad to act as a railroad detective. It wasn't a permanent job, but the D&RG had been robbed too many times lately, and because Matt had worked with them before, they offered him a good fee to make one trip for them. They didn't choose the trip arbitrarily; they had good information that the train would be robbed somewhere between Denver and Colorado Springs.

Matt accepted the assignment but under the condition that no one on the train, except the conductor, would know about him. He had boarded the train in Denver as a passenger, taking a seat, not on the Pullman car, but in one of the day cars, doing so to keep his official position secret. He had turned down the gimbal lantern that was nearest his seat, which allowed him to look through the window without seeing only his own reflection. At the moment he was looking at the moon reflecting from the rocks and trees when the train suddenly ground to a shuddering, screeching, banging, halt. So abruptly did the train stop that the sleeping passengers were awakened with a start.

"Why did we stop in such a fashion?" someone asked indignantly.

"I intend to write a letter to the railroad about this. Why, I was thrown out of my seat with such force that I could have broken my neck," another passenger complained.

Because Matt could see through his window, he saw some men outside, and it gave him a very good idea of what was going on. He pulled his pistol and held it close beside him, waiting to see what would happen next. He didn't have to wait but a short time before someone burst into the car from the front door. The train robber was wearing a bandana tied across the bottom half of his face, and he was holding a pistol, which he pointed toward the passengers.

Although the passengers were shocked and surprised at this totally unexpected interruption of their trip, Matt was not. He had been told to expect a train robbery between Denver and Colorado Springs, and it was now obvious that the intelligence had been correct.

"Everybody stay seated!" the train robber shouted. He was holding a sack in his left hand, and he handed it to the passenger in the front seat.

"Now, if you are churchgoing folks, I know you understand what it means to pass the plate. Just pretend that this sack is the plate that gets passed around in church, only don't hold back on your donations like you do with your preacher. Gents, I want you to drop your wallets into the sack. Ladies, if you got 'ny jewelry, why that would be appreciated, too."

"Look here, what gives you the right to . . ." a man started, but before he could finish the question, the train robber turned his gun toward him.

"This gives me the right," he said.

Another gunman came on to join the first. "How is everything going?" he asked.

"Nothing I can't handle. Is everything under control out there?"

"Yeah," the second gunman answered. "We've got the engineer covered, and we're disconnecting the rest of the train from behind the express car."

"How will I know when you're pullin' the express car away? I mean, what if you fellas leave and I don't know you're gone? I'll be stuck back here."

"We'll blow the whistle before we go."

"There's no need for you to be worrying about that. You two won't be going anywhere," Matt said.

"What? Who said that?"

"I did," Matt replied. "Both of you, drop your guns."

"The hell we will!" the first gunman shouted as he fired at Matt. The bullet smashed through the window beside Matt's seat. Matt returned fire, shooting two times. Both of the bandits went down.

During the gunfire, women screamed and men shouted. As the car filled with the gun smoke of the three discharges, Matt scooted out through the back door, jumped from the steps down to the ground, then fell and rolled out into the darkness.

"Walt, Ed! What's goin' on in there?" someone shouted from alongside the track. "What was the shootin' about?"

"I'm afraid Walt and Ed won't be going with you," Matt called. Matt was concealed by the darkness, but in the dim light that spilled through the car windows, he could see the gunman who was yelling at the others.

"Drop your gun and put your hands up!" Matt called out to him. "I've got you covered."

"I'll be damned if I will!" the train robber replied. He realized he was in a patch of light, so he moved into the shadow to fire at the voice from the darkness. He may have thought he would be shielded by moving out of the light, but the two-foot-wide muzzle flash of his pistol gave Matt an ideal target, and he fired back. A bullet whistled harmlessly by Matt, but Matt's bullet found its mark, and the outlaw let out a little yell, grabbed his chest, then collapsed.

Matt stood up then and moved toward the side of the train to try and get a bead on the one who had been separating the express car from the rest of the train. One of the passengers poked his head out to see what was going on.

"Get back inside!" Matt shouted gruffly.

The passenger jerked his head back in quickly.

The train robber peered cautiously around the corner, trying to see his adversary.

"Mister, you are the only one left alive," Matt called out. "And if you don't drop your gun and come out here with your hands up right now, you'll be as dead as your partners."

"Who the hell are you?" the outlaw called back.

"The name is Jensen. Matt Jensen."

"Matt Jensen?" The outlaw's voice suddenly took on a new and more frightened edge.

"That's my name."

There was a beat of silence, then Matt saw a pistol tossed out onto the ground. A moment later the would-be train robber emerged from between the cars with his hands in the air.

"We can go on ahead, Mr. Engineer," Matt called up. "It's all over now."

"Yeah, but the track ain't clear," the engineer called back down from the cab window. "Look ahead, 'n you'll see what it is that made me stop so fast."

Matt saw that a tree had been felled across the track.

"We're goin' to have to get that cleared away before we can go on."

By now the conductor, hearing the conversation and realizing that the danger had passed, came down to see what was going on.

"I'll get some volunteers to clear the track," the conductor promised.

"You think you can get enough people to volunteer?"

"I'll offer them a refund on their train tickets," the conductor said.

Matt looked at the man he had captured. "What's your name?"

"Dockins," the man replied. "Art Dockins."

"Dockins, you and I will ride in the baggage car with your three friends."

"Are they dead?" Dockins asked.

"Oh, I expect they are," Matt replied easily.

The conductor employed the two porters to load the bodies into the baggage car, while passengers from the train made quick work of the tree trunk that was lying across the track. Within an hour after the train's unscheduled stop, they were underway again.

The sun was fully up by the time they reached Colorado Springs, and the platform was crowded with family and friends who were there to meet the arriving passengers as well as departing passengers and those who were there to tell them good-bye.

"We was held up!" someone shouted as soon as he stepped down from the train.

"Held up?" one of those waiting said.

"No, we wasn't actually held up," another said. "Though some folks did try to hold us up."

"What do you mean, tried?"

"I mean tried. Some men tried to hold us up, only

they didn't get away with it. Three of 'em's dead now, 'n the fourth one is bein' held prisoner in the baggage car."

"You mean one of 'em's still alive? Let's string 'im up. There ain't no better lesson given to would-be train robbers than to see one of their own with his neck stretched."

Inside the car, Matt sat with his prisoner, Dockins, and the bodies of the three outlaws he had killed.

"Oh, Lord!" Dockins said. "They're a-fixin' to hang me."

"No, they aren't."

"Yes, they are. I heard 'em talkin' about it."

"They'll have to get you away from me first," Matt said. He opened the door to the baggage car, then stood there in the opening.

"Mister, is it true you're holdin' one of the train robbers prisoner in there?" someone called up to Matt.

"I am. I'm holding him for the law."

"Ain't no need for you to be a-doin' that. You can turn him over to us."

"I don't think so," Matt replied.

"You'll either turn him over to us, or we'll take him from you."

Matt drew his pistol.

"I don't think so," he said again.

"There's at least twenty of us. There's only one of you. Do you think you can stop all twenty of us?"

"No, that wouldn't be possible. I've only got six bullets in my gun. But before you get him, I'll kill six of you." Matt pointed his pistol straight at the loud mouth. "And I may as well start with you, right now."

"No!" the man shouted, holding out his hands. "Now, just a minute, mister, you got no call a-doin' that."

"Then I suggest you start trying to calm down all your friends. Because I will kill the first person who makes a step toward this car, then I will kill you."

"Hold it, fellas, hold it!" the loud mouth said, talking to the others in the crowd. "Let's just let the law handle this."

"Thanks, Jensen," the surviving train robber said.

By that time the sheriff and his deputy were pushing their way through the crowd toward the mail car.

"Get back," the sheriff was saying. "Get back, ever'body. Make way! Let me an' my deputy through here!"

When the sheriff reached the train, the messenger climbed down from the express car.

"You want to tell me what happened here?" the sheriff asked.

"We were beset by train robbers," the messenger said.

"I had a bank shipment coming. Did they get any of the money?" The question was asked by a very thin, clean-shaven, bald-headed man who had a prominent Adam's apple. This was the banker.

"No sir, Mr. Underhill," the messenger said. "I'm proud to say that the money is all here."

"We got three bodies onboard, Sheriff," the conductor said. "What do you want to do with 'em?"

"They the ones that tried to rob the train?" the sheriff asked.

"Yes, sir."

"I've got a prisoner for you, too," Matt said.

"You've got a prisoner? Who are you?"

"His name is Jensen, Sheriff," the conductor said. "The railroad hired him to look after the money shipment. He's the one that killed the three and captured this one."

"All by himself?" the sheriff asked in disbelief.

"All by himself."

The sheriff turned to his deputy. "All right, get 'em out of the car and lay 'em on the platform," he said. "Let's take a look at 'em."

Soliciting help from a couple of men in the crowd, the deputy soon had the three bodies out and lying on the brick platform. Drawn by morbid curiosity, the crowd moved in for a closer look.

"Hey, Sheriff, I know a couple of them boys," the deputy said. "That's Walt Porter and Ed Stiller. They used to cowboy some for the Bar T."

"Yeah, I know them, too," the sheriff replied. He pointed to the third one. "I don't know that one, though."

"That's Bing Baker," Dockins said. "Me 'n him used to ride together up in Wyomin' some."

"Who are you?"

"Dockins. Art Dockins."

"He's the prisoner we've got for you," the conductor said.

"Prisoner? How come he's not tied up or anything?"

"There was no need to make him uncomfortable," Matt said. "He wasn't going anywhere."

CHAPTER TWO

"The Denver and Rio Grande thanks you," General William Jackson Palmer said to Matt. General Palmer was president of the railroad.

"And, in addition to the agreed-upon fee of two hundred and fifty dollars, I am proud to present you with an additional fifty-dollar bonus."

"General, I thank you," Matt said.

"Let me ask you this, Mr. Jensen. "Do you have any interest in becoming a full-time private detective?" Jefferson Emerson asked. "The pay is good, and you would be a natural for it."

Emerson owned the Emerson Private Detective Agency, and provided contract security service not only for the D&RG, but the Denver and New Orleans, as well as the Union Pacific Railroad. Emerson's headquarters was actually in San Francisco, but he had come to Colorado Springs to discuss the renewal of his contract with the Denver and Rio Grande Railroad.

"Well, Mr. Emerson, I do thank you for the offer,"

Matt said. "But I have the feeling that steady work like that would be a little too confining for me. Over the years I've developed the habit of moving around. I'm afraid if I stayed in one job too long, I'd wither up like a piece of rawhide."

Emerson and General Palmer both laughed.

"Well, we can't have you withering up now, can we?" Emerson asked. "But I wonder if I could call on you from time to time, to handle a specific job for me? At a mutually agreed-upon payment, of course."

"Yes," Matt said. "I see no reason why I couldn't take an occasional assignment."

"That's good to know, but, if you're going to be moving around, how will I get in touch with you, if I need you?"

"Isn't your home office in San Francisco?" Matt asked.

"Indeed it is."

Matt smiled. "Well, that's where I'm heading now. I'll be there within two weeks, so, why don't I just check in with you when I get there?"

"Wonderful!" Emerson said.

San Francisco, California

Lucas Conroy had a fine office on the top floor of the Solari Building on Jackson Street. He had a rich red carpet on the floor, a George Catlin painting on the wall, and a vase, dating from the Ming Dynasty, sat on a table in front of the window. At the moment, he was meeting with a potential client.

"You have to be specific in telling me what you want," Conroy said. "I don't deal in generalities."

"I, uh, have to know just what it is you are willing to do before I can be more specific," Conroy's visitor said.

"I arrange things."

"What kind of things do you arrange?"

"Look around my office," Conroy said. "Everything you see here cost a great deal of money. I can afford expensive things, because my business is very lucrative. And my business is very successful, because I am willing to arrange things that most people won't do, either because they can't, or they are too frightened."

"Does that include things that may not be within the law?" his client asked.

"Yes."

"Suppose someone came to you . . . uh, this is just a question, mind you, but, suppose someone came to you and said that he wanted someone killed?"

"That would cost you a great deal of money."

"I didn't say I was the one who wanted someone killed. I was posing a hypothetical question."

"I have no time for hypothetical questions. If a hypothetical question is the only reason you have come to see me, then I must tell you that this meeting is over. So please, get to the point."

"All right, I will get to the point. I represent a consortium of businessmen. And I believe, that is, the consortium believes, that our businesses, and indeed many businesses that we don't represent, are being hurt by the ruthless practices of someone who is concerned only for his own self-interest. We believe that this person's ruthless business practices put at risk the jobs of thousands of people. He is much too powerful to take on in the courts. We believe the only solution is to have him killed. So you see, Mr. Conroy, that wasn't purely a hypothetical question. Can we arrange to have that done?"

"Yes, you can arrange that. But it is going to cost you a great deal of money."

"You will guarantee success?"

"Of course. I could not stay in business unless I guaranteed my clients success."

"Very good. I would say, then, that we wish to become your client."

"Who is the person you want killed?"

"Actually, there are two of them that we want killed."

"Two? You mean you want to arrange two separate operations?"

"No. The two I want killed are always together, so it will be only one operation. Do you think you can handle that?"

"Yes, I can handle it. But whether or not it is one operation or two separate operations, the fact that you want two people killed will double the cost. A human life is a human life, after all, and one doesn't kill without some compunction."

Conroy's visitor smiled. "I'm glad to see that your misgivings can be set aside, for a price," he said caustically.

Colorado Springs, Colorado

Matt was awaiting his turn in the Model Barbershop on Lamar Street. The barber and the customer in his chair were having a discussion. As it turned out, they were discussing him, though neither of them knew that the subject of their discussion was present at the time.

"Jensen faced down all four of 'em," the man in the barber chair said. "Throw up your hands, or prepare to meet your Maker," he called out to 'em.

"It's you that'll die," one of the three men said. Then the pistols commenced a-blazing, 'n the next thing you know, why three of them bandits was lyin' on the floor of the railroad car, 'n the fourth one got scairt and throwed up his hands."

"That's pretty amazing," the barber said.

"Yeah, well, if you knew Matt Jensen as well as I do, you wouldn't think nothin' of it. I told him, I said, 'Matt, you keep gettin' yourself into situations like this, one of these days you're just liable to bite off more'n you can chew.'"

"What did Jensen say when you told him that?" the barber asked.

"Why, what did you expect him to say?" the talkative man replied. "He said, 'The outlaw ain't been born who can get the best of Matt Jensen.' Yes, sir, that's what he said. And me 'n him knowin' each other as well as we do, why, I figure he's prob'ly right." Overhearing the conversation, Matt chuckled quietly, then picked up the newspaper and began to read.

From the *Colorado Springs Gazette:*

Gillespie Enterprises Acquires Northwest Financials

John Bartmess Gillespie announced this week that his company, Gillespie Enterprises has acquired Northwest

Financials, the largest investment firm between San Francisco and Chicago. In making the acquisition, Gillespie beat out Whitehurst Commercial Development, the Kansas City–based company who was also bidding for the investment firm.

Northwest has its main office in Denver, but there are subsidiary offices in a dozen cities. Northwest has been losing money over the last two years, and it is believed that Gillespie will completely reorganize the institution.

"That'll do it, Mr. Allman," the barber said, taking the cape from his customer.

Allman looked at himself in the mirror, ran his hand through his hair, and smiled. "You done a good job, Milt," he said, handing the barber fifteen cents.

"Hello, Mr. Allman," Matt said as the customer walked by.

"Do we know each other?" Allman asked, made curious by Matt's greeting.

"I heard the barber call you by name."

Allman nodded, then left the shop.

"You're next, sir," the barber said.

Matt lay the paper aside and walked over to get into the chair.

The barber put the cape over Matt, unaware that Matt had drawn his pistol and was now holding it in his lap under the cape. It was a suggestion that his mentor and friend, Smoke Jensen, had made a long time ago.

* * *

"Matt, I have a feeling that, like me, you're going to wind up making some enemies, more than likely, a lot of them," Smoke told him. *"In addition, there will be some men who aren't particularly enemies, but would be happy to kill you just for the reputation. One place where you are always vulnerable is when you're sitting in a barber's chair with a cape tied around you. That's when your enemies will see you as a prime target. But you don't have to be vulnerable there. If you'll just pull your pistol and hold it in your lap, you'll turn the situation around. Then, it will be you who will have the upper hand."*

"That fella that just left here sure gets around," the barber said. "You heard him talking about Matt Jensen, didn't you?"

"Yes, I did."

"Yes, sir, well, Matt Jensen ain't the only one he knows. He's good friends with Smoke Jensen and Falcon MacCallister too. He also knows Wyatt Earp, and he knew Wild Bill Hickock. Yes, sir, that fella really gets around."

"Some men just have a knack of making friends, I suppose," Matt said, swallowing a laugh.

"Find anything interesting in the newspaper?" the barber asked as he began building up a frothy lather in the shaving cup.

"I was just reading about Northwest selling out," Matt replied.

"Yeah, what do you think of that?"

"It doesn't look like they had much choice," Matt said. "According to the article, they've been losing money for the last couple of years."

"I guess that's right," the barber said. "It's just that I hate to see it go to Gillespie."

"Why? What's wrong with Gillespie?"

"Oh, I don't know as there is anything wrong with him. It's just that it don't seem right for one man to have so much money. Why, they say he's as rich as some countries." The barber was sharpening his blade on the razor strop.

"There's nothing wrong with being rich, as long as you have come by it honestly," Matt said.

"Well, yes, sir, I reckon that's true. Maybe I'm just jealous 'cause he's got all that money, and I don't."

"Are you married?" Matt asked.

"Yes, sir, I am. I got me a fine wife, two kids, a boy 'n a girl, and another one on the way."

"And a nice business where you provide a service for people who need that service," Matt commented.

The barber was quiet for a moment, then he chuckled. "You're a pretty intelligent man, mister. You're right. Now that I think about it, I've got all a man needs to be happy."

The barber whistled a contented tune as he began shaving Matt.

After the shave and haircut, Matt walked out front, untied his horse from the hitching rail, then swung into the saddle.

"Spirit, we're going to San Francisco. I know that's over a thousand miles, but you won't have to walk the whole way. I'll find a place for us to catch the train before we get there."

Turn the page for an exciting preview!

THE GREATEST WESTERN WRITERS
OF THE 21ST CENTURY

*Preacher takes on the last of the Aztecs
in his biggest, bloodiest showdown yet . . .*

There are a million ways to die in the Rockies—
and a million predators, natural or otherwise.
But even a seasoned mountain dweller like
Preacher is shocked by the latest horror lurking in
the hills. Trappers are being hunted down like
animals. Captured. Murdered. Mutilated.
Their hearts carved out of their chests. Some of the
victims were Preacher's friends, and Audie and
Nighthawk have gone missing. Preacher is
determined to track them down before they end up
on the chopping block. But nothing can prepare
him for what's waiting at the end of the trail . . .

A secret cult as old as the Aztecs.
A warrior priest with a lust for blood.
And an epic battle that begins and ends—
with the ultimate sacrifice . . .

USA TODAY AND *NEW YORK TIMES*
BESTSELLING AUTHORS
WILLIAM W. JOHNSTONE
with J. A. Johnstone

**The First Mountain Man
PREACHER'S BLOODBATH**

On sale now, wherever Pinnacle Books are sold.

CHAPTER ONE

The man burst out of the brush, eyes wide with terror as he ran, arms pumping, legs moving so fast they were almost out of control. Every few steps, he twisted his head to glance wide-eyed behind him as if Ol' Scratch, the Devil himself, was behind him, closing in.

Might as well have been.

Based on his appearance, the terrified man looked like he shouldn't have been scared of anything. He was tall and rugged, with broad, powerful shoulders that strained the buckskin shirt he wore. His bearded, weather-beaten face showed that he had spent a lot of time on the frontier. He had two flintlock pistols, a tomahawk, and a sheathed knife tucked into the sash around his waist, and he carried a long-barreled rifle. A powder horn and a full shot pouch bounced against his hip as he ran. He was armed for bear, as the old saying went.

But it wasn't a bear that was after him. Even as terrible an engine of destruction as one of those creatures could be, what pursued the trapper was worse.

As he started up a bare, rocky slope, he lifted his frenzied gaze and saw a clump of boulders above him. If he could get in among those rocks, his pursuers couldn't come at him all at once. At least he would be able to put up a fight . . . for a while, anyway. His heart slugged harder as he increased his pace.

He heard them howling as they crashed through the brush behind him. Like a pack of wolves, they were. Sometimes he could face down wolves and make them retreat, if he didn't show any fear. That wasn't going to work. His pursuers were worse than wolves.

With enough of a lead, he lunged into the clump of boulders and turned. His pursuers had reached the edge of the brush, charged into the open, and started up the slope after him. They wore buckskin leggings and tunics and had large necklaces of thick leather decorated with small, shiny rocks draped around their shoulders. They carried war clubs and spears and looked like they knew how to use them.

A man in the rear of the party, urging the others on, was dressed similarly but also sported a headdress styled to look like an eagle's beak. A pair of actual eagle's wings, stiffened so they would remain spread out, was attached to a harness strapped to his back. He carried a spear and shook it in the air as he shouted at his companions.

The trapper flung his rifle to his shoulder. He would have liked to ventilate that eagle-wearing varmint in the back, but he couldn't get a clear shot at the man. He settled for drawing a bead on one of the warriors in front and pressed the trigger. The rifle boomed, and the target went over backwards as the heavy lead ball smashed into his chest.

The war chief or whatever he was yelled louder.

The trapper set the empty rifle close enough that he could snatch it up again and use it as a club, and drew both pistols. Already loaded, all he had to do was pull back the hammers as he planted himself in the narrow opening between two boulders.

Three of the attackers flung spears at him. He ducked one, and the other two bounced off the rocks. The leading edge of the charge was only about twenty feet away.

He leveled both pistols and pulled the triggers. The barrels gushed smoke and flame. Two more attackers went down, and the thunderous explosion of the shots made the others pause for a second—long enough for the trapper to dart back a few feet, drop the pistols, and snatch the knife and tomahawk from his belt.

The gap between the boulders was so narrow only one man at a time could get through it. Of course, the attackers could stand off a ways and chuck spears at him, but the odds of hitting him were small and soon they would be weaponless.

Through the opening, he saw his enemies hesitate, even though their leader was still behind them, exhorting them on.

A grin stretched across the trapper's whiskery face. He had already killed three and was confident he would take more of them with him when he crossed the divide.

A faint scraping sound behind him was the only warning he got. As he turned, he caught a glimpse of a figure hurtling at him from the top of one of the rocks. Somehow, at least one of his pursuers had gotten around him.

The warrior crashed into him, the impact driving him against a boulder. He felt something snap and knew he'd probably broken a rib. Pain shot through him but it didn't stop him from swinging the tomahawk. He felt bone shatter as he smashed it against the attacker's head. The man collapsed.

More warriors crowded around the trapper. He slashed back and forth with the 'hawk and the knife as he tried to clear a space around him, but there were too many of them. One thrust a spear into his right thigh. The trapper yelled in a mixture of rage and agony. Then a war club caught him on the head and dropped him to his knees as the world began to spin crazily around him.

It was no use. They ripped his weapons away from him, along with the shot pouch and powder horn, and bore him the rest of the way to the ground. He writhed and tried to strike out with his fists, but strong hands gripped him and held him down.

He had never been a religious man and hadn't set foot in a church since his ma had made him go back in Pennsylvania, long before he headed west to the Shining Mountains. But he had never considered himself a heathen. Knowing that his tormentors were about to kill him, he begged forgiveness for all his sins—and there were aplenty.

Instead of skewering him with spears or bashing his brains out with their clubs, the warriors picked him up and carried him out of the boulders. The fellow who wore the eagle headdress and wings stood with his arms folded across his chest as he regarded the captive with a look of haughty hatred. He spoke harshly in his gibberish of a language.

The trapper knew half a dozen Indian dialects but had never heard that one before.

The man made a sharp gesture. Several of the warriors swung their clubs, but instead of aiming the blows at the trapper's head, they broke his legs and arms, snapping bones with great precision. He howled, and the cry resounded along the valleys and wooded slopes.

With the trapper completely helpless, the warriors picked him up again and carried him over to a low, squarish rock that had split off the mountain from above and toppled down in ages past. They laid him out on the rock and stepped back.

The war chief moved up beside the rock and sneered down at the trapper. He gestured again, and an old man the trapper hadn't seen before came into view. The old man's face was as brown and wrinkled as a nut. He placed a long cloak made of eagle feathers on the war chief's shoulders and handed the chief a knife.

It was not the sort of hunting knife the trapper carried. The blade was made of flint chipped down to an edge. The handle, also made of stone, had been fashioned into the shape of a man kneeling far forward. The war chief grinned as he ran the ball of his thumb along the blade. A drop of blood welled from the cut as he leaned over the captive.

The trapper's eyes widened and bulged from

their sockets until it looked like they were going to pop out.

The war chief slashed the trapper's buckskin tunic and ripped it aside, baring the man's hairy chest. The trapper screamed as the chief began sawing with the blade.

The screams didn't stop until the chief pulled the trapper's bloody, still quivering heart out of his chest and thrust it aloft with a strident, triumphant cry.

CHAPTER TWO

Two men moved through the woods, each very different from the other. One was a Crow Indian, tall and muscular, with a rugged, middle-aged face that looked like it might have been hewn out of a redwood tree.

The Crow's companion was little more than half his height, a white man in buckskins and coonskin cap. Despite his diminutive stature, he was broad-shouldered and brawny, too, with the upper body development of a much taller man.

As far as his weaponry was concerned, he carried a rifle with a barrel somewhat shorter than usual so he could handle it better. That was the only concession to his height. The two flintlock pistols at his waist were full-sized—as was his fighting heart.

"I don't wish to cast aspersions on the acuity of your hearing or the veracity of your declarations, old friend," the little man commented. "So I have no doubt that you actually did hear shots and screams from this direction a short time ago. But we've found nothing so far, and I begin to wonder if our search might be fruitless."

The Crow regarded him gravely. "Umm."

"Yes, I share your concern over Rawley. He was headed in this direction when last we encountered him, and the man's notorious for his predilection for impulsive, reckless behavior. He easily could have waltzed right into trouble, just as you point out, friend Nighthawk."

The trappers who operated in the Rocky Mountains, from above the Canadian border to the Sangre de Cristo far in the south, knew the little man only as Audie. His full name, the name he had used when he was a professor at one of the most prestigious universities back east, was a mystery. He had given up the academic life and come west to live a much simpler existence on the frontier. As he liked to put it, the dangers of grizzly bears, mountain lions, and hostile Indians were nothing compared to what lurked in the hallowed halls of the Ivy League.

Soon after his arrival in the mountains, he had won friends far and wide because he was able to recite from memory the complete works of Shakespeare and many other poets. Men who spent most of their time alone in the vast wilderness were desperate for any sort of entertainment, so Audie was a popular figure around the campfires.

Somewhere in his travels, he had fallen in with Nighthawk, a deadly, taciturn Crow warrior. An unshakeable bond had formed between the unlikely friends, and they had been trapping together for several years.

Nighthawk pointed.

Audie nodded his agreement. "Very well. We'll continue in this direction for another half hour, and if we don't find any sign of Rawley, we can turn back and return to our camp."

As they moved through the woods, being cautious out of habit and taking advantage of the cover they found, Audie thought back to the previous evening, when Jacob Rawley had shared their campfire.

"There's somethin' mighty odd goin' on in these parts," *Rawley said. "You recall Mike Dickinson? He vanished a* *couple weeks ago. Said he was gonna check some of the* *streams up there in Shadow Valley, toward Sawtooth Cliffs,* *and nobody's seen hide nor hair of him since. Jack Phillips* *found some bones in the valley yonder, though. Human* *bones, he claims."*

"Did you see these skeletal remains with your own eyes?" *Audie asked.*

Rawley shook his head. "Naw, Jack claims he give 'em a *decent burial, even though he couldn't find all of the fella* *they came from. But he found what had to be a leg bone,* *and you recollect that limp Mike had on account of he* *busted his leg when he was a boy? Well, Jack said that leg* *bone he found had a place on it that looked like it'd been* *broke and then healed up years ago."*

"That's hardly conclusive evidence some misfortune befell *Michael. Besides, I'm not sure Jack Phillips has the neces-* *sary skill to positively identify human bones, let alone evi-* *dence of a previous fracture."*

"I'm just tellin' you what he told me, Audie."

"Anyway, even if the bones did belong to Michael Dick- *inson, their existence doesn't necessarily indicate foul play.*

We both know there are a myriad of methods a man can confront his mortality in these mountains."

"Lots of ways to die, you mean?"

"Precisely. And it would require only a few days for scavengers to strip the bones clean."

"You're right about that," Rawley admitted. "But Mike ain't the only one who's disappeared around Shadow Valley and Sawtooth Cliffs lately. There are three or four other fellas I ain't seen in a good long while, and I've heard rumors that even more trappers are missin'. I think it's Injuns." He glanced at the Crow. "No offense, Nighthawk."

"Umm."

Audie frowned. "The tribes in this vicinity have been on the peaceful side in recent years, Jacob."

"Yeah, well, you never can tell when something'll get 'em riled up," Rawley insisted.

"Besides, I don't recall hearing of any tribe that actually lives in Shadow Valley."

"They could've moved in from somewheres else. I reckon the best thing to do is head up yonder myself and have a look around."

"Do you think that's wise? I mean, if there is some sort of unusual depredation going on . . ."

"Mike Dickinson and me was trappin' partners for a couple years. If he ain't dead, maybe I can find him. And if he is"—a grim cast came over Rawley's face—"maybe I can settle the score with whoever done for him."

"You'll do what you think best, of course—"

"I always do," Rawley declared.

And now it appears that Rawley's stubbornness might have led him into more trouble than he bargained for,

Audie mused as he and Nighthawk climbed a ridge. *That is, if Nighthawk is right about what he heard earlier.*

Audie had great faith in his old friend.

They paused at the top of the ridge. To the west as the landscape fell away was a broad valley, and on the far side of that valley, forming its western boundary, were the Sawtooth Cliffs.

It was actually the first time Audie laid eyes on them. Despite their wanderings, he and Nighthawk hadn't been *everywhere* west of the Mississippi.

He had heard of the Sawtooth Cliffs numerous times, though, and usually when anyone spoke of them, it was to mention how ugly and sinister they looked.

That was true. The cliffs ran roughly north and south as far as the eye could see in either direction. They were at least two hundred feet tall, and the rim rose and fell in a jagged pattern that made it look like the teeth of a saw.

They look like the lower jaw of a gigantic predator, thought Audie. *Teeth poised to rend and chew until there was nothing left of their prey* . . .

Nighthawk swept a hand out to indicate the valley in front of them. "Umm."

"Yes, Shadow Valley is a good name for the place," Audie agreed. "It definitely has a gloomy atmosphere about it. Do you think Rawley is out there somewhere?"

Again, Nighthawk lifted an arm and pointed. Audie spotted what the Crow's keen eyes had already taken note of. Dark shapes were circling lazily in the sky some distance away, closer to the cliffs.

"Carrion birds," Audie murmured. "Never a good sign. Do we turn back or do we ignore those black-feathered, foreboding auspices and press ahead?"

Without answering, Nighthawk started down the slope. Audie went after him, catching up easily despite his short legs. He possessed a nimbleness few of the full-sized could match.

In the several hours it took them to cross the valley, the buzzards disappeared. That was a bad sign. It meant the birds had descended to feed. Whatever had caught their attention was no longer alive.

They had reached a point where the cliffs loomed over them when Nighthawk grunted, started moving faster, and climbed a bare slope toward a nest of boulders. Audie hurried to keep up with the Crow's long-legged strides, following him.

Before they reached the rocks, Audie saw what had caught Nighthawk's eye. Buzzards formed a dark mass as they fed on something lying on a rock slab. The ugly birds rose into the air, squawking in protest as the two men approached.

"Merciful God in heaven," Audie breathed as he saw what the buzzards left behind.

It had been a man, and enough of his clothes remained to recognize what Jacob Rawley had been wearing when he'd visited their camp the previous evening. It was the only way Audie could tell who the dead man had been. Not much of his face remained.

The buzzards had been at his chest, too, and that was rather odd. Rawley's buckskin shirt wasn't torn open raggedly as the birds might have done to get at his flesh. It looked like someone had cut a slit in the shirt, then ripped it back. The straight edges of the cut remained, indicating that a blade had been used.

Rib bones were visible through the bloody, shredded flesh. Nighthawk leaned forward, studied the mutilated trapper for a moment, and then pointed at Rawley's chest.

Stepping closer, Audie grasped instantly what had caught Nighthawk's interest. "Good Lord. It looks like someone reached in there and *pried* those ribs apart. Why in the world—"

"Umm." Nighthawk clenched a fist and thumped it lightly against his own chest.

"Yes. Oh, my, yes. Even if the buzzards had picked it apart, there would be *something* left." Audie swallowed hard. "The conclusion is inescapable. Someone cut poor Jacob's chest open, pried those ribs apart, reached in there . . . *and ripped out his heart!*"

CHAPTER THREE

Preacher heard singing in the night, somewhere up ahead of him. He reined his rawboned stallion to a halt and told the big, wolf-like cur who padded alongside, "Stay, Dog."

The mountain man swung down from the saddle, looped the packhorse's lead rope around a nearby sapling, and took his long-barreled flintlock rifle—already loaded and primed—from its sling attached to the saddle. He moved forward through the darkness with his thumb curled around the rifle's hammer so he could cock it in an instant if he needed to.

The men he heard sounded peaceful enough, if a mite tipsy. Carrying on like that at night wasn't the best idea—drawing too much attention to oneself never was, on the frontier—making Preacher suspect some jugs of tanglefoot were involved.

No one could ever accuse him of drawing attention to himself. On the contrary, the big mountain man was famous for his stealth. On several occasions during his longstanding hostilities with the Blackfoot tribe, he had slipped into the enemy camp in the middle of the night, cut the throats of several, and then slid back out without ever being noticed. None of the survivors had even known he was there until the bodies were discovered the next morning.

Because of that, some of the Blackfeet had taken to calling him Ghost Killer. Others called him the White Wolf because of his deadliness.

The song's ribald lyrics ended in laughter as Preacher saw the glow of a large campfire up ahead. The party that had made camp had to be a large one. The men didn't seem to care about the size of the fire or the loudness of their singing. The fire would keep animals away, and a large, well-armed group of men didn't have to worry much about being attacked.

Still, such boisterousness went against the grain for Preacher. There was a time and a place for everything and nighttime in the wilderness wasn't for loud singing.

He was close enough to pause and call out, "Hello, the camp!" A fella didn't just waltz in unannounced at night. That was a good way to get shot.

The men fell silent.

After a moment, someone responded. "Who's out there?"

"They call me Preacher."

"Preacher!? Well, the saints be praised! Come on in, you old he-coon!"

The voice was familiar. "Is that you, Miles?"

"Aye, 'tis!"

Preacher hadn't seen Miles O'Grady since the previous year. He had always gotten along with O'Grady and figured if the Irishman was part of the group, they were all likely to be friendly, but he kept his thumb on the flintlock's hammer just in case as he strode forward and stepped out of the trees into the circle of light cast by the campfire.

A quick head count told him there were fifteen men in the bunch. He looked around, saw several familiar faces in addition to O'Grady's broad, ruddy one, and nodded to his acquaintances. It seemed a little odd to him, seeing all of them together.

Most fur trappers were, by nature, solitary creatures, content with their own company except on those rare occasions when they attended a rendezvous. If they partnered up with anybody, only two or maybe three would be in a group.

In the early days of the fur trade, large parties had been common. But like anything else, the customs had evolved over time.

O'Grady moved toward Preacher and stuck out a hand. "Last I heard, you were over in the Wind River country."

Preacher shook his hand and drawled, "Yeah, but I didn't have much luck there. Decided to see how the plews are over here. Looks like you fellas had the same idea." He paused, then added meaningfully, "At the same time."

O'Grady's mouth quirked. "Well, that's not exactly why we're all here together like this. It's because of what's been happening over in Shadow Valley."

Preacher frowned and shook his head. "I hadn't heard of anything goin' on over there."

"Well, it seems like 'tis not a very healthy place to be these days. Sit down, warm your bones by the fire, and I'll tell ye all about it."

"Let me get my horses and my dog," Preacher said. "I left 'em back in the woods a ways . . . until I found out what all the celebratin' was about."

"'Tis not celebrating we are," O'Grady said with a sigh. "More like trying to hold off the darkness with the power of song."

Preacher thought about the situation as he fetched Horse, Dog, and his pack animal. O'Grady, like most Irishmen, was given to bouts of melancholy. Whiskey would just make it worse. Maybe that was all that was going on.

Preacher brought his trail partners back to the camp, unsaddled the big gray stallion, and took the supplies off the packhorse. He picketed both animals, although he knew from long experience that Horse would never willingly stray far from his side. Neither would Dog.

He joined the other men and sat down on a log with several of them. O'Grady offered him a jug.

Preacher shook his head. "Not right now. I'd rather hear about whatever it is that's got you fellas spooked."

One of the men said, "I ain't ashamed to admit I'm a mite scared. You don't know what's goin' on in this part of the country, Preacher. It ain't safe no more."

Preacher grunted. "Shoot, I don't think these mountains were ever all that safe. If you don't have Injuns wantin' to kill you, bears and cougars and lobo wolves are always around. Not to mention avalanches and floods and forest fires. Seems to me like there's always been a million ways to die once you get west of the Mississipp'."

"Yes, but this is worse than usual," O'Grady said. "Nigh on to a dozen men have disappeared around here this year."

"What do you mean, *disappeared*?" Preacher asked with a puzzled frown.

"Just that. Vanished. Dropped off the face of the earth like they never existed. Most of us know someone that's happened to, and the rest have heard stories."

The men sitting in a circle around the campfire nodded solemnly.

"That's not the worst of it, though. We've found bodies"—the Irishman shuddered—"and the things that had been done to them."

It must have been pretty bad to affect O'Grady, thought Preacher.

Although he hadn't been in the mountains as long as Preacher had, Miles O'Grady was a veteran trapper who had been in his share of fights.

"Indians have been known to torture captives," Preacher pointed out. "Hell, one time a bunch of 'em planned on burnin' me at the stake."

"Yeah, I've heard the story," O'Grady said. "Reckon we all have."

"I haven't," one of the other men said.

Preacher didn't know him, couldn't recall ever having seen him before. The stranger was young, probably in his early twenties. Of course, Preacher couldn't hold youth against a fella. He hadn't even been shaving yet when he lit a shuck from his family's farm and headed off to see the elephant.

"Then you don't know how Preacher got his name." O'Grady seemed glad for an excuse to change the subject. "By the way, Preacher, this youngster is Boone Halliday."

Preacher reached over to shake hands. "Boone's a pretty well-known name back in Kentucky."

"I know. That's where I'm from. In fact, my ma named me after Daniel Boone." The young man grinned. "I reckon that with a name like that, I couldn't help but turn out to be a trapper and a long hunter, right?"

Preacher wasn't sure Boone Halliday could make that claim just yet. He appeared to be pretty wet behind the ears, which in his case stuck out rather prominently from the sides of his head. Boone had a shock of brown hair falling down over his forehead under the wide-brimmed, brown felt hat he wore. Actually, he looked more like he ought to be behind a plow somewhere instead of wandering around the high country.

But every mountain man had to start somewhere, Preacher supposed.

"Tell me about your name," Boone went on.

Preacher shook his head and waved a hand. "I disremember how it got hung on me."

"Well, I don't." O'Grady leaned forward eagerly.